MISS MATCH

Visit us at www.boldstrokesbooks.com

MISS MATCH

by
Fiona Riley

2016

MISS MATCH

ISBN 13: 978-1-62639-574-9

THIS TRADE PAPERBACK ORIGINAL IS PUBLISHED BY
BOLD STROKES BOOKS, INC.
P.O. BOX 249
VALLEY FALLS, NY 12185

FIRST EDITION: MAY 2016

CREDITS
EDITOR: RUTH STERNGLANTZ
PRODUCTION DESIGN: SUSAN RAMUNDO
COVER DESIGN BY G. S. PENDERGRAST

Acknowledgments

Without the encouragement and support of Bold Strokes Books, this wild ride would never have taken place. I feel privileged to be in the company of such amazing, talented, and creative authors. It is my absolute pleasure to be able to say that I have made friendships with many of you along this journey that I know will last a lifetime. I can't wait to learn from you and am looking forward to the many opportunities in which you will undoubtedly astound me with your brilliance. In case I am unable to form words when those times occur, please know that I thank you in advance and I probably want your autograph.

I'd like to thank Ruth Sternglantz for her undying patience, for sharing her genius, and for writing the most hilarious critiques in the margins of my manuscript that I have ever read. I have learned more about writing and editing from you than I thought was humanly possible. I imagine you will forever be reminding me to limit my use of exclamation points, but I just can't help myself, I get so excited!!!! Thank you for fielding my late night emails and always taking the time to explain things to me, no matter how big or small they may be. You have an undeniable gift and I am grateful that you share it with me.

To Toni Amato who took a hundred thousand words and helped me make sense of them, I am forever in your debt. You taught me to feel all of the words I put on the page as though they would be my last, and you changed my life in the process. I hope you are proud of the final product, because without you, this would just be a pipe dream. Thank you, thank you, thank you.

Also, thank you to all of my friends and family who have acted as sounding boards to all of my nonsense and for all being crazy enough to inspire my characters. You are bottomless pools of resource for me and my imagination.

To the real Myrtle the Sea Turtle at the New England Aquarium—you are gorgeous and graceful. Thanks for hanging out with me while I researched. It was fun getting to know you.

Lastly, to my wife Jenn for being a literal saint during this whole writing process—I would still be talking about this story had you not encouraged me to sit down and write it. Thank you for always helping me to live in the moment and reminding me to laugh always. You are the funniest person I know, and I will continue to use your effortlessly hilarious daily dialogue as fodder for my future works. You are the best.

Dedication

For Jenn.

You are the best part of my day, every day. You are my loudest cheerleader, my best beta reader, my truest friend, and the absolute love of my life. Life with you is what inspires me to write stories of love, passion, and adventure. I am forever grateful for the chance to learn with you, live with you, and love with you. Thank you for always seeing the potential in me and encouraging me to take all of the great leaps that have gotten us to this point in our lives today. I love you to the moon and back.

CHAPTER ONE

Lucinda Moss had crossed and uncrossed her legs a dozen times in the past thirty minutes. She doodled on the pad in front of her for a moment as Richard Thomas wrapped up his presentation.

"Any questions?"

"Comments, actually." Lucinda, the first woman to be appointed the head of advertising and marketing for Clear View Enterprises, Inc., raised an eyebrow at Richard, making sure he could see her disappointment before she voiced it. She knew that Richard loathed working for a woman, especially one younger than him. He was one of the loudest grumbles when she came into her new position and his lack of preparation for this presentation clearly demonstrated the glaring absence of respect for her intelligence. "This is the same projected plan you had for the Devereux commission last month, isn't it? This client warrants a more aggressive marketing structure to pursue its higher-end consumer population. How will your recycled, passive approach serve an office full of sharks?"

Brian Edgars coughed to her right, flipping through his notes quickly. Undoubtedly checking to see if Lucinda was correct in her criticism of Richard's proposal. He frowned at his notebook, obviously not liking what he found. She liked that Brian was so reliably thorough. He was a generation older than her with years more experience, but he had been one of very few who had embraced without hesitation her promotion and the direction with which she was taking Clear View. She respected Brian's opinion and knew he believed in the structural changes she was implementing. It was nice to have a confidant in a sea of naysayers.

"I think the general scheme would suffice for Levonbaum and Carlyle," Richard answered, narrowing his gaze and focusing just to the right of her eyes, "with a few adjustments of course."

"Why don't you try your final pitch again," Lucinda said, standing abruptly. "Claire will help you iron out whatever details you may need."

The ten other men and women in the room begin to pack up their things as Lucinda's heels clicked closer to the exit of the conference room. She glanced back once to flash a quick smile to a blushing Claire Moseley, just one of a few handpicked employees that she knew would absolutely flourish with the right direction and nurturing. Claire was a little younger than Lucinda, in her late twenties, with shoulder-length auburn hair and a quick wit. Lucinda had quickly promoted the junior executive after observing her dynamic and tenacious interaction with Richard on a particularly challenging client case a few months earlier. What really impressed her about Claire though was the way she handled Richard's intimidation and bullying at the end of the meeting when he thought everyone was out of earshot. As an unseen observer, Lucinda's chest swelled with pride when Claire easily sidestepped his antagonistic comments about her perceived lack of experience with a series of well-volleyed retorts and sarcasm. It was a shame the rest of the marketing execs missed the learning experience.

Lucinda smiled to herself as she walked through the corridor toward her office. She was eager to be done with the Richards of this place: stuck-up, self-consumed, and bigoted little shits left from the old regime.

Her assistant met her at her office door with a hot coffee and a yogurt. Amanda had worked with Lucinda for almost five years, easily transitioning to the increased responsibility with every promotion Lucinda had earned. Without Amanda, Lucinda wasn't sure she could juggle it all—Amanda made sure Lucinda never missed a meeting, a workout, or a paper clip. She placed everything on Lucinda's enormous desk and asked how the morning's meeting went.

"The usual, Amanda. Boring. But thank you for the coffee." Lucinda smiled as she settled into her chair, powering up her laptop. Today was Amanda's first wedding anniversary. Lucinda fondly remembered the first and only time Amanda was late to work—she had floated into the office in a dreamy haze, announcing she had met the love of her life at a bus stop in the rain. It warmed Lucinda's heart to see Amanda still so in love after all this time even if it made her wonder if she would ever find such happiness. "I think I'm all set for the rest of today's meetings, so why don't you take the rest of the day off?"

"Are you sure?"

Lucinda chuckled to herself before opening her bottom left drawer and pulling out a bottle of champagne with a decorative gold ribbon around the neck. "I'm sure. Here, this is for you and Tom. Have a good night, okay?"

Amanda nodded quickly, taking the bottle from Lucinda and forcing a quick hug on her boss. The contact was unexpected, and Lucinda patted her awkwardly before Amanda broke away, thanking her again for the free afternoon.

Lucinda let out a content sigh before returning to the project outlines and photographs of a new client's building specs that were patiently waiting on her desktop for her attention. Hours later, Brian knocked at her door as she began packing up at the end of the day.

"You are mighty popular with some, Miss Moss," he teased gently as he closed the door behind himself, before sitting on one of the chairs in front of her desk. "And not so much with others."

"Can't win 'em all, Edgars," she replied coolly but with a small smile, happy to have a chance to chat with Brian about the meeting earlier. "What's up?"

"I was curious about your pairing of Claire and Richard."

She looked at him expectantly, waiting for him to continue.

"We both know that Richard is an entitled ass, but this client is a relatively big fish and he has much more experience working this type of crowd than Claire does. Aren't you worried that assigning Claire as co-lead will exacerbate the already rocky office dynamics?"

"It's time people get comfortable with the idea that I'm not going to tolerate subpar performance. Claire has more intuition in her pinky finger than Richard has in his whole body. This is a good opportunity for her to flex her muscles and really get involved on a high-priority client. I expect great things from her."

"And this is why you're the new chief. I'm interested to see their final pitch." Brian nodded as he stood slowly, calling behind him as he closed the door, "Have a good night, Lucinda."

Lucinda leaned back in her desk chair, slouching low enough to rest her new Louboutin heels on the expansive oak desk in front of her. The sunset perfectly illuminated the Boston skyline, casting shadows in harmony with deep orange hues, making a beautifully haunting portrait of her metropolitan playground. Her corner office had floor-to-ceiling windows on two of its sides, which, if she stood close enough to the glass, made her feel like she was standing in the sky, not limited by the confines of gravity or her mortality.

As the last sliver of orange slipped beneath the skyline, a memory of Dominic crept into her thoughts. Nothing in particular incited such recollections: sometimes it was a smell, a sound, the texture of a fabric, a perfectly trimmed goatee. Her exchanges with Brian of late brought memories of Dominic to the forefront of her mind. No matter how good a friend Brian had been during these transitional months, she missed her best friend. Dominic's unexpected and sudden death had devastated her in more ways than just derailing her professional dance career. He was the brother she never had, the one who had rescued her from the foster system by teaching her to direct her pain into dance—Dominic had helped Lucinda find an identity. He gave her some stability. He probably saved her life. It was no surprise that she struggled to form relationships with people following his death—both personal and professional ones.

Brian was the closest thing she had to a friend these days, but he was no substitute for Dominic. How badly she wanted to pick up the phone and tell him all about her feisty new junior executive and how much she hated the way Richard sort of made eye contact with her ear when he addressed her. She could almost hear his carefree laugh in response to the conversation she was desperate to have with him. What she would give to have one more moment instead of just a memory.

Her phone rang loudly, catching her off guard.

"Hey, Luce. How are you?"

She could hear the smile in her little sister's voice. "Hi. I'm good. You excited?"

"Yeah, maybe a little nervous too." Connie paused before asking nervously, "You're going to be there, right?" She sounded more concerned about Lucinda actually showing up to the wedding than at the prospect of being married.

"Of course! I wouldn't miss your wedding for anything in the world. I promise." Lucinda's reply was confident but she was less than thrilled at the prospect of dealing with all the emotions this event would likely stir up. Connie and Dominic had been her world for as long as she could remember, and Connie growing up and getting married was never something she thought she would have to experience without Dominic by her side. Life was moving on without him, and she sort of hated it.

"Good. Okay, I have to go do rehearsal stuff, see you soon!"

"Bye, Connie."

Lucinda adjusted her skirt as she stood and closed her laptop, then shuffled the photos into their folders, effectively ending her long day. She frowned as she shrugged on her tailored blazer, realizing that her fridge was empty and thus, nothing was waiting to quell the angry rumble of her stomach when she got home. "Well, takeout it is, I guess," she mumbled to herself as she packed her bag and walked to her office door, glancing back once before flicking off the light and closing the door.

❖

"Ms. Monteiro." Claudette Frost's sneer was as legendary as her love of old money. "I expect better results for the money we are dumping into this ludicrous company."

"Mrs. Frost," Samantha Monteiro replied with her utmost diplomacy, although it was wearing thin, "you need to understand that I can only bring the women to Alec—he has to be the one to make the connection. I can't do it for him."

Alec Frost was a typical wealthy playboy searching for someone to drag to his boring society family dinners: tall, handsome, and filthy rich, but with a hot temper and a propensity for womanizing and hard partying. Finding someone he liked physically wasn't hard: tall, blond, and thin. Most of the women Samantha set him up with were eager for the life of leisure his money promised, but everyone had a breaking point, and his antagonistic nature coupled with his short fuse eventually landed eight crying women in her office.

She frowned, trying to retain her professional timbre. "He has to meet me halfway if he ever expects to get further than a half dozen dates with these girls."

"Really, it's a wonder you came so highly recommended to me," Claudette scoffed. "Obviously, you and Mr. Stanley have been mismanaging Alec's female prospects."

"I understand your frustration, really I do." Samantha turned to address Alec directly, who up until this point was distractedly playing with his phone. "We'll try one more time, Alec, but please, stick to the plan we lay out for you. The system works, but you have to follow the guidelines."

Alec glanced up from his phone. "Maybe if you gave me something to work with, I could actually get somewhere with one of them."

Samantha had reached her quota of insults from this family. "You know what, Alec," she snarled, "why don't you—"

Andrew Stanley appeared in the doorway of her office and interrupted before Samantha had a chance to give them a piece of her mind. "Why don't you let us give you a call next week with another list of ladies and a plan for a mixer meet-and-greet, free of charge."

Claudette stood, smoothing out her Chanel pantsuit and pulling Alec from his slouch to a standing position as she glared at Andrew. "Make this one count." She punctuated her statement with an angry gesture to Andrew and Samantha before she stormed out and dragged her overgrown brat behind her.

It took Samantha a good twenty minutes to calm down after they left. Her leisurely stroll to get coffee next door turned into an hour-long retail therapy trip that did nothing to calm her throbbing head but did result in the acquisition of two lovely pairs of Jimmy Choos and a pair of Prada sunglasses that begged her to take them home. Back at her desk, she contemplated her purchases with satisfaction.

"Samantha?" Her partner's annoyed voice called from his office, echoing through the now-empty conference room separating him from her.

"Yes, Andrew," she replied sweetly, hoping to suppress the building irritation she could sense in his tone.

He leaned against her door frame, half-hidden behind a large box filled with files and papers. "Samantha, seriously, what gives?"

"You'll have to be more specific. I'm obviously involved in a few things here." She motioned over the endless paperwork on her desk.

"You know how important you showing face at the Lundsteins' wedding is—all that hard work, Sam!"

She pulled the box out of his arms and lowered it to the couch by his side. "Honestly, you know how much I hate those things, can't you go in my place? You look so dapper in a suit."

"Of course I look great in a suit," he said, "but that doesn't excuse you from attending. You have to go." He nodded his head as if agreeing with himself, crossing his arms and puffing out his chest.

Samantha knew he was right. Ever since her dramatic breakup with her cheating fiancé and the hush money campaign to keep it from the public eye six months ago, she had been shirking her duties. She needed to show face for the sake of their business or it would flounder, like her unfortunate love life.

"Ugh, fine, I'll consider it."

"Well consider it very seriously, because I already mailed your affirmative reply. You ordered the fish."

"Andrew!" Now it was her turn to scold. "What were you thinking?"

"I was thinking about *you*. And your job, and my job. And how much you need this."

She wanted to argue back for the sake of arguing, but her long day was catching up with her. She leaned wearily against the desk behind her, "Fine. Thank you, Andrew."

He flashed her a bashful smile as he stepped out of the doorway, returning thirty seconds later with a long black dry-cleaner's bag draped over his arm.

"Well, good, because I bought you a new dress for the occasion, and a matching suit for me." He smiled apologetically as he handed her the garment bag.

She didn't know whether to chastise him for his omniscient prediction of her concession or hug him for planning on going with her. She settled for a weary smile and appreciative arm tap as she walked toward the door, flicking off the light and following him to the elevator.

❖

The couch was closer than the bedroom and the wine was closer than last night's leftovers, so both won out in Samantha's fatigue. She eyed the garment bag draped over the arm of her couch. The dress was probably gorgeous, complementing her olive skin, accentuating her curves. Making her beautiful was Andrew's specialty. It was why he was one of her closest friends, and not just her business partner. He was the only reason she had maintained any sort of professional success of late.

As she settled into the couch, swirling the cabernet sauvignon in her wineglass, she glanced down at her briefcase. Inside were the dossiers of two millionaires looking for their perfect mates, begging for her attention, expecting her to make a feast out of crumbs. Samantha and Andrew ran a Boston-based high-end dating service for the blue bloods of the Greater New England area. Many members of the social elite found themselves later in life in search of love, having consistently put their business successes ahead of their personal accomplishments. And one day they—or their elderly parents—realized it was time to start looking for a perfect mate to match their well-manicured lives.

Samantha had become known in the matchmaking industry for taking particularly complex clients who were so regimented in their professional lives that fitting another piece into an already established puzzle was nearly impossible. She had practically run her brand on making the impossible possible. Her business, Perfect Match, Inc., was booming. She and Andrew had a waiting list of up to six months for in-office meetings, with webcam interviews slotted out eight to twelve weeks. She had more head shots, essays, applications, and questionnaires to sort through than she knew what to do with.

Trouble was, she couldn't seem to garner the same type of enthusiasm for the business that she had in the past. She pushed Alec's folder aside, reaching for Sheldyn "Shelly" White's instead with a small smile. Shelly was significantly less outgoing than Alec, average in height and weight, sweet natured and quiet. But nerdy, socially awkward in groups of greater than two people, and she struggled to make conversation around beautiful women.

Alec and Sheldyn were her two biggest clients and polar opposites, remaining single for a few very different reasons—the handsome but self-consumed prince with a violent temper, and the mild-mannered computer genius with crippling social anxiety. Oh, and each with millions upon millions of dollars at their fingertips.

Samantha tossed the file back onto the table, leaned back, and rubbed the bridge of her nose as she reclined on the couch. She rested the wineglass on the table to her right as she slowly pulled off her fake eyelashes and placed them gently on the tabletop. She was done trying to make the impossible possible tonight. It was time to finish her drink and try to sleep, something that for once seemed like it was not far off.

CHAPTER TWO

Samantha smiled sadly as she looked around at the Lundsteins' wedding celebration; it was everything Mrs. Carol Lundstein wanted for her son, and nothing that Nathan, the groom, wanted at all. Even the monogrammed napkins were not his taste, or that of his lovely bride, Constance. They both would have preferred a small, quiet ceremony without the pomp and circumstance of this grand display. Nathan was appeasing his mother, and Constance was dutifully fulfilling the role of obedient daughter-in-law. This was not their party—this was Carol's. But, oh, what a party Carol could throw.

Samantha could tell from the number of seats that this wedding had at least two hundred and fifty guests. It was a five-course feast with expensive wines, champagne flowing freely, and gift bags that would give the Oscars a run for their money. It was all decadence and frills. Breathtaking, really. The reception hall was gorgeous: the lighting, the flowers, the centerpieces, the ice sculptures—all flawless, the best that money could buy.

"Did you really think eighteen months ago that we would be here?" Andrew mused as they made their way to their table. "Soft-spoken son of a self-absorbed mother bred on old money falling for a poor girl from a broken family. It's the stuff fairy tales are made of."

"Honestly? No, never." Samantha remembered the day when this unlikely match was made—a true pairing against all odds. After three months of searching, Nathan had still not found what he was looking for, until a pretty UPS delivery girl literally fell out of the elevator into their office. Nathan had thrown down the head shots he was holding and bolted to the elevator to help her, saving the contents of the box and keeping her from getting hurt.

"He was her knight in shining Brooks Brothers and she was his damsel in an ugly brown uniform," Andrew said as he pulled out Samantha's chair. "You saw it though, you saw that connection and jumped on it. You really do have a talent, Sam."

They were seated off to the right of the dance floor, far enough from the seven-piece band to hear each other speaking. The table had filled in quickly: Samantha and Andrew were accompanied by Constance's best friends from high school and college, Sarah and Franny, a few single friends of Nathan's, a cute married couple that were expecting, and one empty seat to Samantha's right. When the two single guys went to sit, they had fought over the chair next to hers, but she'd cleared her throat in annoyance and shot them each a quick glare. She didn't feel like spending her evening brushing off horny late twentysomethings when just being here was difficult enough.

Andrew excused himself to the restroom—and, Samantha suspected, to troll the cute, rich gay boys—effectively abandoning her at the table. Could the evening get any worse? But her pity party was interrupted by a waiter escorting a woman to the table. And she was positively stunning, tall and blond, in a gorgeous dark blue dress perfectly tailored to her lean build, with matching pumps.

"Right here, Ms. Moss, can I get you something to drink?" He smiled warmly and pulled out the chair next to Samantha for the new guest.

"Champagne please, lots. Thank you." She smiled, her voice sounding smooth and melodious.

The waiter nodded and pushed in her chair, looking expectantly over at Samantha to see if she needed anything as well.

"I'll have the same, thank you." She broke out of her trance, smiling at the waiter before he turned to go.

"How many glasses in are you?" the new woman leaned in and asked playfully.

"Um, this is my second, but I do confess to drinking on the ride here." Samantha paused, adding quickly, "I wasn't driving."

"Ha. So I have some catching up to do. Good to know." She laughed. "Also, glad to hear you abide by the rules of the road. I'm Lucinda, by the way." She extended her hand toward Samantha.

"Hi, I'm Samantha. And I'm so glad you aren't some creepy guy, because you just saved me from having to politely reject that cretin over there." She nodded subtly toward one of Nathan's friends on the far side of the table who was leering at a woman standing by the ice sculpture.

Lucinda laughed as she watched him lick his lips and smooth his eyebrows before standing to stalk the unsuspecting woman. "Glad to help." She smiled and accepted the champagne flute that the waiter brought over, turning in her seat to face Samantha. "Cheers to deflecting unwanted sexual advances from strangers?"

"I'll drink to that." Samantha clinked her glass with Lucinda's before taking a hearty sip, maintaining the eye contact Lucinda had initiated.

Lucinda's bright blue eyes flashed and she winked playfully before asking, "So, what brings you to the misfit table?"

"Misfit table?"

"Yeah, misfits," Lucinda repeated, quirking an eyebrow at Sarah and Franny before standing.

"Ef you, Moss!" Franny snapped before tapping Sarah on the shoulder and pointing to Lucinda.

"Hey, Luce!" Sarah's face lit up and she waved, walking around the table to embrace Lucinda, shortly followed by Franny.

Samantha watched the three obviously long-time friends with interest. People watching was an occupational hazard.

"Hey, girls, how are things?" Lucinda asked, hugging the women and smiling.

"We're good. Franny here has some pre-med boy toy, but she has yet to introduce me to one of his classmates." Sarah rolled her eyes, shoving Franny playfully.

"As if you would even be interested in some bookish nerd," Franny chided.

"Hey, I love a man in uniform." Sarah giggled, looping her arm into Lucinda's. "I mean, scrubs are a uniform, right, Luce?"

"Yeah, I think that counts." Lucinda nodded and looked past her friends to the bride and groom who were making rounds at the tables on the other side of the room. "They're very cute together, huh?"

"Yeah," both Sarah and Franny replied simultaneously with a dreamy air and immediately burst into laughter.

Sarah nudged Franny. "Let's go sign the guest book. See you, Luce." She smiled and hugged Lucinda again before skipping off with Franny toward the reception table.

Lucinda resumed her seat next to Samantha, who could barely contain her amusement. "What?"

"Well, first off," Samantha said, "I'm still trying to get over the fact that you called me a misfit."

"Oh, that? That was more for the oddballs at the other end of the table. I don't know you well enough to call you a misfit. Wait," Lucinda challenged, arching a perfectly plucked eyebrow, "are you offended because it's true?"

"I've been called worse things before, I guess." Samantha smiled and sipped from her flute. Conversing with Lucinda was easy; something about her was warm and welcoming.

"So, how do you know the happy couple?" Lucinda asked.

"I was there when they met," Samantha replied quietly, sipping her drink again.

"That is an understatement," Andrew supplemented from over her shoulder. "Don't you think?"

"Ah, you're back"—Samantha winked at Lucinda before turning back to Andrew—"and surprisingly chatty for someone who abandoned me at the misfit table."

Andrew furrowed his brow in confusion before training his eyes on Lucinda. "Andrew Stanley." He surveyed her curiously. "I know you, don't I?"

"Mmm, it's possible. Lucinda Moss, nice to meet you."

"Uh-oh, don't look now"—Andrew scowled as he looked toward the dance floor—"but it's getting awfully cold in here."

"I should have known that bitch would be here." Samantha's gaze settled on the ash-blond-haired woman approaching their table with a determined stride. She drained the contents of her glass and took a deep breath as though she was preparing herself for a fight.

❖

Lucinda leaned back and watched Samantha closely; stress lines sneaked across her flawless complexion as the woman in question got closer, slowed by another guest attempting to engage her in conversation.

"Well, if it isn't the notorious Miss Match," the woman quipped with a venomously saccharine smirk as she finally approached their table. "What a pleasant surprise. Are you using this opportunity to assess potential prospects for your little dating-game resource pool?"

Lucinda watched as Samantha visibly clenched her jaw before she swallowed the emotion and smiled sweetly.

"Mrs. Frost, how have you been?"

Mrs. Frost quirked an eyebrow, obviously irritated her barbs were so easily cast off. "It's positively lovely that Andrew can be your date at such a wonderful event. I applaud you, Mr. Stanley—everyone loves a supportive gay friend."

Andrew allowed a small smile to break his otherwise masklike expression. "I have always appreciated the particular charm you bring to our interactions, Mrs. Frost." And just like that, the mask returned and Andrew sipped his drink before turning and walking away.

"He's delightful today, isn't he?" Mrs. Frost snarled at Andrew's quick dismissal.

Samantha turned to face the unpleasant woman fully. "I find his company a lot more appealing than that of most others, Claudette. I haven't seen Alec yet today. I suppose he's off somewhere *assessing* for himself?"

As a deep scowl ripped across Claudette Frost's plastic-surgery-altered face, Lucinda cleared her throat and stood from the table.

"Hi, I'm Lucinda Moss, it's a pleasure to meet you." She extended her hand to a surprised Mrs. Frost, who took her hand suspiciously, clearly caught off guard. Lucinda smiled once more and turned her attention back to Samantha.

"Samantha, shall we?" Lucinda asked while stepping between the women and ushering Samantha in the general direction of the guest book.

Samantha smiled and linked her arm with her savior, before nodding curtly back at Mrs. Frost's angry expression. She leaned in and tucked her arm tighter into Lucinda's elbow as she whispered, "That's twice today you saved my life…Who are you?"

Lucinda nudged Samantha in the ribs with her elbow. "I just have a habit of being in the right place at the right time, I guess. It looked like you needed a distraction and I was afraid her face would get stuck like that."

The guest book was adorned with gold script and long flowing ribbons. A quill and ink bottle sat nearby with a wedding planner's assistant policing it to ensure no profane scribbles would mar Carol Lundstein's perfect memory book. The attendant guarding the book looked up and smiled broadly before stepping forward to shake Samantha's hand. "Ms. Monteiro, it's so nice to see you again. Another perfect match, I see—congrats."

"Hey, Lisa, it's good to see you. Has Mrs. Lundstein been nice enough today?" Samantha had recommended Giovanni, her favorite wedding planner, and his team to help manage Mrs. Lundstein's requests.

Lisa looked around quickly. "She had him personally hand count the number of flower petals that were sprinkled in the church after being told by her numerologist that one thousand was the number of luck and fertility or something." She paused and looked at Samantha with a grin. "Giovanni will never forgive you for introducing the happy couple."

Samantha caught Lucinda arching a curious eyebrow at that remark, and she hoped her complexion mostly hid the blush she felt forming under the amused look Lucinda was casting at her. "I'm a matchmaker, it's what I do. I work in the industry of perfect pairings."

Lucinda's smile evolved into a devilish grin. "Ah, Miss Match. I see."

Samantha pulled her arm from Lucinda's and crossed it playfully across her chest, feigning an expression of annoyance. "And just how do you know the happy couple, Ms. Moss?"

The smile on Lucinda's face faltered a little as she contemplated her answer. "She's my—"

"Sister. I'm her sister." Constance O'Malley Lundstein swooped in and wrapped her arms around Lucinda's waist, finishing Lucinda's sentence before kissing her on the cheek. "I'm so glad you made it, Luce."

"Connie, you look beautiful! Spin for me?" Lucinda extended her arm and took Connie's hand, twirling her gently on the spot.

"Sister?" Samantha hadn't known about any female family members—the two older brothers, yes, but no sisters. She frowned slightly at the new information and wondered how it had gone unnoticed.

"Mm-hmm." Connie hummed distractedly as she continued to twirl and dance happily with Lucinda, who was looking equally as distracted and giddy.

Lucinda hugged Constance, whispering something into her ear and kissing her cheek before looking back at her confused tablemate. "Little Connie O'Malley was the biggest pain in the butt any girl could ever ask for." She winked and smiled back at Connie in response to her scoffing noise. "I lived with her family for a while when we were younger," she explained. "They took me in as their own, so—"

"So she's my annoying older sister," Connie said with a nod. "And, Luce, I see you met my fairy godmother, Samantha Monteiro."

"Well, that's a little dramatic, Connie," Samantha replied modestly. "I didn't save you from dropping those boxes. That was all Nathan."

"Well, that's *sorta* true"—Connie reached her hand out to touch Samantha's arm affectionately—"but you made everything else fall into place for me to get to know him, so I am very grateful."

"How has everything been today? Not too much stress, right?"

"Giovanni has been an angel, throwing himself on all the fires before we even notice them. Carol is very pleased, so everything is going pretty well. Have you seen her yet?"

"Not yet, but I'm sure we'll cross paths eventually. Just as long as you two are having fun. Make sure you send that handsome man over for a dance with me at some point tonight, okay?"

"I will—thanks again, Samantha." With tears in her eyes, Connie turned back to Lucinda and reached for her hand before asking, "You'll stay, right? Don't leave without saying good-bye."

"You know I would never leave without dancing with my baby sister," Lucinda replied quietly, and this time Connie let the tears fall as she hugged her sister and waved before heading back to meet up with her groom.

Chapter Three

Lucinda traded gentle barbs and jokes with Samantha at the table until Andrew reappeared in a much more chipper mood. The Frost woman had been dealt with, as he put it. Lucinda actually quite enjoyed his snarky commentary and found herself leaning toward Samantha's plate so she could hear what he had to say.

"I haven't seen Alec yet," he said to Samantha in between bites of his filet mignon, "but I'm sure he's having his way with some pretty girl on the waitstaff." His lip curled in disgust.

Samantha turned in her seat to include Lucinda in the conversation. "Alec is the less-than-charming son of that fabulous woman you met earlier, Claudette Frost."

"So I take it you are in the business of perfect pairings too, Mr. Stanley?" Lucinda asked with a small smile.

"Really, Sam? Really?" Andrew teased. "You used that line on her?"

"That line, as you call it, is part of our marketing slogan," Samantha countered before reaching for her water. "And I didn't use it on her, it came up in conversation."

"It's true. She's got no game," Lucinda said before sipping her champagne and winking at Samantha, who huffed in protest.

Andrew laughed next to her and almost choked on his food. "I love her, Samantha. Can we keep her?"

"I think anything can be negotiated," Lucinda replied with a wink before returning to her own plate.

"So," Andrew asked, "although I am already smitten with the idea of employing you, I ought to inquire, what is it you do, Ms. Moss?"

"Lucinda, is fine, by the way." She smiled back before adding, "I do consultation on marketing and public relations."

Andrew's eyes widened momentarily. "You work for Clear View, that's how I know you."

Samantha turned to face Lucinda, her expression bleak. "You work for Clear View?" Her tone sounded both accusing and hurt.

Lucinda couldn't figure out how a perfectly nice evening was suddenly spiraling into such an uncomfortable exchange. "Yes. Yes, I do." This didn't seem the time to correct Andrew and add that she was a division head.

Samantha removed her napkin from her lap and folded it on the table before she stood and walked toward the bathrooms without another word.

Lucinda shot a look at Andrew. "What's that about?"

He sighed and rubbed his forehead before replying quietly, "Why do you suppose she's upset, Ms. Moss?"

Lucinda didn't appreciate Andrew's tone or the use of her surname. She reached for her champagne, swirling the contents while she thought about his redirected question. Then it dawned on her. Samantha Monteiro and Andrew Stanley—the names clicked. "You were clients of Clear View, weren't you?" She watched for Andrew's reaction.

"You could say that."

"When?"

He looked at her with mild surprise. "Earlier this year. You didn't know?"

Lucinda had a moment of clarity, remembering a case of deep-seated betrayal and an extensive cover-up with confidentiality agreements and payments exchanged. She hadn't worked the case directly, but heard it was handled with kid gloves. The owner of a major company was caught up in a love triangle that would negatively impact her business. She had everything to lose. It was one of the last cases under her predecessor's management before she had been promoted. All she knew was that it had been wrapped up in record time; both parties involved agreed to a settlement and confidentiality agreement. The final number had been high, the business owner bending to sacrifice more than was usual for these cases to bury it quickly.

She put down her glass and was quiet for a moment. The details were fuzzy, but she remembered the perpetrator's name as clearly as the vileness of the betrayal; someone had joked that he was nothing as wholesome as his surname would suggest. "Eric Campbell." Lucinda sighed. "I didn't make the connection."

Before Andrew had a chance to comment any further, Lucinda was up and leaving the table, headed in the direction that Samantha had fled.

❖

Samantha washed her hands and fixed her makeup for the third time since retreating to the bathroom. She was still paying off the immense debt that Eric had inflicted upon her business with his little infidelity. She was still licking her wounds when Andrew had forced her to come here tonight. But she knew he had been right. She had to move on and face whatever was around the corner if she planned on saving her business.

Maybe it was the surprise that Lucinda, someone she actually enjoyed talking to, probably knew all along about her dark little secret, or maybe it was too much champagne, but Samantha couldn't shake the feeling of sadness that swept over her. She hated the tears that threatened to fall. She hated feeling trapped. But mostly, she hated the idea of going back out there.

The door behind her opened and closed quietly as she dug in her purse for her phone. This was as good a time as any to text Andrew and let him know she was going to need a stronger drink than champagne if he expected her to stay. She was typing furiously into the phone when she became aware that there was someone leaning next to her by the sink, watching her silently. The bluest eyes she had ever seen looked back at her, apologetically, in the mirror's reflection. She stopped typing and put her phone back in her purse, glancing up at Lucinda's mirrored reflection once more before turning to go.

"Wait, please."

Samantha pulled her arm away from Lucinda's soft touch around her wrist, but Lucinda resisted gently.

"Samantha, I didn't know. I swear. I didn't know. I've just recently been appointed the head of advertising and marketing. Your case fell under the management of my predecessor. I didn't put two and two together until just now."

Samantha sighed, wanting to believe the earnest expression in front of her. But every bit of anxiety she had about attending this wedding revolved around keeping her own failed relationship and subsequent hush agreement under wraps. Who would ever employ an unlucky-in-love matchmaker? "Lucinda, I can't. I can't let people find out, it would ruin me."

Lucinda nodded, her thumb gently stroking along Samantha's wrist. "I didn't handle the account back then, but now it's part of my job to keep a lid on the story. You can trust that I'll make sure your business stays private."

Lucinda's tone seemed so genuinely empathetic that Samantha's typical defensive reaction was alarmingly delayed. Normally, physical contact when she was angry was a trigger for an outburst, but she felt surprisingly soothed by the soft touch on her arm, even stepping closer.

"Sorry, I have no idea what's wrong with me today."

Lucinda dipped her head to catch Samantha's gaze. "Hey, I don't know you that well or anything about what you've been through, but you seem perfectly fine to me."

"Thanks—congrats on the promotion, by the way."

"Um, thanks? Kind of not the point, but I'll take the praise, I suppose." Lucinda smiled.

"I figure it's only fair since I sort of stormed away from you at the table. I have better manners than that usually."

"Okay, so, you'll come back out there with me? Because that creepy guy is back at our table and he keeps giving me eyes…" Lucinda teased as she gently tugged Samantha's hand toward the door.

Samantha chuckled and rolled her eyes before nodding and allowing Lucinda to guide her out of the safety of the bathroom and back into the events unfolding at the reception.

❖

When they returned to the table, the final dishes had been removed and the bride and groom were about to cut the cake.

"I took the initiative to order more champagne for us—I figured we could use it." Andrew handed each woman a glass. Lucinda nodded and smiled, a silent agreement passing between her and Andrew to agree to move on.

Lucinda watched as multiple photographers and videographers hung from strategically placed furniture to both blend in with the background or scale it for the perfect shot. Samantha smiled and laughed easily next to her, bumping elbows and clinking champagne flutes conspiratorially making comments about the onlookers as they watched the cake cutting and the circus feats unfold in front of them. Connie and Nathan were perfectly polite and no cake was smeared in anyone's face, which was both well received and booed by the slightly inebriated wedding crowd. As the cake was cleared and the music began again, the guests began to trickle back to their seats.

"Hey, I've been meaning to ask," Samantha said to Lucinda. "Why aren't you sitting at the family table with Constance?"

"Why? Are you disappointed in being my tablemate?"

"What? Um, no, I—"

"Relax, I'm just teasing." Lucinda nudged Samantha and replied a little more seriously, "Connie and I are close, but I've never really gotten along with her brothers. We have a complicated relationship."

Complicated was putting it lightly: Lucinda had been a foster child with the O'Malley family from age eleven to seventeen. When Connie's mother died unexpectedly from cancer, Lucinda's placement with the family ended. Connie's brothers resented her addition to the family even though it was temporary but Connie didn't see it that way. Connie had always treated her like she was blood, and that's all that mattered to Lucinda.

"Well, well, Samantha, don't you look lovely?" A tall dark-haired man with a square jaw leaned down and crooned into her ear.

"Alec. How are you?" The distaste must have been evident in her reply, because Lucinda turned and appraised him with suspicion.

Andrew was engaged in conversation with some cute waiter and was oblivious to the exchange.

"Oh, you know me, staying out of trouble." He winked suggestively, making Samantha recoil reflexively. "And who is this stunning lady in blue? You must introduce me."

Of course he would want to meet Lucinda—she was just his type. Samantha was surprised by how much this infuriated her. She cast a quick apologetic glance at Lucinda before speaking tersely. "This is Lucinda Moss. Lucinda, this is Alec Frost."

Lucinda extended her hand to Alec. "I met your mother before. She's charming." Samantha turned her face away to hide her grin.

Alec shook Lucinda's hand and let his gaze drag slowly over her body. "You are positively beautiful in that color. Would you care to dance?"

"We'll see if you can keep up," Lucinda challenged before finishing her champagne and handing the glass to Samantha with a wink as she was pulled to the center of the dance floor.

"I sure hope she isn't swayed by his well rehearsed sweet talk," Andrew sneered from behind Samantha, startling her from her staring. "It would really taint my opinion of her."

"Ugh. I know." She crossed her arms over her chest, turning back to watch the dance floor intently. "Who's the new boy?"

"His name is Ben, he's a Virgo, I'm in love." He laughed and wrapped his arms around his friend's waist, gently resting his chin on her shoulder. "Thanks for coming tonight, Sam. I know it was hard."

"You were right," she murmured quietly before kissing him sweetly on the cheek. "I needed to get out."

"Whoa, are you seeing this?" Andrew shifted, releasing her waist and standing up straight, eyes locked on the dance floor.

A crowd formed a loose circle around Alec and Lucinda. The band was playing a slow song and they moved together in easy harmony. It was obvious that Alec's pedigree included ballroom training, but compared to the way Lucinda moved with such effortless fluidity, he looked like a novice.

Samantha watched as Alec twirled Lucinda, his hand lingering a little too long below her hip, undoubtedly an intentional misplacement. She smiled when Lucinda shifted her hip away from his hand, slowing on the next turn to stop one of the wedding attendants walking by. She whispered something with a smile and nudged the attendant toward the stage. Samantha was impressed by how flawlessly Lucinda resumed her position with Alec in one flowing movement, returning her arm to Alec's back and her hand to his. A curious expression was plastered on Alec's face as they turned around on the dance floor, giving Lucinda an opportunity to wink at Samantha as she mouthed, "Watch this."

The song ended and another started immediately, this one fast and upbeat, the tempo starting at a moderate pace and moving to a fever pitch. The singer cheered out into the crowd and raised her arm, encouraging the guests to get up to their feet. The other dancers on the floor slinked back as this was not a typical wedding song, and many couldn't keep the pace the beat required. Samantha watched as Lucinda flashed a quick smile to Alec and waited for him to initiate the movement. Alec narrowed his eyes, grabbing her more aggressively, and dramatically moved her across the floor. Samantha could tell that his beat was off and that Lucinda was humoring him for a chorus or two before she pushed him away and proceeded to embarrass the hell out of him.

She moved in tight circles around him, shifting away when he reached for her. She turned and dipped to the ferocious tempo of the song, stalking toward him and sliding against him suggestively before slipping away. Samantha marveled at Lucinda's ability to keep Alec's eyes focused on her in frustrated concentration while she maintained a teasing smile plastered on her face. Samantha would have laughed if she hadn't known about Alec's volatile temper—she watched, half concerned, half entranced by the controlled boldness Lucinda displayed. She was like a current of angry water moving around him with natural grace. As the song wound down and her movements slowed to match the music, Samantha watched Lucinda reach for his hand as she forced him to twirl her to a finish. She stepped away from him as the crowd applauded and headed straight toward Samantha, grabbing her champagne flute from the table and taking a quick swig with Alec in close pursuit behind her.

"What was that?" Alec growled behind a false smile as he grabbed Lucinda's arm and pulled her tightly to his chest.

"Keep your hands to yourself next time, Mr. Frost." She shoved off him so quickly and forcefully that he lost his grip on her and stepped back to maintain his balance. She turned and exited the ballroom, heading toward the balcony overlooking the gardens below. Alec stood there for a moment, stunned, before walking in the opposite direction and getting lost in the crowd of onlookers.

Samantha had never seen anyone move like that. She felt her mouth gaping.

"Yeah, that's the look most people get when Lucy dances." Connie placed her arm around Samantha's waist before resting her head on her shoulder.

Samantha reached down and gently squeezed Connie's hand. She opened her mouth to ask a question, but closed it again, not sure what she had meant to inquire about.

"Lucy was a professional dancer for a while. I'd tell you that that was her best performance, but I'd be lying." Connie smiled sadly, looking out at the terrace for her sister. "She's amazing. She doesn't dance as much anymore, so you should feel lucky to have seen it."

"God that was hot. And I am very gay, so good Lord…" Andrew sputtered next to her, interrupting Connie's trance. Nathan joined them, hugging Samantha and Andrew as Samantha watched Connie slip out onto the balcony after Lucinda. She felt in that moment that she should have followed.

❖

Lucinda took a deep breath and leaned against the balcony. This was the picture-perfect location for a wedding: sweeping, flawlessly manicured gardens and acres of gorgeous green lawn with a large, beautiful reception room lit immaculately with the setting sun's glow through the dozens of French doors on the west side of the building.

Everything about today had been perfect; Catherine O'Malley would have been positively ecstatic that her kind and forgiving daughter was marrying a wonderful man. Lucinda missed Catherine on days like these, days filled with memories and hopes for the future, and her heart hurt because she realized Connie must miss her too.

"Hey, Luce, what're you thinking about?" Connie's soft voice brought Lucinda back to the beautiful bride before her, illuminated by the sunset.

"Just you, peanut, thinking about you." She pulled Connie into a hug. "I was thinking about how proud I am of you and how proud your mom would be too."

Connie sniffled and pressed her face against Lucinda's neck, snuggling close and nodding. "Yeah, I miss her."

"I know, me too." Lucinda held her close and kissed the top of her head, gently rocking her in her arms.

"I'm so grateful for the day you came to us, Luce," Connie murmured, letting herself be held by her sister.

Lucinda nodded and took in a deep breath, remembering the day she ended up on the O'Malley doorstep with just four sets of clothes, two pairs of shoes, and a favorite stuffed animal. She had been an undernourished, quiet, fearful, and stoic little girl haunted by nightmares and a heart of pain when she showed up to her fourth foster home in four years. Prior to being fostered by the working class O'Malley family in the South End of Boston, she had been a displaced orphan lost in the system. Keeping a child in the bad economy that plagued Boston at that time was just not something anyone could really do. But what Catherine O'Malley lacked in funds she made up for in love and encouragement; she was the person who initially saw Lucinda's love of dance and placed her in her first class. That class changed her life forever.

"You and your mother were the first real family I ever had," Lucinda said.

"I think about her when I see you dance." Connie leaned back and looked up at Lucinda with sad eyes.

"You know, your mother would chastise us for moping around out here and not enjoying the moment."

Connie looked up with wet eyes. "Will you come back in and dance with me? Just like old times? Before you go?"

"You bet, peanut. Let's wow the crowd."

"You already did that earlier." Connie nudged her sister playfully. "I saw what you did to the Frost kid."

"Ha! You saw that?" Lucinda smirked and looped her arm with Connie's. "He was getting a little too touchy-feely. I needed to prove a point."

"I don't know how well the message was received"—Connie winked—"but his mother didn't look too pleased when I passed her on the way out here."

They weaved their way through the crowd to the dance floor and started to slowly move with the music, laughing and joking just like when they were younger. After a while Connie smiled and looked over Lucinda's shoulder, watching the guests as they began to wind down their evening.

"You know," Connie said, "I think she likes you."

"Hmm, what's that? Who likes me? Franny?" Lucinda twirled them so they had switched positions.

"No, Franny hates you because you always make fun of her," Connie countered. "I meant Samantha."

Lucinda cruised the crowd until she found Samantha standing by their table and talking to a few guests as they walked by. "Well, what's not to like?"

"She's single, you know—I think so, anyway."

"Mm-hmm, single and probably straight, but thanks." Lucinda spun Connie in place before pulling her into a tight hug at the end of the song.

Connie hugged her back and kissed her cheek. "I'm just saying, you should have seen her face when you were dancing. She was captivated."

"Good to know." Lucinda glanced back at Samantha, the other woman's eyes finding her own in that minute. Lucinda smiled and waved.

"Thanks for coming tonight," Connie said.

Lucinda's heart melted a little. "Anything for you. I'm going to find Nathan and head out. Call me when you get back from the honeymoon, okay?"

"Of course. I love you."

"I love you too. Have fun." Lucinda pecked her on the cheek. "And tell Franny, I hate her too."

❖

Samantha let out a tired sigh as the night wound down and the dinner guests began to leave. Quite a few of the social elite were present tonight, many of whom had utilized Andrew and Samantha's services at one time or another. She greeted many happy customers, now couples, and ruffled some little kid's hair. It was a good showing for her professionally and a positive personal uplift as well.

As Samantha and Andrew stood to leave their table, Giovanni wandered over with a happy grin. "Samantha, Andrew, darlings... Thank you for the referral."

"How'd it go?" Andrew asked.

"The mother was a total nightmare control freak," Giovanni said. "That woman is out of her fucking mind."

"See, Giovanni, this is why you're the best," Samantha said. "You handle everyone with such charm and poise."

"Yeah, well, thanks. Business is good, no?"

"Business is booming, yes." Andrew nodded in agreement. "Speaking of which, Miss Monteiro, you ready to retire this old gay of yours? I'm exhausted."

"Mm-hmm. Let's hit the road, I've had enough work for one day." Samantha bid Giovanni good-bye before retrieving her purse from the table. "Let me just run to the ladies' room first. I'll meet you by the valet."

The wait was pleasantly short considering the healthy line filtering out of the reception hall. Samantha washed her hands and checked her makeup one last time, then rummaged through her purse for her phone.

"Leaving without saying good-bye, Ms. Monteiro?"

Every hair stood up on the back of Samantha's neck. It took all her self control not to let the involuntary shudder ripple through her. Just as she was turning to face Claudette, she was interrupted by the perfectly timed Lucinda Moss.

"Mrs. Frost—it was a pleasure meeting you tonight. Please send my thanks to your son for the dance." She smiled and turned, effectively blocking Claudette's response by moving her body and ushering Samantha forward with a hand placed gently at her lower back. "Samantha, I was wondering if I could ask your opinion on something before you leave."

Once they were around the corner and safely out of earshot, Lucinda let out the laugh she was stifling. Samantha shook her head in amazement and reached forward to touch Lucinda's forearm. "How do you do that? I mean, where were you, waiting in the wings?"

"You seem to always be getting yourself in trouble. I just have good timing."

"Yeah, I'll say. Ugh. Thanks. Again."

"Look, if you happen to find yourself in need of any more saving"—Lucinda reached into her purse and pulled out her business card—"feel free to give me a call. I'll see what I can do." She winked, leaning forward to press her lips to Samantha's cheek and squeeze the hand that was on her forearm. "It was a pleasure meeting you, Samantha."

And with that, Lucinda Moss walked out of Samantha's life just as quickly and seamlessly as she had come in.

A few moments later, Andrew stalked up behind her, draping his jacket over her shoulders. "Well, well. A blush on you is a rare thing. To whom do we owe this honor?"

"Hmm? Oh, it's nothing," Samantha replied a little too quickly.

He glanced down at the card in her hand and grunted, "Hmph."

"What?" she asked, adjusting his coat on her shoulders and nudging him in the ribs.

"By the way"—he smiled and waved to the valet as he spoke—"you have lipstick on your cheek."

Chapter Four

In the three weeks since the Lundstein wedding, Sheldyn White had been in Samantha's office four times. Each time she appeared more and more depressed over her inability to find a match. Samantha flipped through a new folder of applicants and tried to find a suitable match for her. She was such a sweet girl, but her anxiety and stress in social situations scared off all the girls she was interested in. And that list was already shorter than she would have liked, because Shelly had eliminated some applicants after reviewing the background checks Logan, Samantha's private investigator, had run.

Shelly had shown some small progress with their individual meetings and seemed to respond well to her, but it had taken a lot of work on her part. She had taken her to a few nice restaurants and walked her through the routine: pull out the chair for the girl, make eye contact with conversation, sip your water, don't chug it. Shelly knew what she had to do—she could recite the rules backward and forward—but she was just so damn anxious! It was infuriating and heartbreaking for Samantha, because she was a real catch and she would find her a great girl, but first she had to get her to relax.

She leaned her elbows on her desk and rested her forehead on her hands as she tried again to clear her mind and think of an alternative solution that might help. Her phone rang, and she reached blindly for it, knocking her Rolodex off the desk along with two or three folders. She cursed quietly and answered.

"Hey, I have to run out and do an errand," Andrew's voice said, "can we rain check lunch today?"

"Yeah, Andrew, that's fine. I think I'm going to get out of the office for lunch and clear my head. I'll be back later, okay?"

"Sure, sounds good. Everything all right?"

"Yeah, it's fine. I'm just banging my head on the desk over this Sheldyn White thing. I think I need a change of scenery."

"I gotcha. Okay, see you in a bit, ciao!"

Samantha hung up the phone and bent over to pick up the papers from the floor. She put the Rolodex back and shuffled the papers into the necessary folders before something caught her eye. She reached for the phone. If only this idea would work.

❖

Lucinda smiled at Claire Moseley's proposal. She was more than pleased with the results of the Richard-Claire pairing on the Levonbaum & Carlyle project. Claire had suggested a new angle for dealing with the client's demands that was fresh and innovative. She'd taken lead on the second pitch attempt and secured the client's final approval, further obliterating Richard's undeveloped original plan. The result of the final contract with Levonbaum & Carlyle had been a huge success and generated a few new referrals from smaller firms that caught the buzz.

Claire was currently tackling a new client working on promoting an innovative brand of software for smartphones. It was a low-stress job with a manageable timeline, but Claire was already way ahead of schedule and had gone above and beyond the client's request in her research. She had a great idea for market research at an upcoming tech conference in the area next month, and she was pitching the proposal to the new client on Friday—the specs she gave Lucinda were fantastic. Claire had really done her homework on this one. Lucinda could see this client being successful and retaining their services on the launch of the product. It would be a big win for Claire and her team and an even bigger win for Clear View. Now, if only she could wrangle Richard Thomas and a few other stragglers to get it together, she would have a lot fewer stress headaches and long nights at the office.

"Lucinda?" Amanda paged through on the office phone. "I was about to go to lunch, but you have a client here in the waiting room."

Lucinda reached for her tablet; she didn't remember having someone scheduled for today. "All right, Amanda, you can head out. Please send the client in."

She stood at her desk, smoothing out her vest and adjusting her feet into her heels. She realized she had locked the door behind her earlier after the morning meeting because she'd felt the need to stretch after last night's vigorous dance class, and the last thing she wanted was to have her receptionist walk in and see her on the floor. She pulled open the frosted glass and oak door to the waiting party.

Samantha Monteiro's smiling face greeted her with a raised eyebrow. "Do you always lock your office door?"

"Samantha, this is a pleasant surprise." She stepped back and extended her arm in gesture for her to enter. "Please, come in, come in."

Samantha looked around the room, taking in the bookcases that matched the large oak desk. "Your office is incredible, the view is amazing." She wandered over to the floor-to-ceiling windows and looked out at the skyline, letting her fingers lightly dance on the glass.

Lucinda closed the door and took a quiet moment to appreciate the way Samantha was dressed in a tight black pencil skirt and light purple blouse under a matching black blazer, her back to Lucinda in this moment. She was speaking more to Samantha's perfect curves than anything else when she replied, "Yeah, it is a great view, isn't it?"

Lucinda's line of sight settled at a more appropriate level by the time Samantha turned around and they smiled at each other.

"How do you get any work done? I would just stare out my window all day long."

"Some days are harder than others. I had blinds put in to combat the gray and the rain. I find those days to be the hardest—it's so damn gloomy when two of your walls are weather dependent."

Lucinda leaned against her desk, crossing her ankles in front of her as she waited for Samantha to explain why she was here, not that she minded at all.

"I feel like I should come clean." Samantha traced her fingers over the back of the leather chair in front of her, looking shy. "I sort of sweet-talked your receptionist into letting me wait for you. She put up a good fight, but I have my ways."

"I was wondering how I had an unplanned lunch meeting... tricky, tricky." Lucinda waved her index finger at Samantha. "So, to what do I owe this pleasure?"

"I would say I was in the neighborhood, but that's sort of a lie. I came to ask a favor."

"Does this favor include lunch?" Lucinda replied with a sly smile. "Because I'm starving."

Samantha beamed. "Yes, actually. I think I owe you at least that much. Can I take you to lunch?"

Lucinda smiled as she held open the door for Samantha.

"So, where do you want to go?" Samantha asked as the elevator started its descent. "I'm not sure what's around here."

Lucinda hadn't had a social lunch in months. She did frequent a few restaurants for working lunches, but they were all very formal and stuffy. "How do you feel about sushi?"

"Sounds great. I love fish." Samantha grinned.

"Good to know." Lucinda added with her eyebrow raised as she held open the elevator door for Samantha. "How's Andrew?"

"He's good. He went out with one of the waiters from the wedding the other night—Ben, I think, was his name."

Lucinda nodded and led Samantha to the door of a small restaurant tucked out of sight around the corner from her office. "This place is cute, it's small, but I think you'll like it."

"I'm sure it's perfect."

They settled into a booth in the corner and ordered some food, Lucinda requesting some warm green tea to start. The waitress brought their tea and told them the meal would be there shortly. Lucinda smiled and nodded before pouring each of them a small cup.

"So," she hedged, "what brings you by?"

"Yeah, about that, I was coming to ask for a favor," Samantha replied shyly.

"A favor, huh?" Lucinda leaned back. "Are we at the point in our relationship where we give each other favors yet?"

Samantha flushed and cleared her throat. "Listen, I'm totally stumped here and I need some help." She leaned forward, tracing the outline of her place setting with her free hand. "I was hoping maybe you could be my savior again, once more."

Lucinda considered this a moment; coming to Samantha's aid at the wedding had been mostly about being in the right place at the right time. Mostly. Although if she were being honest with herself, she had made it a point to keep a watchful eye on Samantha after their initial introduction at the table. She was fascinated by this matchmaker—beautiful and poised, effortlessly social, and encouraging without being condescending. It seemed that everyone that crossed Samantha's path was happy to see her. She had a warmth that resonated with Lucinda. And she was gorgeous. That helped.

Lucinda watched Samantha's hand slowly making circles and tapping her fingers gently on the smooth surface. She settled into her chair and crossed her legs, slowly sipping her tea. "All right, I'm intrigued, what did you have in mind?"

"I have this client. She's great, sweet and gentle, but she suffers from terrible anxiety. Every time I get her in a room with a pretty girl, she freaks out. Spills her drink, stutters, just shuts down. She's been in my case file for months, but I haven't made much headway." She took a sip of her tea. "I've tried getting her into relaxation classes, on prescription meds, hypnosis, everything. I'm just stumped."

Lucinda nodded, listening patiently. Samantha had such a soothing tone to her voice, like honey. She waited before speaking, but when Samantha didn't continue she asked, slightly confused, "What is it you wanted me to help you with?"

"I was hoping you would spend some time with her."

Lucinda laughed, startling her lunch partner. "Samantha Monteiro, did you just indirectly call me ugly?"

"What? No! No, far from it! I mean, that's not what I meant to say at all." Samantha backtracked furiously. "I was hoping you would teach her to dance."

"Dance? You want me to teach her to dance?"

"I feel like she needs confidence and grace—God, she could use some gracefulness. I saw the way you dance. I asked around a bit, and I think you could help her. She just needs someone to take the time with her, you know?"

Lucinda couldn't suppress the wide grin that spread over her face, "You asked around about me?"

"Yes, Lucinda. I like to do my homework before putting myself out there for potentially embarrassing interactions."

Lucinda smiled, smaller this time. "Well then, I'm sure you found out that I don't do private lessons anymore."

Samantha pouted slightly, nodding her head before adding, "Well, that's why I was hoping to ask for a *favor*. Do you think you could make an exception just this once?"

Lucinda focused on Samantha's perfect pouty lips. She reminded herself of why she got out of the private dance business: creepy couples trying to recruit her for threesomes, inappropriate touching by her clients, dislike of being alone during such intimate activities. So many other reasons circled around her head, but she was drawn back to the pleading face in front of her, drawn to the nervously moistened lips as she watched Samantha sip her tea while she waited. She considered Samantha's word choice; maybe Samantha owing her a favor in return wouldn't be all that bad.

"All right."

"All right?" Samantha sounded surprised, like the answer came too easily.

"Yes, all right, but we have to set up some ground rules."

"Anything." Samantha let out a sigh of relief. "What are your terms?"

"Well, first off, you must be present for the initial sessions. I'm not going to be alone with this girl only to find out she has some weird dancer fetish you don't know about."

"Okay, that's fair."

"Also, the lessons have to happen at my studio, after I have completed my other classes, when I have time in my schedule."

"You have a dance studio?"

"I do. I like to keep active and it helps me clear my head. We host classes most nights of the week and have free dance training for neighborhood children on the weekend and in the summer. So, like I said, only at my studio and when I have time in my schedule, okay?"

"Okay, done. What else?"

"If at any point I feel uncomfortable or she is no longer making progress, I can terminate my involvement and recommend a different, less amazing, but completely competent instructor."

Samantha laughed at her lack of modesty, appreciating that she was being a good sport about this. "Those terms are perfectly agreeable."

"And one last thing." Lucinda flashed her that same wicked grin from the wedding a few weeks ago.

Samantha leaned back and crossed her arms, a smile on her face as she drawled, "Yes?"

"You have to come with me to a fundraiser event next weekend and act like you're enjoying yourself." Lucinda sipped her tea, keeping her eyes on Samantha, watching her mull over the request.

The idea of spending one-on-one time with Lucinda was exciting. This could be very fun. What did she have to lose?

"All right"—Samantha reached her hand out to Lucinda—"deal."

Lucinda shook her hand firmly, leaning back and recrossing her legs.

The food arrived shortly after and they fell into easy conversation about nothing, laughing and joking as they traded food and poked at the decorative radish flowers on the plates.

"So, are you seeing anyone these days?" Samantha asked quietly, letting her gaze settle on the surprised face in front of her.

"No. Actually, I'm not." She chose a salmon roll from the sushi and countered, "Are you?"

Samantha resisted the urge to roll her eyes—the idea of dating was horrifying. But for some reason, she didn't mind Lucinda asking. In fact, she liked being able to announce her single status to her newfound friend. Talking to her was easy.

"No. For the time being I'm avoiding all romantic interactions that are not work related."

Lucinda nodded and looked toward the window of the restaurant. "I can appreciate that."

"Speaking of which…you know, I'd be more than happy to put you in the system and see what turns up if you wanted."

"Ha! You're going to find me a perfect match, huh, Ms. Monteiro?"

"Well, I can always try." Samantha pointed her chopstick at Lucinda before gambling on her next statement. "We have an extensive portfolio of lovely ladies looking for their mates."

Lucinda choked on her tea, coughing into her hand while trying to gain composure. "Huh. People sometimes assume I'm straight. What gave me away?"

Samantha covered her giggle with her hand before adding, "I told you, I have an eye for detail. The way you always hold the door for me, the tone you use when speaking with women versus men. Also, I saw you checking out my ass in the reflection in the glass at your office."

Now it was Lucinda's turn to blush. She shrugged and looked up at chocolate eyes, "I told you it was a beautiful view."

❖

Samantha was still smiling when she returned to her office twenty minutes later. Lucinda Moss was charming and funny and beautiful, and Samantha thoroughly enjoyed her conversation style.

"You're awfully chipper. How was lunch?" Andrew leaned into her doorway, watching her hum to herself lightly as she moved things around her desk.

"God! Andrew! You scared me." She brought her hand to her chest and sat heavily in her seat.

"Well?"

"Well, what?"

"How. Was. Lunch?"

"Umm, fine," Samantha answered as she flipped open the laptop. "Why?"

"You were smiling like a buffoon when I got here and humming quietly to yourself, so did you have a date or something?" He slinked into the room and sat at the edge of her couch, leaning forward excitedly.

"A date? No."

"Omigod." He pointed his finger at her, his eyebrows lifting to his hairline. "You got laid."

"Andrew, please." She frowned. "I'm happy because I think I figured out a solution for our friend Sheldyn White."

"Oh." Andrew sat down properly on the couch, clearly disappointed. "Well, what did you figure out?"

"We just need to focus some of that nervous energy into something Sheldyn will enjoy and find useful at the same time. I had lunch with Lucinda Moss and—"

"Aha!" Andrew exclaimed, jumping off the couch and pumping his arms in triumph. "I knew it."

"Knew what?" Samantha glared back at him.

"You like her. I knew it." He did his impression of an end-zone dance in his pristine Tom Ford pants.

"Andrew, focus," she chastised. "I'm trying to tell you I think I can fix our problem."

"And just how is Lucinda Moss going to fix our problem with Ms. Afraid of Her Own Shadow?" Andrew challenged, crossing his arms and flopping back onto the couch like a disciplined child.

"She is going to give her private dance lessons."

Andrew crossed one leg over the other. "Is she giving you private dance lessons too?"

"Huh, what? No. Why do I need dance lessons?"

"Because"—he smiled smugly—"I have a feeling you would take anything she had to offer."

"Andrew." Her tone was a warning, but she couldn't stifle the flush she felt rising to her cheeks.

"Oh please, Sam. You two spent the whole night of the wedding making eyes at each other."

"First off, you are completely delusional. Secondly, I like men, remember? And thirdly, this is strictly for the betterment of our business."

"Uh-huh." Andrew rested his chin in his hand. "It wouldn't be the first time you dabbled, remember Adriana and cheer camp? How about the first three years of college?"

Samantha swallowed hard and averted her eyes.

"Yeah, I thought so." Andrew stood to leave. "You think she's hot. Because she is. So good for you," he called over his shoulder, closing the door behind him as he left.

Chapter Five

G reat class ladies!" Lucinda encouraged her students. "Next week we try something different."

The women filed out slowly and Lucinda ran a quick broom over the floor, smoothing out the surface and picking up any loose debris. This night had been more fun than usual; she had a good group of ladies that really challenged her to choreograph fun exercises. They spent most of today polishing their routine, so it had been a relatively easy night for her. She patted dry her forehead and checked her makeup again in the mirror. Tonight she was meeting Sheldyn White and seeing Samantha again. *She was seeing Samantha again.* The thought made her smile.

They had talked twice over the phone since their lunch, coordinating their schedules and making sure the studio would be available. Tonight she would assess the situation and determine if dance could indeed help this poor soul. Lucinda rolled her neck and stretched her arms over her head before reaching to the side, stretching her obliques and loosening her lats. She took a quiet moment to lean forward on the barre before getting *en pointe* and slowly winding herself into a controlled spin. She let her mind wander as her body went through the familiar motions. Dancing had been her escape from the harsh reality of her life growing up. It soothed her. Even though she eventually got into the professional competition circuit with Dominic, her stance remained the same: she danced for herself, she danced for the feeling. She did not dance for some dollar-store plastic trophy and bad lighting.

Her ankle clicked painlessly as she shifted position into another slow stretch. Years ago, she had taken a bad spill after a particularly arduous workout in prep for a competition. She had partially torn a few ligaments in her ankle and foot that required her to be immobilized in a boot. The follow-up with the doctor had been positive, but he warned her there was bone bruising that needed to be watched closely; although the ligaments eventually healed, her ankle still clicked from time to time.

She often wondered how some wounds could heal so seemingly completely. The click was a reminder, like a scar—it was a reminder of her mortality, a reminder that there had once been pain and loss, but she had moved on. Lucinda often considered that when she had to overcome other obstacles. Losses. Pain. The body healed, that's what it was made to do—bend, break, rebuild. She wasn't so sure about the heart though. The heart was so much more fragile than the bones she danced on. Bones were strong and protected all the organs they enclosed, bones were walls. But what protected the wounded heart? Would the heart ever heal from all the pain life inflicted? Did that feeling of loss ever go away? Or would she scar over, her heart clicking like her ankle, reminding her that it had been rebuilt but was forever changed? She considered whether this scarred, changed heart would ever beat as vibrantly as it had before she had known such pain. But then again, she wasn't sure she knew a life without it.

"Where did you go, just then?" Samantha Monteiro's voice played like music to Lucinda's ears as she opened her eyes from her stretch. The smile was automatic.

"Just enjoying the moment…stretching is very relaxing for me," she replied quietly, turning and leaning against the barre to face her guest. "You look nice."

"Oh, thanks." Samantha blushed.

"Where's your client?"

"She's on her way, I'm early. I just wanted to make sure you had everything all set."

Lucinda stepped forward and spread her arms out wide. "Just me, the barre, and the floor, ready and waiting."

"Well, let me tell you a little about our friend." Samantha crossed the floor, dropping her purse by the bench in the back before walking slowly back to Lucinda in the middle of the room, her heels clicking with a loud echo on the perfect hardwood floors.

"No, thank you. No preconceptions. The less I know the better, because then I can hone in on her physical responses to movement. I don't need to know what makes her tick beyond that." Lucinda saw that the quiet confidence of her words halted Samantha a few feet away. She watched Samantha's face, choosing her next words carefully.

"Let me show you," Lucinda said. "Let me show you what I mean." She took Samantha's left hand in her right, stepping closer and guiding Samantha's other hand to her waist, holding her hand in place with her own.

"Just relax. Move with me. Let me lead."

She spoke quietly, letting her gaze meet Samantha's. She had such beautiful brown eyes; Lucinda let herself get lost in them as she moved in a gentle circle on the floor. She felt Samantha's tense stance start to loosen as she slowly turned them, melting even more as she slid her hand off Samantha's and pressed it hesitantly to her lower back.

Samantha broke eye contact and blushed, looking over Lucinda's shoulder and tucking her chin as Lucinda pressed her palm flat against her back, repositioning the gentle grip she had with her right hand. She smiled as she felt Samantha take a short, almost inaudible breath. She held them close like this, moving slowly as she listened to Samantha's breathing, occasionally feeling the ghost of that breath across her collarbone. Lucinda liked the feeling of having Samantha this close. She fit perfectly in her arms, moved so well with her.

Lucinda stepped to the side, hooking her arm behind Samantha's back and pressing her weight into her hands, turning her slowly and dipping her backward. Time slowed to a stop as she held Samantha in extension, letting her eyes trace the contours of Samantha's jaw and perfectly tanned neck. She didn't realize at what point she'd started humming but when Samantha looked into her eyes, she stuttered the tune to a halt. She smiled at the embarrassed dimple Samantha was flashing and pulled her back up, easing her close again before twirling her gently on the spot. She let her hands slide slowly down Samantha's arms before lightly clasping their hands together, keeping her gaze intently locked with her dance partner's. She was reading her, feeling her, seeing her up close.

"That moment, when you feel free," Lucinda said softly, "when you don't think, you just move and react…that's the moment I wait for, that's the moment I need to see, to feel. That moment tells you everything."

Samantha nodded subtly, her fingers curling gently in Lucinda's palms as she dropped her gaze to their hands.

"I think your client is here," Lucinda whispered, threading her fingers between Samantha's for a moment before squeezing gently, releasing their hands, and stepping back, increasing the space between them and nodding toward the door.

❖

When Lucinda had calmly told her that she didn't want any background information on Shelly, her first instinct was to object— after all, she knew Shelly the best of the two of them. But the self-assurance of her statement stopped Samantha in her tracks. It was oddly refreshing to be gently commanded. She found herself watching Lucinda's movements as though she was some fragile piece of art, paying close attention to the details of her breathing, the way her collarbone moved as she spoke. She was drawn to her. It seemed like a perfectly normal occurrence for Lucinda to reach out and touch her, pull her into such an intimate position, and lead.

She found herself hanging on Lucinda's every word. Lucinda spoke softly, with clear meaning. She did not wax poetic about dance; she just lived it. When her hand settled comfortably on Samantha's hip, it felt like a natural extension of herself, like it was made to rest there, to guide her. And when Lucinda shifted her weight into their joined hands and dipped Samantha back, her heart raced. The closeness of their position, Lucinda's eyes intently tracing her face—it was exciting to be so closely admired. The look in Lucinda's eye was one that she was familiar with, one that she looked for when matching her clients. She was sure of it: Lucinda was attracted to her. What surprised her was she felt the same thing for Lucinda.

When Lucinda started to hum, seemingly absentmindedly, Samantha thought she might faint. Lucinda cradled her in position, a firm and confident hand at her lower back, controlling every tiny movement. It was intoxicating. She had seen the small smile on Lucinda's perfect mouth when she had involuntarily gasped as they first started dancing—she knew she was staring at those same lips while Lucinda hummed. It was reflexive; she couldn't help herself if she tried.

When Lucinda noticed her gaze and stopped humming, a part of Samantha mourned the loss of the melodious sound. After a brief pause, she was brought upright. Thankfully though, she was held close. A little more time this close wasn't so bad, right?

When Lucinda spoke, Samantha was frozen in her spot, her hands lightly clasped with Lucinda's, feeling far too out of breath for the amount of activity they had just done. She understood what Lucinda meant before, she could feel it. She was listening to her body, feeling the way she moved with her hands and hips. Lucinda was reading her body language as fluently as if it were the only tongue she knew.

And just like that, it was over. Lucinda gently squeezed her hands and stepped away as Shelly came into the studio and broke their trance. Samantha had never been so disappointed about someone's punctuality than she was in that moment.

Lucinda Moss could tell from across the room that Sheldyn White was a heartbreaker in the rough. She was a petite five foot four and thin, with soft, wavy brown hair. She wore dark-rimmed glasses and fidgeted nervously by the door, waiting for her arrival to be noticed. Her clothes fit well but were wrinkled, and she scuffed her shoe nervously on the floor as Samantha introduced them. Lucinda was going to like this woman, she could tell, but she could also tell she would be a little work.

"Hello, Ms. Moss, it's nice to meet you." Her eyes darted frantically across Lucinda's face as she extended her hand.

"Ms. White, may I call you Sheldyn?" she asked quietly, using her tone to sooth her nerves.

Sheldyn's beautiful green eyes stopped their nervous movement and she looked at Lucinda fully. She nodded. "Shelly. I prefer Shelly."

"Good, well, let's start by you calling me Lucinda."

"Hi, Lucinda, nice to meet you." She glanced over at Samantha for approval. She nodded and smiled, and Shelly appeared to relax infinitesimally.

"So, Shelly, I hear we have some work ahead of us. Have you ever danced before?"

"Um, like in a class? No."

"Okay. Well, let's get you out of that heavy coat and see what we can do. Ready?"

She looked over at Samantha again, like a child waiting for approval from her parent. Lucinda walked toward the surround sound system in the corner and watched their interaction in the glass. Samantha smiled warmly and whispered something quietly to Shelly that made her smile. Lucinda selected basic ballroom music, turned the volume up so it was a little more than background noise, and walked back to her clients, nodding to Samantha as she passed her.

Samantha leaned against the wall and observed. She couldn't help the smile that felt like it was permanently etched on her face. Her cheeks were beginning to actually hurt. Lucinda had weaseled her way under Shelly's defenses and around her anxiety. They were facing each other, hands in position, and moving slowly, a few steps left then right, forward then back. Lucinda was actually getting Shelly to laugh and make eye contact. She hadn't stuttered in fifteen minutes. She only stepped on Lucinda's foot twice, and from what Samantha could see, she was beaming. Her favorite part was definitely when Lucinda taught Shelly how to twirl her.

She would demonstrate herself first, then tentatively take Shelly's hand and guide her through it. After a few tries Lucinda coached Shelly on where to put her other hand, to lightly graze Lucinda's body: back to abdomen to back. Shelly was obviously nervous at first. She started to move with a blocky, uncoordinated movement and pulled her eyes from Lucinda's. She finished the spin herself and stepped back into position with her, saying something quietly that snapped her eyes up to Lucinda's again. Lucinda nodded slowly, cleared her throat, and started to hum.

Samantha was amazed at what happened next: Lucinda danced with Shelly, one whole dance, no missteps, no misplaced hands, and she got her to spin her with near perfect accuracy from the start to finish of one song. When they separated, Lucinda glowed and congratulated Shelly: she patted her shoulder, made direct eye contact and smiled, uttered calm but encouraging words, her hand squeezing hers…and Shelly didn't flinch. She just smiled and blushed and shook her head in disbelief. She had successfully danced with a beautiful woman and not hurt her, spilled anything on her, or embarrassed herself. Pride poured off Shelly, and Samantha couldn't have been happier.

And yet, she felt oddly jealous at the same time. She felt a yearning to feel the positive physical reinforcement that Lucinda so freely gave to Shelly. The envy was unexpected and she quickly tried to stifle the emotion. She wasn't quite sure what was coming over her.

They all met in the middle of the room and compared schedules for the following week. Shelly was significantly more relaxed but tensed visibly when out of physical contact with Lucinda. Samantha noted that everyone seemed a little more at ease under Lucinda's touch, herself included.

Shelly excused herself but not before stuttering a grateful good-bye to Lucinda, who graciously accepted and nodded her head lightly.

Lucinda walked to the stereo, shutting off the music and reaching for her bag as Samantha attempted to shrug on her overcoat.

"That went fantastically well, don't you think?" Samantha called out, struggling to get her arm in the sleeve of her jacket.

"Yeah, she's great." Lucinda smiled and nodded, walking toward Samantha.

"Well, you were great, she was a good listener." Samantha corrected playfully.

"Let me help you before you hurt yourself." Long pale fingers closed around Samantha's wrist, gently pulling down the sleeve of her coat.

Samantha fussed with her scarf and a few buttons until warm hands closed upon hers and gently brushed them away. Lucinda kept her gaze while she slowly tucked Samantha's scarf beneath the flap of her overcoat, buttoning each button with care, only breaking their eye contact when she reached the last one. She reached up and smoothed out the scarf as it lay beneath the collar of the coat, the warmth radiating off her hand like fire along Samantha's jaw. Samantha blinked her eyes closed, took a deep breath.

"I'll call you about this weekend. We're still on, right?" Lucinda practically whispered the words, as she forced herself to step back and remove her hands from Samantha. She wanted to touch her face, she wanted to kiss her lips, and she had a feeling that she could, but it didn't feel right, not yet.

"Yes, of course," Samantha replied quickly, maybe too quickly. "We made a deal."

Lucinda felt her face light up as she stepped toward the door and motioned for Samantha to join her. She shut off the light and locked the studio before they exited to the street. "Do you need a ride? Or…?" Lucinda looked around the busy street before them.

"I'm all set," Samantha replied. "I'll hail a cab. I don't live far from here."

"Hmm, good to know."

Samantha reached out and touched Lucinda's forearm. "Thanks again for tonight. I'll talk to you soon."

Chapter Six

A ndrew, it's not a date." Samantha grunted in frustration. "I'm her guest at a fund-raiser, that's all."

"Whatever, Sam. You called me to help pick out an outfit, not the other way around."

"That doesn't even make sense. Why would you ask for my help with an outfit?"

"Well, if I was going on a date and I felt insecure, then maybe I would." He smirked and dodged the pillow she threw at his head. "You know, I think this is good for you, dating again, I mean," Andrew added as he reclined on her bed, examining his fingernails in the light.

"Andrew, for the last time…Oh yeah, this is it," Samantha mumbled to herself, the angry sound of hangers sliding across metal suddenly halting. She turned around with a huge grin on her face, holding up a purple satin dress and matching pumps.

"Oh, my." Andrew grinned like an idiot. "First you dazzle in red and then you stun in purple? This is a situation now."

"What? I can't help it if I happen to have the perfect complexion for such vibrant color palettes." Samantha winked. "I look great in purple."

"I know. I bought you that dress and those heels. You are welcome, again, by the way. Maybe I should dress you for every occasion that you spend with Miss Moss."

He hopped off the bed and snatched the dress from her hands to hide behind it.

"Andrew!" She laughed and swiped at him. "Stop fooling around and help me pick out some earrings."

"Now we're talking, bring on the bling!" He hung her dress on the door to the closet before prancing to the jewelry on her dresser.

Samantha knew she was lucky to have such a good friend who just so happened to have great taste. Having him with her to quell some of her nerves over tonight was a blessing…and a curse, because she was nervous and he knew it.

Lucinda pulled in front of Samantha's apartment building and laughed to herself. Samantha lived a few streets off the main strip of downtown Boston, in a towering building with lots of windows and a perfect view of the Commons. Everything she could ever possibly need was within walking distance. She was in the hub of the city, a stark contrast to Lucinda's residence in the quiet suburban part of the city. A doorman quickly jogged to Lucinda's driver's side to valet her car. He was older, very handsome, and smiling broadly as he took in her sparkly midnight-blue 1970 Dodge Challenger, complete with a white racing stripe up the middle and black leather interior.

"Wow, nice car! You must be Ms. Moss, no?"

"That I am," she affirmed as he helped her out of the car. "And you are?"

"Mario," he replied with a nod of his head and a gentle shake of her hand. "I'm the doorman for Ms. Monteiro. She told me you would be arriving."

"Well, I'm pleased to meet you, although I'm not used to having warnings sent out about my arrival," she joked with him as he led her through the massive glass doors of the building.

"Ah yes, well, she wanted me to let you know she would be right down. Please make yourself comfortable." He gestured to the ornate seating area in the lobby, as the phone rang at the desk behind them. "Excuse me…" He indicated to the phone and she nodded.

Lucinda was walking toward the couch when the ding of an elevator caught her attention. She turned toward the noise and caught her breath. Samantha stepped through the doors and into the lobby. She was positively gorgeous in an off-the-shoulder purple dress and sky-high heels. She was checking her phone and adjusting her shawl when she looked up and caught Lucinda staring. Lucinda probably should have looked away, but she couldn't. She just smiled and raised an eyebrow. Samantha was dressed to kill tonight and Lucinda couldn't be happier.

"Hey," Samantha purred as she stepped toward Lucinda, "you look great." Samantha's gaze traveled over Lucinda's black dress and pumps. Lucinda was glad she'd decided on the smoky eye tonight with a hint of dark blue glitter. Samantha's eyes lingered on Lucinda's lips before connecting with her gaze.

"Thank you," Lucinda replied with a smile. "You look fantastic in purple." She stepped forward and kissed Samantha's cheek. "Are you ready to be bored out of your mind?"

Samantha blushed as Lucinda pulled back, keeping her hand resting lightly at her hip. "I was told to pretend to have fun the entire time and I am totally prepared." She flashed a bright, cheesy smile.

"Perfect. Shall we?" Lucinda turned and offered her elbow to Samantha, who hooked her arm into it easily and rested her hand on Lucinda's forearm. The ease of their contact now made Lucinda's heartbeat pick up.

Mario hung up the phone and motioned for another man, younger but dressed in the same uniform and hat. The two men held the doors for Lucinda and Samantha and rushed to open the driver's and passenger's doors. Samantha turned to look at Lucinda before whispering, "This is your car? Seriously?"

Lucinda smiled and winked as she patted Samantha's hand that clasped her forearm before walking toward Mario. She loved the reaction she got from women when they saw her pull up in the muscle car. Once she and Samantha were seated in the car, doors closed, Lucinda shifted in her seat to face Samantha with a sly smile. "Whatsamatter? Not your style?"

Samantha scrunched her face. "I didn't say that, it just surprised me is all."

"Well," Lucinda challenged, "what kind of car did you think I'd drive?"

"I hadn't given it much thought." Samantha chewed her bottom lip while she glanced around the car. "Maybe something black and sleek, something mysterious."

"This isn't mysterious enough for you?" Lucinda started the car and shifted into first gear, revving the engine before pulling away from the curb.

"Actually, it's extremely mysterious, and intriguing, and..." Samantha focused on Lucinda's right hand shifting and left foot pressing down on the clutch as they cruised down the street. "Wait, is this car a manual?"

"Yes, it is. Classic car, classic engine." It was completely refurbished, the interior revamped and modern, the black leather interior embroidered with dark blue stitching and equipped with a stereo system fit for a dancer's taste in fast, loud music. "I sort of inherited this car."

Samantha traced the smooth lines of the dash, feeling the vibrations of the engine through the warm surface. "How do you do that?"

"Hmm? Do what?" Lucinda replied as she put her blinker on and slowed the car into the turn.

"Drive in heels."

"I was a dancer. I can do everything in heels." Lucinda smiled. "I'm not one to let inconvenient footwear mar a good time. You learn to forget about them."

"You still are a dancer," Samantha supplied quietly. "You still are."

A lopsided grin appeared on Lucinda's face as she surveyed her passenger with a raised eyebrow. "Of sorts, I guess...." Her voice trailed off as she turned her attention to the road.

Samantha let her gaze settle on Lucinda's ivory complexion. Pain etched her features.

They drove in amicable silence for a few moments and Samantha let her nerves settle into the comfortable leather seats. She broke the silence first. "So, tell me about this extravaganza we're going to."

"Ha. Well that's generous of you. It's a fundraiser for the aquarium."

"Are you a regular contributor?"

"Me? Not particularly." She flashed an impish grin before adding, "Mostly I just love fish."

Samantha felt the blush creep across her face as she coughed out a nervous laugh, waiting for Lucinda to elaborate.

"A close family friend is speaking tonight. I try to come and support him as often as I can. Plus, I love when the aquarium is closed to the public. Walking around it at night in near darkness feels magical to me."

Samantha could see the draw of quiet, unobstructed viewing, how it would feel positively otherworldly. "I like that way of thinking. That sounds tranquil. And romantic."

Lucinda pulled up to the building and put the car in neutral, letting it idle for the valet before facing Samantha fully. "I really appreciate you coming tonight. You know, I would have helped you with Shelly even if you'd refused, right?"

"I was hoping, but I'm glad you asked me to come." Samantha ducked away from Lucinda's scrutiny as the valet opened the car door.

❖

The function room was simply and beautifully decorated in off-white with modern angles and reflective stainless-steel encased pieces of the ocean's floor on exhibit throughout the large open space. The rectangular room held seating that fanned toward a stage; waiters wandered around with beverages and appetizers. A long table with pamphlets and gift baskets ran along the east wall, manned by attractive men and women in matching uniforms, likely representing the aquarium. A projection screen stood in the middle of the center stage with a podium set off to the right. The lights were dimly lit and bright blues and greens reflected off the walls displaying pictures of ocean life. A gently swirling image ran across the projection screen like a screensaver, broken up periodically by photographs of scientific explorations and live-action images of water samples in slides under microscopes. Samantha found herself smiling as she appreciated the murmur of voices around her, talking excitedly about the upcoming presentation.

Lucinda led her gently by the arm past a few people in expensive suits and dresses and toward a reserved section off to the right of center stage. People were taking their seats and filing down the aisles as they made their way to the front. A waiter intercepted them en route and offered things to sample—Lucinda ignored him, her attention directed toward the stage, while Samantha politely declined the food but accepted the wine with a smile.

"Hey, Luce, red or white?"

Lucinda glanced back at her with an unreadable expression.

"Red or white?" Samantha repeated, motioning toward the glasses on the waiter's tray.

"Um, white. Sorry. You surprised me." She admitted, taking her glass.

Samantha quirked a curious eyebrow as she stifled a grin. "Because I called you Luce? Does that bother you?"

"No, not at all. I like it." Lucinda's lips formed a smile on her glass, sipping the cool wine before turning her head toward the stage again.

Samantha felt a warm flush through her chest as she sipped her own glass. She let herself believe it was the alcohol, but her eyes continued to focus in an envious way on the way Lucinda Moss's lips touched the glass. She got the distinct impression Lucinda was letting herself be admired, the twinkle in her eye when Samantha stopped staring at her mouth and looked up all but confirming it. There was a definite flirtation brewing between them. She liked it.

"That guy in the suit over there, with the dark-rimmed glasses, he's speaking tonight." Lucinda pointed to a handsome man shuffling some papers at the podium. He had jet-black hair and a strong jawline. He looked both nervous and annoyed as he fidgeted with the microphone pinned to his lapel. "He's giving a quick lecture on the effects of pollution on marine life to kick off the night. He's an important featured guest here, and a good friend."

Samantha nodded and glanced at the speaker. He sipped a bottle of water and straightened his tie before looking up at the audience and waving to Lucinda with a broad smile.

"He's such a dork." She laughed and waved back. "Come on, let's get into our seats before they dim the lights and we trip over everyone's blatant displays of wealth."

Samantha looped her arm with Lucinda's as they moved toward the second row. She heard Lucinda mutter a name to the aisle attendant who nodded and motioned for them to sit in the reserved seats to his left. "You must be something special to get these magic seats," Samantha teased as they were seated.

"The most special." Lucinda winked back flirtatiously.

The quiet voices around them increased to a low rumble as the remaining seats were taken and the overhead lights flashed. The emcee thanked the audience for their attendance and generosity during the night. She informed them that after the presentation the aquarium would be open for their enjoyment and that food and drinks would circulate throughout the facilities. A silent auction would be held by something called the Touch Tank and live music would be performed every thirty minutes in the Jellyfish Room. She added regretfully that the sea lion exhibit was closed because Jacques and Cousteau were under the weather, but that all other exhibits were open. When the applause quieted down she introduced the featured speaker, Massimo Andiamo, and stepped off the stage.

Massimo cleared his throat and greeted the audience. He had a soothing, deep voice, demanding attention. Samantha was enraptured by his presentation. He spoke of climate changes affecting the marine world and how each individual in the room could positively change and limit the amount of waste generated. She shivered and rubbed her hands in her lap at the sight of rubber tires and dead sea creatures wrapped in discarded plastic that flashed across the screen.

"Are you cold?" Lucinda leaned over and whispered quietly, her forehead creased with concern.

"A little, I guess." Samantha adjusted her shawl. She wasn't sure if it was the cool air in the room or the damning visions on the screen that were making her shiver, but Lucinda's concern felt like a warm blanket.

"Here, let me…" Lucinda reached across, her eyes asking permission before she took Samantha's cold hands in her own, gently rubbing her thumbs along each knuckle.

Samantha let the heat and strength of Lucinda's hands ground her. They were so warm, her hands, as though she had held them by the fire. Suddenly the images before Samantha weren't as overwhelming anymore.

They sat like that, hands together for a while, before Lucinda opened her hand and repositioned Samantha's so she could intertwine their fingers lightly. She kept her eyes on the stage but could feel the quick glance from Samantha at her bold move. She smiled to herself when she felt Samantha flexing and curling her fingers into a more comfortable position as she slid her other hand underneath in a cradling motion. Massimo was winding down his lecture, but Lucinda was content to stay like this for as long as necessary—she liked the feeling of Samantha's hand in her own. It fit perfectly.

"He's fascinating," Samantha said quietly as they separated their hands to applaud. "That was great."

"Yeah, he's really passionate about this stuff, it's sort of infectious." Lucinda chuckled and shifted on her feet to nod toward the stage. "Would you like to meet him?"

Massimo was surrounded by a few important-looking people in suits. A photographer in the background shot candids of him talking and shaking hands while a small group of admirers began to form. When Lucinda stepped closer, he looked up between handshakes just long enough to make eye contact with her and beamed. "Excuse me a moment, gentlemen, I have to talk to this lovely lady." Before he reached them, he adjusted his glasses with a shy smile and swept forward, wrapping his arms around Lucinda, spinning her on the spot, and laughing. "Lucy, it's been too long. You look great."

Lucinda laughed and smiled as he finished the spin and placed her down gently. "Thank you, Massimo, you look pretty good yourself."

"Tell me, tell me, how are you? How have you been?"

"I'm good. Been busy, you know"—she winked—"staying out of trouble."

"Mamma asks about you." He added with a frown, "You should call her, you know, she misses you."

"I know, I miss her too. I will, I promise." Lucinda added quietly, "Massimo, this is my friend, Samantha."

"Ah yes. It's very nice to meet you, Samantha. Sorry about all of that. I haven't seen Lucy in a long time." He shook her hand and bowed his head. "Did you like the presentation?"

"I will never look at a plastic water bottle the same ever again," Samantha answered solemnly.

Massimo turned to Lucinda and asked, "Will you be around for a bit? I have to do some meet-and-greet nonsense. Can I catch up with you lovely ladies later?"

"Yes, Mass, we'll be around," Lucinda replied happily. "I'm sure we'll end up by the new wing eventually."

Massimo kissed Lucinda's cheek as he squeezed her shoulders once more. He looked at Samantha and added quietly before turning back to his colleagues, "I want to hear all about how you two met."

Samantha quirked her eyebrow and glanced over to Lucinda who shrugged. She could think of worse things than someone assuming that Samantha Monteiro was her girlfriend. "Come on," Lucinda said, "let's go get lost in the ocean."

Chapter Seven

Lucinda asked Samantha if she had ever been to the aquarium before and she was embarrassed to admit that she hadn't. She had considered taking her niece and nephew here a few times, but it seemed that all they wanted to do when they were here was shop and look at electronics. To be honest, she didn't have much experience with children; she barely had a relationship with her brother, so she didn't see them very often anyway. They lived in New York; close enough to visit if need be, but far enough away to forget about almost entirely. Just like the rest of her family.

"Well, I am honored to give you a special guided tour of the aquarium and I promise to give you all the inside scoop on the exhibits," Lucinda said as they walked through the main doors.

Samantha took in the penguin exhibit in front of them. It was set below eye level into an open-water alcove with rock faces and small cliffs from which the penguins could propel themselves into the water below. She scanned the enclosure and let her mind wander back to the greeting between Lucinda and Massimo. Their exchange was familiar, loving, and yet also a little sad. She wondered about the pained look on Lucinda's face on the drive here tonight—it had been fleeting, but it had been there. There was something mysterious about Lucinda that intrigued her; she had so many questions for this woman. Being here tonight was her chance to find out those answers. All she had to do was ask, right?

"Do you come here a lot?" That was a start.

"I've been here quite a few times. Not as much recently, though." Lucinda leaned in and whispered, "Don't tell the others, but the southern rockhoppers have always been my favorite because they have that cool punk-rock hair thing going on." She pointed out the bright yellow feathers coming off its head. "But, if we are being totally honest, I have a huge soft spot for the little blue penguins over there. They're the smallest penguin species in the world."

Samantha nodded, listening to Lucinda's facts about penguins as she wandered closer to the enclosure. These little guys were tinged blue and positively adorable. Their habitat was different from the rockhoppers'—there were an abundance of nest-like burrows and some sand. Lucinda explained that these penguins preferred a warmer climate and lived almost exclusively in Australia and New Zealand.

"They're so cute," Samantha gushed as she watched one groom another. She turned to find Lucinda watching her with amusement.

Lucinda waited until Samantha was ready to move on. She explained how the aquarium was divided into sections all surrounding one large center tank. Large was an understatement. The tank made up the entire center of the building. The structure was surrounded by sloping ramps that wound around the tank until they reached the top. Each ramp connected to a few smaller connected hallways with exhibits on the far walls: Gulf of Maine crustaceans like the rare blue and white lobsters found locally; Amazon Rainforest exhibits with brightly colored tree frogs, enormous anacondas, electric eels, and ferocious piranhas.

The Pacific Reef community was Samantha's favorite, filled with coral reefs and brightly colored tropical fish. She listened closely as Lucinda explained how the fish blended in with their tropical environments to avoid predators; even the eels had bright yellow stripes and green eyes. Samantha stood close to the glass, watching as a shark slowly wound his way under a coral formed ledge into the vicinity of an unsuspecting blue and white fish. The fish sensed the approaching predator and quickly switched directions, bulleting forward toward the glass before turning sharply. Samantha jumped and gasped, reaching back instinctively before bumping into Lucinda.

"Hey there, you okay?" Lucinda's hands fell to Samantha's hips to steady her; they were so close now that her breath skated across Samantha's shoulder.

Samantha blushed and gently bit her lower lip. "Sorry, I totally thought that thing was going to jump through the glass." She moved to step forward but Lucinda dug her fingertips into her hips slightly before releasing her grip.

"It's fine. I don't mind at all." Lucinda smiled and licked her lips as she stepped back and motioned toward the larger center tank. "I want to show you my favorite spot in the whole aquarium."

Samantha hesitated for only a moment before taking the hand Lucinda reached out to her to lead her. She let her fingers loosely entwine with Lucinda's as they weaved past a few people and up the remaining length of the ramp. The opening at the top of the tank was absolutely breathtaking. Glass barriers around the tank reached just a little above waist height, so all patrons, large and small, could get a view of the tank below. A small platform at the north end of the tank was partially submerged in water; Lucinda explained that this little shelf was where the divers and staff climbed into the tank to do daily cleanings and feedings. Also, it was where aquarium staff would give daily lectures on the tank's inhabitants and a few of its bright stars.

Lucinda guided Samantha to the eastern edge of the tank, a less populated area, and walked her up close to the barrier so she could lean forward and look down. "Here, this is my favorite spot."

Still holding Samantha's hand in her right while pointing down with her left, she said, "From where you're standing, you can see the whole coral reef and all the fish, but through there, there you can see down to the Pacific Reef tank and the reflection of the brightly colored fish on the tank walls permeates through the space. It looks like a hidden rainbow, how the light bends with the curved glass. One exhibit spilling into the next—like total harmony."

Samantha squeezed Lucinda's hand. An announcement rang out overhead about the silent auction, and the few remaining people around them started to filter down the ramps.

Lucinda's thumb soothed over the knuckles on Samantha's hand as she explained more details of the tank. "There are over two hundred thousand gallons of water, over twenty feet deep and forty feet wide. There are sharks and stingrays and hundreds of fish."

Samantha turned from the tank to face Lucinda. "Is that how you know so much about the aquarium? From knowing Massimo?" She found it hard to utter well-formed sentences under Lucinda's intense gaze.

"Sort of. I spent some time here when I was younger, back when Massimo was a budding biologist. I sort of grew up with his family and have been coming to his lectures ever since."

"That's why you came tonight? To hear him speak?" Samantha asked quietly, her eyes flickering to a stray blond hair across Lucinda's forehead. She was resisting the urge to brush it back.

"I told him I would support him by bringing an attractive date so he could be flanked by beautiful women in all the pictures—you know, so he didn't feel like such a nerd."

Samantha smiled at that statement and couldn't stop herself before replying, "Is that what this is? A date?"

Lucinda faced Samantha fully, adding quietly, "It can be, if you want it to be."

Samantha let the words settle over her as she thought about it. Her right hand moved as if of its own volition, carefully brushing that stray hair to the side, her fingers lightly grazing Lucinda's temple. Lucinda's eyes fluttered closed momentarily and she gripped the glass barrier with her free hand.

"Yes," Samantha breathed. "I would like that."

Lucinda took a half step, closing the distance between them as she released the rail and reached forward to touch Samantha's jaw with her thumb. "You look beautiful tonight," she murmured. "Absolutely radiant." She curled her fingers slightly, coaxing Samantha forward, and closed her eyes as she pressed their lips together.

The kiss was slow and soft. Lucinda cradled Samantha's face, her fingers sliding gently along Samantha's hairline while her thumb stroked her jaw. Samantha let herself melt into it, into the feel of warm and soft, and she let Lucinda lead. Their lips slid against each other slowly, gentle and tentative until Samantha pressed forward, increasing the pressure. She wanted to feel the kiss entirely, she wanted to feel everything. Lucinda smiled through the kiss and stepped even closer, so their hips were touching, and Samantha's hand slid from Lucinda's shoulder to wrap gently around her biceps as her heart started to race a little faster.

A sudden, loud spitting noise jarred them apart. Samantha jumped back from Lucinda and looked around, alarmed.

"Relax," Lucinda said as she pulled Samantha closer by their clasped hands and pointed down into the tank at the largest sea turtle Samantha had ever seen. "That's Myrtle, just being a perv."

Samantha blinked, her mouth slightly agape as she watched this behemoth move around the water with a grace that seemed contradictory to her size, ducking her head periodically and spitting air and water out when she resurfaced. Samantha unclasped her hand from Lucinda's to put both hands on the rail as she leaned forward to get a better look. Hundreds of small shimmery silver fish skated along the tops of the coral, darting in and out of holes in the rocks and seaweed-like filaments. Myrtle circled the tank once more before diving down again, disappearing into the ripples of the clear water, her shape distorted by the schools of fish swimming below.

Lucinda stepped up behind Samantha, placing one hand at her lower back, the other on the rail next to her as she explained, "Myrtle the sea turtle is the star of the Ocean Tank. She came in 1970 and has been here ever since. She's more than five hundred pounds and thought to be about eighty years old. And quite the practical joker, it seems."

Samantha let her eyes close at the soft voice behind her, her heart racing again when she felt gentle lips press quickly to her skin before pulling away. She missed their warmth and absently reached her pinky toward Lucinda's fingers on the railing. She smiled as those fingers laced with hers, and looked down to admire the pale fingers between her own darker ones. Samantha turned slowly so her back was to the tank and then smiled at the appreciative look on Lucinda's face as she let her eyes drag slowly over Samantha's body.

"Thank you," Samantha said quietly.

"Hmm?" Lucinda's eyes locked on the dark ones in front of her. "For what?"

"Thinking I'm beautiful. Teaching me about all things aquatic..."

"It's nice to share my useless knowledge with someone," Lucinda quipped. "And of course I think you're beautiful. I think you're gorgeous." Lucinda paused a moment. "Hey, wanna play with some sharks before we see Massimo?" She flashed an impish grin.

Samantha scrunched her nose. "Sure, I guess. But I have to pee first. All this water is distracting."

"Ha. Okay, come on, I'll take you."

They walked back down the ramp until they were on the second floor and Lucinda pointed out the bathroom to Samantha. She told her she would be waiting over by the center tank when she was all set.

Lucinda walked to the edge of the ramp and leaned against the cement rail so she was facing the twelve-foot glass panel in front of her. She was just above the floor level of the giant tank and could see all the fish swimming in schools, skirting around enormous stingrays that obscured almost all of the glass, their tender white underbellies ghosting over the slightly clouded surface of the pane. She observed the reef that made up the center of the tank and climbed its way up to the top. Eels poked out periodically and a large nurse shark slinked across the sandy bottom. Her mind wandered to another time when she was in a similar position, lounging against the ramp's border, staring aimlessly at the glass. It had been a few years prior, after a pretty awful fight with her last girlfriend, Grace. That relationship had been so damn toxic; she couldn't believe it lasted as long as it did. Maybe that's why she hadn't dated anyone since, something she found herself reconsidering since meeting Samantha. She had secretly wanted tonight to be a date—to have the chance to kiss Samantha like she had wanted to the other night at the dance studio. And now that she had a new memory to help wash out the older, more painful one, she felt a little better about being here. Just a little. There was a lot about this place that gave her peace. She always found comfort at the aquarium; she could get lost in thought and imagine how weightless she would feel in the center tank. It was the only place she felt truly safe other than on the dance floor with Dominic. She came here to clear her head—she came here to find herself. She'd come here after Dominic died and tried to make sense of everything that had happened. She never quite found what she was looking for though. Her quest for peace had fallen short; it was the first time the tranquility of the aquarium had failed to help her find answers.

"You're thinking about him. I can tell." Massimo's calm, deep voice alerted her to his presence. She nodded and glanced over to him as he perched himself in the space next to her.

"This place reminds me of Dominic. Every place does," she added sadly. "But this place in particular."

"I know. Every time some idiot raffle winner gets inside the tank to feed the fish or scrub the glass I think of that day he almost scared that guy to death with the fake shark fin." Massimo laughed. "My parents had to donate a whale skeleton to patch up the relationship with the head marine biologist just so Dominic could resume his diving therapy. My little brother was always up to something."

She smiled at the memory. Dominic was always getting into trouble. He was a total pain in the ass, but he could always make you smile when things got too serious or too heavy. He had started the scuba-diving therapy when he was younger. It was typically used to help rehabilitate paraplegics and those who suffered from neurological disorders, but he used it for a different reason. He had crippling stage fright and would hyperventilate. His mother hated the idea of medicating him because it affected his performance, memory, and balance. Some high paid shrink recommended he try diving to help him focus and control his breathing when he was nervous.

He did well with it and then was encouraged to practice his breathing where he would be in front of lots of people. Dominic was the one who suggested he try to do both at the same time. He had been coming to the aquarium since he was little and felt like it was the perfect mix: control your breathing and be on display.

How many thousands of eyes would see him in the forty-minute session he did underwater? Helping to clean the tank and practicing his breathing, calming his nerves, being careful and mindful of the living creatures while settling into himself. It was genius.

"She's very pretty, by the way," Massimo added with a wink and crooked smile. He nodded toward Samantha who had emerged from the bathroom and was chatting with a waiter at the top of the ramp. As if sensing she was the topic of conversation, she looked up, making eye contact with Lucinda and smiling before returning to her own discussion.

"Yes, she is. Just a friend though, Mass."

"But you want more, no?"

Lucinda looked into his hazel eyes and nodded subtly. "I do."

"Well, Luce, if there is any person in this world that can get the girl, it's you. In fact, I'll be disappointed if you don't."

She smiled and looked over his shoulder as the woman in question approached, holding two glasses of white wine.

"Massimo, sorry, would you like a glass? I sort of ran out of hands." Samantha handed one to Lucinda, whose fingers lingered on her own longer than necessary, distracting her from his reply.

"Oh no, no, thank you. I'm not much of a wine guy." He smiled knowingly. "But I am hungry and I refuse to sample the shrimp cocktail. It's a travesty to pass around seafood in an aquarium. Can I treat you ladies to a late dinner?"

"Well that's up to Cinderella here, I'm just the lowly pumpkin driver."

"Huh? Yes, sure, that sounds great," Samantha answered.

"Lucy, I have to run over to the new wing to grab my jacket and briefcase—meet you by the sculpture?"

"Yeah, Mass, sure."

He chuckled to himself and rubbed Lucinda's arm affectionately before turning to go.

Samantha sipped her wine and watched him walk away. "Is that how it is with everyone you're friendly with?"

"What's that?"

"They all use nicknames like Lucy or Luce. But you introduce yourself as Lucinda. Is that intentional?"

"Mm-hmm," Lucinda purred as she stepped closer, watching as Samantha sucked her bottom lip into her mouth. She trembled as Lucinda's fingers danced along her hairline, her eyes fluttering closed.

"Stop that." Lucinda dragged her thumb across Samantha's lip, pulling it from her teeth before pressing a kiss to them and whispering, "They're terms of endearment for me, so it's special." She kissed Samantha slowly once more and pulled back, while still staying close.

Samantha opened her eyes. "Well, I feel very special then."

"You should." Lucinda contemplated leaning back in to suck on those full lips again when she was interrupted by an unwanted guest.

"Well, you two look mighty cozy." Claudette Frost's voice was as warm as dry ice. "I hear you're using Ms. Moss here to assist with that White mess. Dating the help, are we, Samantha?"

Lucinda watched Samantha stifle a lip curl before turning to address Claudette. "What do you want, Claudette?"

"I want you to do the job you've been paid to do and find a match for my darling son. Perhaps fewer…distractions would be advised. What will your clientele think?" Claudette smiled and walked away.

Although Lucinda doubted Samantha would let her professional poise falter, her body language suggested that she was considering following Claudette.

Lucinda placed a soft but firm hand on her forearm, holding her back. "It's not worth it," Lucinda stated quietly, her tone not quite matching the death glare she was casting at the back of Claudette Frost's head. She was trying to remain calm, but the thinly veiled threats against Samantha put her on edge in a way she hadn't been in years.

Samantha let out a huff, Lucinda's contact seemingly grounding her. "Who the fuck does Frosty the Snow Bitch think she is, calling you *the help*?"

"Hey." Lucinda's tone was firm as she ducked her head to catch Samantha's eyes. "It's really adorable that you're upset about me and my feelings, but it's not a big deal. I'm sure Alec spoke volumes about me embarrassing him on the dance floor at the wedding."

"Of course he fucking ran back to Mommy." Samantha grumbled and attempted to pull her arm out from Lucinda's grasp, unsuccessfully. "And it does matter."

Lucinda paused at Samantha's comment, touched by the sentiment even though it was obscured by Samantha's palpable anger. She loosened her grasp on Samantha's arm, stroking the skin with her thumb until Samantha looked up at her. "Thank you for that. I don't want to cause you any trouble, Samantha."

Samantha let out a slow, angry breath. "I'm here with you tonight because I want to be, Luce. I don't care who knows it."

Lucinda saw a mix of emotions flash across Samantha's face, "Come on, let's grab our stuff and head to the front. I'll take you to pet the sharks another day."

"Promise?" Samantha teased as she scrunched her face in mock disapproval.

"Oh yeah, absolutely. It's a definite now." Lucinda slid her arm to Samantha's waist and walked her down the ramp.

CHAPTER EIGHT

Samantha wandered around the gift shop, looking at the magnets and collectable snow globes featuring some of the aquarium's most popular exhibits: penguins, seahorses, stingrays. Lucinda was retrieving their purses and her shawl from the coat-check area and had left Samantha to her own devices. She let her fingers dance over delicate pieces of colored sea glass that hung from fishing line to make a beautiful wind chime. She found a fact book on the aquarium and thumbed through the pages with one hand while her other ran over her lips, remembering.

The last time she had been attracted to a beautiful blonde was in high school during a cheer camp stint between junior and senior year. It was a relationship that was fast and intense and raw. She'd kept in contact with Adriana for a while during senior year but eventually they lost touch. They crossed paths again in college at a cheer competition and rekindled the flame over one crazy weekend, but Adriana ended up marrying her college sweetheart—some guy—and Samantha dabbled a bit before she eventually crawled back to what was comfortable and socially accepted, dating men. It wasn't that she denied her desires; it's just that she hadn't really found another woman that piqued her interest like Adriana had. Until now.

She liked kissing Lucinda Moss. She liked feeling special enough to use a nickname with her if she chose to. She liked that Lucinda was affectionate but respectful of her space. She liked the darkness in those blue eyes when they tracked down to her lips. She liked how completely comfortable she felt in Lucinda's presence, even if she made her nervous sometimes, but it was a good sort of nervous, like butterflies nervous. She liked that Lucinda was able to step right back into the soft, tender moments they shared before they were interrupted as if seeing Claudette didn't faze her. Maybe it didn't, and that made Samantha feel that much more appreciated, like she was worthy of Lucinda's attention and affection.

At the same time though, she had to admit to herself that she was a little anxious. Claudette's influence in certain circles was significant and her tone had been threatening. It was true that Samantha wasn't ashamed of being caught kissing Lucinda Moss, but she wasn't exactly looking for a fight either. She needed to maintain as many contracts as possible to repair the damage her break-up had done to the company's finances and reputation, a fact she intended to keep under wraps. The spectacular failure of her relationship was not something she could afford getting out. It could literally ruin her. And the idea that the woman who knew all of her secrets was currently also making her question whether she should be dating again at all...well that was a totally different struggle altogether.

She couldn't deny her attraction to Lucinda. But Lucinda also had the power to expose her secrets to the world. Secrets that at this point had closed her off almost entirely from engaging in any sort of relationship with another person. Should she really even consider dating with all of the consequences it might bring her? Was opening up to Lucinda really the smartest choice here? If she had learned one thing in her matchmaking business, it's that timing was everything. The real question was whether she could resist her growing attraction to Lucinda before it was too late. Maybe it already was.

"Find something you like?" Lucinda asked her quietly as she stepped up next to her.

"Yes, I have." That was true, she really did like Lucinda, "But about this? Just looking."

"You're cute. I'll keep you." Lucinda smiled and stepped closer to Samantha, her hand affectionately resting at Samantha's waist.

Samantha turned and ran her fingers along Lucinda's elbow. "I'm ready whenever you are," she said as her eyes continued to dance over the toys and books surrounding them.

Lucinda nodded and draped the shawl over Samantha's shoulders, shuffling the purses to one arm as she slid her hand into Samantha's. Samantha repositioned their hands into a more comfortable position to entwine their fingers. She liked playing this game with her, learning which way was most comfortable. Lucinda seemed to prefer to hold with her left hand, Samantha's right. It was convenient that Samantha was left-handed—they fit so well that way. The thought settled in her stomach with a warm flutter.

They moved slowly through the doors to a large bronze statue of a sea turtle suspended above a few large fish, swimming in tandem. It was beautiful and well over eight feet tall. Samantha leaned in to examine the fine details carved into the seaweed at the base. Her attention was drawn to the gold-plated plaque attached to the base of the statue. "This statue is brought to you by the generosity of the Andiamo family," she read aloud. "This statue is from Massimo's family?"

Lucinda nodded, her eyes trailing over it. "Yes, it's a few years old now."

"How did you meet them?"

"Well, she danced into our lives, didn't you, Luce?" Massimo supplied as he walked up.

"Something like that." Lucinda laughed and quickly changed the subject, "Where to, Mass?"

"How about a little Italian tonight? We're right by the North End and I have been dying to try a new place Silvia recommended." He creased his brow in thought. "Speaking of which, I should probably call my lovely wife and tell her I'm escorting two beautiful women."

❖

They hailed a cab and took the short ride to Boston's North End. Lucinda loved the juxtaposition of trendy nightspots and restaurants scattered amongst the historic sites of the American Revolution and the likes of Paul Revere's house. It was one of her favorite places to unwind after a dance competition with Dominic because of all its charm and energy.

Massimo held Samantha's arm as she navigated the cobblestone streets on very high heels, while Lucinda walked by their side laughing at their conversation and smiling to herself. It had been a long time since she'd had so much fun. She had missed Massimo's quirky sense of humor and she absolutely loved Samantha's naturally husky laugh. She looped her arm into Massimo's and let him lead them to a small Italian bistro tucked behind an ivy-covered trellis at the side entrance of a bakery, the kind of place you would walk right past if you didn't know it was there.

They were seated in the back in a round booth with Samantha in the middle. Massimo ordered white wine, a martini for himself, and a few seafood appetizers as they chatted about his presentation. He told Samantha about his love of all things aquatic and how he advocated for inner-city education at the aquarium. At some point between glasses of wine, Samantha slid her hand into Lucinda's under the table and pulled them onto her lap. She let her fingers trace the lines in Lucinda's palm as she spoke animatedly with Massimo about her work and her partner Andrew. She told them that Andrew had been a close friend since high school who had reconnected with her shortly after college. They started the business as a side project originally but it got away from them and took off on its own.

Lucinda listened with half attention as she focused on the things Samantha was doing to her hand, gliding her fingers up to the tips of Lucinda's and slowly dragging her nails back down to the center of her palm. Lucinda almost dropped her wineglass the first time as she shuddered, her stomach knotting with each swipe of Samantha's fingers. If Samantha noticed, she didn't let on, or let up, continuing to slowly manipulate Lucinda's hand with her own. After a particularly slow drag, Lucinda closed her fingers around Samantha's before releasing them and turning her palm over so it was resting on Samantha's thigh.

She gently squeezed the muscles underneath her hand and was rewarded with a slight pause in Samantha's conversation with Massimo as she sucked in a short breath. Massimo was mid-laugh and missed the exchange before excusing himself to the restroom. Samantha wore a sly grin as she sipped her wine, eyes directed out to the restaurant. Lucinda took it as a taunt and a challenge which she countered by sliding her palm up slightly so her fingers could work the hem of Samantha's dress a bit. That got an immediate response.

Samantha set her wineglass down and licked her lips before turning to face Lucinda. She arched her eyebrow, let her eyes drop to Lucinda's lips, and spoke directly to them. "I like the way your hand feels in mine."

Lucinda pushed up the hem of Samantha's dress a little. "And how about the way it feels on your thigh?"

"Yes, that too." She leaned forward, stopping just millimeters from Lucinda's lips.

Lucinda closed the distance, this time letting her teeth catch Samantha's pouty bottom lip and tugging a bit before soothing it with her tongue.

Samantha moaned against Lucinda's mouth and parted her lips in response. Lucinda nibbled her lips once more before pulling back, leaving Samantha in a haze with bruised red lips. She knew their tablemate would be returning soon enough.

Samantha seemed to understand and nodded, turning her face away to gain some composure. Lucinda squeezed her thigh once more and slid her hand up to her knee to give each of them a chance to breathe. She wanted to keep touching Samantha's leg, all of her really, but if she was going to get through the rest of this dinner she had to cool off. The flustered look Samantha wore betrayed a similar state.

Dinner was easy and fun. They kept their hands to themselves and stayed out of any real trouble. They talked about work and Massimo's new wife, Silvia. He had an upcoming sea voyage that would take fifty days and she was already starting to worry. Lucinda did her best to ignore the worry she too felt, instead nervously toying with her napkin as Massimo reached for the check. After

Dominic's death, she had shut down from all of her relationships, withdrawing into herself. Reconnecting with Massimo tonight had been a pleasant change of pace, but even the slightest notion that he might be in danger made Lucinda feel anxious. She had had enough loss.

❖

They took a cab back to the aquarium and parted ways with Massimo. Samantha had overheard him tell Lucinda that the family missed her, as though Lucinda had somehow lost touch with him. It struck Samantha as odd considering how friendly they were together. Their interaction was effortless and she could see the affection between them.

Samantha noticed the sad look in Lucinda's eyes as she watched Massimo walk away.

She stepped closer, reaching out and touching the crossed arms Lucinda had over her chest, holding her emotions in. "You okay?" Samantha asked quietly.

"Yeah. I'm fine." Lucinda shook her head and stood up taller, uncrossing her arms and flashing a weary smile at Samantha. "I'm good."

"You don't have to be, if you aren't."

"I'm with you, and I couldn't be happier about that." Lucinda's small smile satisfied Samantha for the moment and she let it go. She would pursue it later, if the circumstance arose. "You ready to go home now, Cinderella?" Lucinda joked and smiled, seemingly easing the sad cloud off her shoulders.

Samantha paused, and watching the moonlight reflect off Lucinda's beautiful blond hair, she reached out and ran her fingers along it lightly. "Let's go, pumpkin driver," she said with a grin, pulling gently on a loose curl and letting it spring back up.

Lucinda laughed and waved the valet forward with her classic car, opening the door for Samantha before walking to the driver's side and slipping into her seat. She pulled away from the aquarium, casting one last glance in the rearview. Samantha watched her look back like she had left something behind and she frowned to herself again. Something was haunting Lucinda Moss and she had no idea what.

❖

They drove back to Samantha's high-rise in peaceful silence, Lucinda reaching her hand from the shift to Samantha's lap when she wasn't changing gears. Touch was important to her; she needed it to feel grounded. She appreciated the comfortable quiet she was having with Samantha; it let her think about tonight's unexpected dinner. She considered how Massimo had encouraged her to reach out to the family and to call him soon. It made her stomach knot with emotion. She needed to be better about this. She really needed to reconnect with them. She hated the way just talking to Massimo made her want to cry. She wanted to blame it on the wine, but she had stopped drinking hours ago. No, this was deep seated and festering. She missed them. She missed the family. She missed Dominic. Lucinda wondered if she would ever again risk exposing herself to the vulnerability of losing someone so important. The tired but content sigh from Samantha next to her drew her attention back to her passenger. The warm hand holding her own challenged her to be brave.

When they pulled up to the valet she squeezed Samantha's hand and put the car in neutral. She reached into the back and retrieved her purse before climbing out of the car and walking toward her passenger door, beating the attendant to the door and waving him off politely as she lent a hand to Samantha, helping her out and through the doors to her building.

Samantha had a permanent blush on her cheeks as she ducked her head to avoid the eyes of the night concierge and tugged Lucinda through the lobby to the safety of the elevator before saying, "You know, I can walk myself up."

Lucinda grinned wider, waiting for the elevator doors to close before whispering into Samantha's ear, "As if I would kiss you good night on the sidewalk outside."

"As if."

"I'll at least walk you to your door, like a gentlewoman." She winked and pressed her lips to Samantha's briefly as the doors opened behind them.

Samantha broke the kiss to step out of the elevator and wrapped her fingers in Lucinda's, pulling her down the hall with haste. When they got to her door she slowed, not sure what was going to happen next. Should she invite Lucinda in? Say good night? Offer to make coffee?

Before she could panic any longer, Lucinda turned her gently on the spot and walked her silently backward until she could feel the wall behind her. Lucinda pressed against her, hand on her hip, the other brushing the hair off her face as she pressed a hard kiss to Samantha's lips. The force of the kiss caught Samantha off guard and she gasped, opening her mouth in surprise. Lucinda took the opportunity to suck Samantha's bottom lip between her own, running her tongue along the flesh until Samantha leaned closer and deepened the kiss. Their lips moved against each other slowly, like an elegant dance, before impatience set in. Samantha opened her mouth wider, dropping her purse to the floor as she slid her hands into Lucinda's hair, pulling her face closer.

Lucinda's tongue teased at Samantha's drawing out a low moan from her throat. All Samantha could feel was the heat of Lucinda's mouth on her and the hand clutching at her hip, holding her firmly in place against the wall, fingers kneading softly into her flesh. They kissed like this for what seemed like forever, until Samantha couldn't breathe without gasping. Lucinda smiled against her lips, short of breath herself, before pressing one final kiss against the corner of her mouth.

"I got you something," she whispered as Samantha blinked her eyes open slowly, her jaw still cradled in Lucinda's hand. Samantha's hands slid down from Lucinda's now messy hair to her shoulders, where they clasped loosely behind her neck.

"Oh yeah?"

"Yeah." Lucinda leaned forward to kiss her again, one firm kiss as she guided Samantha's hands between them. She held

Samantha's hands with her right while the other pushed Samantha's hair behind her ear. Her fingers slowly traced down Samantha's face, resting at her collarbone, playing with the soft material of her dress. Samantha was warmed by the touch, her eyes fluttering closed as she felt Lucinda's fingers slowly dance along the bone. Samantha's eyes opened at the sensation of Lucinda stepping back a few inches, giving her room to breathe.

Lucinda reached into her purse and pulled out a small bag from the aquarium gift shop with a shy grin.

Samantha blinked and took a deep breath in before exhaling slowly and taking the bag. "What is it?"

"Just a little thank you for coming gift."

Samantha reached into the tissue paper and pulled out a multicolored glass figurine of a sea turtle. "I love it," she said, leaning forward to kiss Lucinda once more. "Thank you."

Lucinda pulled Samantha into a tight hug, kissing her temple as she released her. "I'll talk to you soon?"

Samantha nodded and bit her lip as she watched Lucinda step back, her hands dropping away slowly. "Have a good night, Luce."

Samantha keyed into her apartment and slumped against the closed door. She let out a contented sigh as she headed to her bedroom to undress, realizing she was getting in over her head with a beautiful woman she couldn't keep her hands or mouth off.

CHAPTER NINE

L et me get this straight," Andrew asked incredulously as he shrugged off his coat. "You're trying to tell me you're this blissfully happy and nothing happened?"

"Yes. It was fun," Samantha replied nonchalantly as she picked a polish color from the rack. "I learned a lot about the ocean and sea mammals and I had a great time."

"Samantha, you are many things, but a good liar is not one of them."

She rolled her eyes and shook the polish, holding it up to the light to examine the color. She had woken up smiling this morning, and nothing seemed to shake her good mood—not the influx of angry emails from Claudette Frost, not the dog walker in the Public Garden who couldn't wrangle the wild poodle that almost knocked her to the ground during her run, not even that slimebag at the coffee shop who always hit on her while also invading her personal space and spitting on her. Not a single thing could foul her mood as she remembered her good-night kiss and the little turtle figurine that was currently residing on her kitchen island.

The nail technician waved her over to the chair as Andrew fussed with his hair in the mirror nearby. She smiled and handed over the color, settling into the massage chair while the tech prepped the station. Andrew slumped into the seat next to her, reaching for a discarded *People* magazine on the shelf when her phone buzzed. She apologized to the technician and reached into her purse to shut it off, pausing as she looked at the screen. Lucinda was calling.

"Hello." She smiled.

"Hey. How are you?"

"I'm good. You?"

"I'm good. How'd you sleep?"

"Um, not bad." She turned in her chair so her back was angled toward Andrew. "Good, I guess. Good."

"What are you up to today?"

"Well, Andrew and I are having a girls' day, you know, manicures, pedicures, hopefully some cocktails."

"Sounds delectable. What salon do you guys prefer? I'm always in the market for a good recommendation."

Samantha smiled and put her feet into the warm water in front of her. "A place on Newbury Street called Perfect 10, it's great. Andrew and I try to get here every few weeks to decompress."

"Sounds fun. I won't keep you. Have a great day with Andrew. Tell him I said hello."

"Sure. Are we still on for Tuesday?"

"Absolutely, I'm looking forward to it."

"Ahem." Andrew cleared his throat dramatically as Samantha put her phone away. "That was her, wasn't it?"

Samantha glared at him and rolled her eyes.

"Whatever, Sam, you were grinning like a kid at Christmas that whole phone call. What'd she say?"

"She just called to chat."

Andrew smiled and folded the magazine on his lap, facing his friend fully as he lowered his feet into the basin below him. He flicked on the massage setting on the chair and tapped his fingers along the seam of the seat. "You really like her."

Samantha frowned, letting his statement wash over her. "I don't know. She's…different."

"Different like Adriana?" he asked quietly. "That kind of different?"

Samantha's frown deepened and she knew she was blushing. "Yeah, maybe. I don't know."

Andrew cocked his head to the side and settled into his chair. "Tell me about her. What's she like?"

Samantha took a deep breath, appreciating Andrew's non-chalance but not being fooled by his fake inattention. "She's great. She's smart, funny, attractive, and easy to be around. I don't know what it is, she's just…I don't know."

Andrew nodded and looked as though he was about to ask a more leading question when the receptionist from the salon stepped up to their chairs, holding a bottle of champagne and two glasses. "Excuse me"—she read from a card in front of her—"Ms. Monteiro and Mr. Stanley?"

Samantha's eyebrows rose. Andrew shot her a confused glance before answering, "Yes?"

"This is a gift from Myrtle, she says to enjoy your day."

"Myrtle?" Andrew scoffed. "Who the hell is Myrtle?"

Samantha chest warmed as she cleared her throat and thanked the receptionist, accepting the champagne flute with a smile.

"Why do I have a feeling this has something to do with a certain enchanting blonde?" Andrew sipped his glass, his eyes twinkling as he added, "I will say she has excellent taste."

"Yes. She does." Samantha beamed as she fished out her cell to fire off a quick thank-you text and then relaxed further into the pampering she had planned for today.

Lucinda couldn't quite keep her attention on the stack of work on her desk. Her eyes kept tracking over to the panoramic glass windows to her right. Outside the sun shone and the view was incredible. She was thinking about Shelly White's dance lesson tonight and her beautiful handler. She hoped Samantha might show up early. In fact, she was counting on it.

Lucinda had a meeting with Claire Moseley to discuss a new client in fifteen minutes—a new client that they had obtained through Claire's hard work on that software campaign earlier in the month.

Claire was prompt as always and came well prepared. "This new client is a PR nightmare," Claire reported. "Alleged sexism in the workplace."

Lucinda tapped her pen on her desk. She loathed spinning for these kinds of clients. "We have, unfortunately, dealt with this particular problem before."

Claire paused a moment before responding. "Yes, of course. But this client is a lesbian-owned magazine and their male editor was released from his duties after multiple infractions."

"Claire, you have a solid plan and an excellent team. I have every faith in you." Lucinda leaned back into her chair. "Tell me about Richard."

"He's been..." Claire was careful with her word choice. "Resistant."

"By all means, feel free to elaborate."

"He's difficult. He's resistant to leadership that isn't his own. He hands in his project portions late and I think he's sleeping with an intern." Claire shrugged and worried her bottom lip, obviously debating what she should say next. "Not that that has any bearing on the project, but it's sort of distracting because she hovers outside our planning meetings with coffee all the time."

Lucinda tapped the tips of her fingers together before leaning over her tablet and pulling up a new screen. "Is that why he isn't on this project team list?" She already knew the answer, but she wanted confirmation.

"Yes. His actions are distracting to the rest of the team and honestly I think he hates women, so this really isn't the ideal PR position for him."

"Fine. I agree with your decision." Lucinda looked back up to a nervous Claire, fidgeting in her seat, the confidence she'd displayed during her presentation waning.

"Claire. You are very good at what you do. You're an excellent executive here and you need to give yourself more credit." Her voice was stern but calm; she wasn't reprimanding her, she just wanted her to step up. "I love your pitch and your team. I want you to be full chair on this—but you need to start believing in yourself, or no one will follow your lead. Do you understand what I mean?"

"I understand, thank you." Claire sat up taller, smoothing out her blazer before standing. She reached for her papers and ran her hands through her hair nervously. Lucinda knew what she wanted to ask.

"I'll handle Richard. I'll make sure it's done anonymously. Come to me if anything else like this arises. I need to know that the staff I employ are as qualified as they appear to be. We're in the business of fixing problems, not making them. Agreed?"

"Yes, Lucinda."

She smiled and dismissed a nodding Claire with a wave as she reached for her phone. It was time to clean house. Starting first with Richard Thomas.

Brian Edgars was in her office an hour later. He had some progress reports from the last quarter to go over before the end of the day.

"How much do you know about the internship program we do here?" Lucinda asked as she scanned through the spreadsheets in front of her.

"Not much. I know that legal uses them, and marketing used them too until you took over. Why?"

"One of them seems to be carrying on some type of relationship with our friend Richard." Lucinda's tone was laced with irritation. "Richard is already on thin ice. By no means should he be fraternizing with an intern."

Brian nodded in agreement. "What do you plan to do?"

"Richard and I are having a meeting tomorrow. I met with all the executives at the end of last quarter for the quarterly review. I explained to them that we would be monitoring all of them individually and with peer evaluations on their projects in the coming months. I had Amanda pull all his accounts from the past year and collect all the self-evaluation surveys we require each team to complete before, during, and after the project is finished. So far the reading material is positively enjoyable." She turned to the next spreadsheet. "As far as the dating-the-intern thing is concerned, I think we ought to find someone from Human Resources to address that. This should probably be monitored closely, but it's a little out of my range." She glanced up at Brian. "Can you look into that for me?"

"I'll handle it. Let me know how the meeting goes tomorrow."

Lucinda returned her attention to the spreadsheets. "Last quarter was great, Brian—these look good."

"These are the best numbers we've had since the shift in management. All your hard work is paying off, Lucinda." Brian stood and offered her a congratulatory grin. "Do whatever you need to do to keep it that way. The board supports your decisions."

After Brian left, Lucinda pulled out her file on Richard and stuffed it into her bag. She would look at it later, between her class and her private lesson tonight if she got a chance. She was hoping she wouldn't.

Chapter Ten

Samantha tapped her fingers anxiously on the door of the cab. Traffic was slow and heavy. It had been gorgeous all day, but a freak rainstorm had come out of nowhere in the last hour, making the roads miserable. She wanted to be there already. Shelly wouldn't arrive for more than an hour, but Samantha had been hoping to catch the end of Lucinda's class. She wanted to see how Lucinda was with the rest of her students. She glanced at her phone again to check the time and continued with her useless annoyed tapping.

She hadn't been able to get Lucinda out of her mind all weekend. She'd spent the better part of Saturday indirectly talking about her to Andrew. She smiled as she remembered the champagne surprise that helped her relax and open up a bit. Andrew was patient and understanding, didn't push too hard, but didn't let her get away with any real shit either. He wanted to know all about the mysterious Lucinda Moss. She did too, but she was more interested in spending time with her to figure it all out. Which is precisely why she was contemplating getting out and walking. The studio wasn't too far and this damn traffic was infuriating.

When the cab finally pulled up, she had to sprint through the torrential downpour in order to stave off looking like a drowned rat. She pulled open the studio door and hopped quickly inside, shaking the moisture off her coat and hair the best she could. It was quiet. The last class having obviously ended, there was only a low hum of music in the background. As Samantha walked into the room she saw Lucinda stretching on the floor by the mirrors, reading over some papers in front of her. Samantha stopped and leaned against the doorway, taking the moment to watch Lucinda's long, lean torso extend over lithe legs. She was gorgeous, all straight lines with gentle curves and lean muscle, perfectly feminine and strong. Samantha watched as Lucinda pulled her hair loose from its tie and tousled it lightly, cracking her neck and rolling her shoulders as she leaned forward once more, bringing her head to her knee. Samantha stood there for another moment or two before clearing her throat.

Lucinda smiled up at her and leaned back onto her hands, shaking her hair before scooping it back into a tight ponytail. She stood up in one graceful movement, gathering her papers as she rose.

"Am I interrupting something?" Samantha asked, only vaguely concerned, her attention drawn to the subtle dance beat playing over the speakers in the background.

"Ha, no. Just reviewing some paperwork. I have a meeting tomorrow that has been sort of burning in the back of my mind all day." She smiled warmly, depositing her papers back into the folder and into her bag on the side of the room. "I'm glad for the distraction though."

"Do you want me to come back later when Shelly comes? I don't want to hinder your meeting prep."

Lucinda sipped her bottle of water, dragging it over her bottom lip before winking and saying, "Nah. I'm good." She dropped her bottle and stepped forward, meeting Samantha's approach. "How are you today?" She let her hand wander to the sleeve of Samantha's jacket, pulling at the cuff idly.

"I'm good." Samantha let herself get lost in Lucinda's eyes for a moment.

"Is it weird if I tell you I missed you?" Lucinda asked boldly, stepping a little closer, pulling harder at Samantha's sleeve.

"Is it weird if I tell you the same?" Samantha wondered if the light flush in Lucinda's cheeks was from dancing or from her being this close. Samantha hoped it was the latter.

Lucinda leaned forward, her hand sliding up Samantha's arm to cup her face gently. "You look great," she whispered as she pressed a quick kiss to Samantha's cheek.

Samantha reached out and pulled Lucinda close, nuzzling her cheek before turning to capture Lucinda's lips with her own. Kissing Lucinda Moss felt oddly like coming home.

Lucinda smiled into the kiss, wrapping her arms tightly around Samantha as their lips moved slowly against each other's. Samantha sighed quietly and melted into her embrace, her jaw loosening and opening slightly, inviting Lucinda in. Lucinda deepened the kiss and let a low moan escape her lips as Samantha slid her hand under the front of Lucinda's shirt, playing with the skin exposed below the hem. She sucked gently on Samantha's tongue, letting her hand slide into Samantha's hair. Samantha broke the kiss, panting for breath as Lucinda's lips slipped along her jaw, leaving warm openmouthed kisses along the way. A low whimper tumbled from Samantha's pouty mouth as Lucinda sucked softly on the spot below her ear, teasing it lightly with her teeth.

"Luce…" Samantha almost growled as Lucinda's other hand traced up her side, brushing against the curve of her breast. She flattened her palm against the warm skin under Lucinda's shirt and scratched lightly before gently pushing her away, and Lucinda's lips released Samantha's neck. Lucinda looked almost hungry as Samantha stuttered, "God…*fuck*," and pressed another searing kiss to Lucinda's mouth before stepping back. "You're trouble."

A pleased smile formed on Lucinda's mouth as she leaned back, trailing her finger along Samantha's jaw before swiping it across her bottom lip. "Is that so?"

Samantha's eyes fluttered closed at the teasing contact on her kiss-plumped lip and she nodded. "Yup, big trouble."

"You started it."

Samantha watched Lucinda shyly for a minute before daring to engage in normal conversation. "What's the plan today?"

"Well, I thought I might teach Shelly how to dance, but I've been working on something new for her. Will you humor me and try it out?"

Samantha arched an eyebrow skeptically. "Something tells me this is somehow you leading me into a trap."

"Is that really what you think of me?" Lucinda feigned offense, dramatically placing her hand over her heart. "As sneaky?"

Lucinda led Samantha into the center of the floor and gently clasped their hands while settling her palm above Samantha's hip, guiding her movements forward and backward in rhythm with the beat of the music.

"I noticed that Shelly does best with verbal distraction. If I engage her in a topic that she enjoys she allows the natural momentum I stir up to lead her." Lucinda pressed her hand more firmly into Samantha's hip, eliciting a dip in the movement that allowed her to turn them slightly. "My goal today is to talk less and touch more, to see if I can get her to relax into her natural movement. Everyone has rhythm—some people just have it hidden under binary code."

She smiled and abruptly changed their direction, pressing her palm into Samantha's as she increased the pace of their feet. "For instance, you have a very sensual, natural sway. When you aren't fighting it." She teased a blush from Samantha's cheeks as she pulled her closer.

Samantha let out a quiet gasp as Lucinda slipped a strong leg between her own and pressed against her slightly.

"Don't fight me. Let me lead you," Lucinda whispered into the shell of Samantha's ear, her tongue punctuating the last word with a quick swipe. Samantha crumpled into her grasp, allowing herself to be moved like a plaything as they glided across the floor.

Samantha's heels made her the same height as Lucinda, if not a hairbreadth taller, so when Lucinda dipped her lightly during the next turn, Samantha was able to pull herself upright quickly and dip her head to catch Lucinda in an unexpected kiss.

"I won't fight." She pressed herself more fully onto Lucinda's thigh. The pretense of dancing quickly slipped away as Lucinda's hands dropped from position and ran almost greedily along Samantha's curves. Samantha started to backpedal toward the mirror behind them as Lucinda's lips met hers again more forcibly. They hit the barre before the glass and Samantha grabbed the wood to steady herself as Lucinda rolled her body against her. Lucinda watched Samantha's eyes flick toward the door of the studio and then to the clock. They had plenty of time.

Lucinda pulled back just enough so their noses were almost touching, pressed up against Samantha again, and then rolled her hips back and away in a taunting circle. Samantha arched her back and pressed her chest forward as Lucinda again closed the gap with a new body roll, this time clamping one hand onto the white-knuckled grip Samantha had on the barre behind her. Lucinda slipped her other hand between Samantha's back and the barre, guiding her more fully onto her thigh as she rolled forward again, in time with the nearly forgotten music playing in the background.

Samantha's eyes fluttered closed at the pressure of Lucinda's leg. Her shallow breathing came out in short pants as Lucinda continued to dance against her at the barre, punctuating her rhythmic movements with featherlight kisses along Samantha's jaw and the corner of her lips, always pulling back when Samantha leaned forward to catch Lucinda's lips with her own.

"Fuck," Samantha muttered after a particularly aggressive thrust brought Lucinda's thigh hard against her center, Samantha's tight skirt barely resisting the contact. Lucinda rewarded her reaction with a hot mouth, no longer teasing, pressed against hers as she swallowed the profanities her movements stirred loose. Samantha's hands left the barre in a flash, gripping at Lucinda's neck as she pulled her even closer, effectively grinding against Lucinda, forgetting the music's rhythm for her own carnal needs.

Lucinda hissed as Samantha nipped at her bottom lip, tugging her close with less than gentle teeth before soothing the bite with a warm tongue. Lucinda met the aggression with a firm hand on Samantha's side, her thumb digging into the soft flesh on the underside of Samantha's bra, gently scratching a blunt nail over the area. They broke apart from their heated make-out session to gasp for breath as Samantha again glanced warily at the door, her heart pounding against her still heaving chest.

Lucinda's eyes followed hers in the mirrored reflection, silently cursing herself for not locking the door. She took a slow, steadying breath and pulled back slightly, increasing the space between them. She was getting riled up too quickly. This really wasn't the place— although the idea of fucking Samantha against this dance barre was extremely appealing, she wanted it to be a little more private. She pressed a firm kiss to Samantha's lips before stepping back and kissing Samantha lightly. She looked positively stunning, lips red and swollen from kissing, eyes dark with desire. Lucinda wanted nothing more than to give Samantha everything her eyes were asking for, just not at the expense of Shelly walking in.

"Not here," Lucinda whispered. "I want to, just not here."

Samantha straightened her skirt and fixed her hair. She took a deep breath and closed her eyes as she slowly exhaled. Lucinda watched her curiously, wondering what she was thinking. She took a step closer when Samantha blinked open her eyes and pressed a soft kiss to her lips, hoping they were feeling the same way. She squeezed Samantha's hand gently and stepped away just as Shelly opened the studio door and greeted Lucinda with a warm smile. The growing feelings she had for Samantha would have to wait; now it was back to business as usual.

❖

The session went well. Shelly was able to relax after fifteen minutes of easy conversation and movement. She started to initiate movement on her own as she eased more and more into her role as female lead. Lucinda added a few counts for her to think about when she got nervous or felt out of tempo. The rhythmic counting soothed her, just like talking about her work did. By the end, she was actually laughing and stepping out of the scripted movement.

Samantha clapped and chuckled along as they wound down their session. Shelly released Lucinda's hand and swept over toward Samantha, pulling her into the position she had been practicing. It was a clumsy start, but Samantha picked up on Lucinda's verbal cues. Shelly twirled her to the right and stepped carefully so as not to step on her shoes.

"Shelly, this would be a good time to practice going to your left," Lucinda interjected. "Samantha doesn't know the steps, so you can practice your leading." She stood behind Samantha, her hands hovering over Shelly's.

Shelly initiated a spin to her left that was off beat by a step. Lucinda brought them back to the starting position and told them to try again, this time placing her hands on Shelly's clasped hand and Samantha's hip.

"Again."

She pushed Samantha's hip forward and into the movement before gently pulling back and digging her fingers into the soft skin above her hipbone to initiate the spin backward. When Samantha cued to the motion, Lucinda stepped back, allowing her to rotate in place, their eyes locking as Samantha's back faced Shelly in the final rotation. The gaze was unmistakably lustful. When the spin was complete and correct, Lucinda ended the session, applauding Shelly's marked improvement.

"Shelly, next time we'll have you run through the entire dance with Samantha, if she's agreeable to it." Her eyes flicked quickly to Samantha, who nodded, slightly out of breath. "That way you can practice your leading with some distractions. Practice your counts, okay?" Lucinda smiled warmly as Shelly pulled on her jacket and said good-bye.

She strode to the sound system, taking long steps. The music was off in an instant and Lucinda moved hurriedly toward the side of the studio where Samantha was pulling on her jacket and adjusting her purse. Lucinda scooped up her gear and pulled out her keys, waiting for Samantha to make eye contact with her before she asked, "Would you like a ride home?"

"I would love one."

Lucinda hooked her arm into Samantha's before leading her to the door to lock up. The rain had stopped but the ground was damp. The air smelled like fresh rainfall and it was eerily quiet. They walked in silence to Lucinda's car. She opened the passenger door and waited for Samantha to sit before walking to the driver's side, pausing to take a deep breath. She slipped into the seat and glanced over at her passenger once more before pulling away from the curb. She recognized the surrounding buildings and found her way to Samantha's apartment without difficulty.

Lucinda grabbed her bags and purse as the valet opened her door and ushered them inside. They walked to the elevator in silence, Samantha pausing to check her mailbox on the way. She shuffled some envelopes in her hand nervously as the elevator pinged in front of them. A concierge was in the car already with a few bags, obviously having come from the parking garage below. They stepped into the elevator and rode quietly up as the man tried to engage them each in conversation. Lucinda's mind was elsewhere, but she was willing to bet it was in the same place as Samantha's.

When they finally reached Samantha's floor after what seemed like an eternity, Lucinda paused and held the elevator door, not wanting to be too forward.

"Why don't you come in?" Samantha offered shyly and walked to her door, unlocking it and stepping over the threshold. As the elevator door chimed closed behind them, Samantha pulled Lucinda through the door by her shirt, the time for niceties obviously being over.

The door was barely closed and locked behind Lucinda before Samantha pushed her up against it with a bruising kiss.

"Watching you being held by another woman was torture," Samantha whispered hotly against Lucinda's mouth, her hands tugging at the waist of Lucinda's loose fitting shirt.

Lucinda deepened the kiss immediately, as she pulled Samantha against her thigh like before, this time more forcibly, and then gently rocked against her. Samantha gasped into Lucinda's mouth as she slid her hands under the soft cotton tee and scratched lightly at the taut stomach muscles that moved with every roll of Lucinda's hips.

Lucinda's eyes rolled into her head at the sensation of warm hands running over her abs. She tugged back on Samantha's hair, pulling her chin up before she lowered her mouth to the soft exposed skin of Samantha's neck, licking and sucking gently as she palmed Samantha's ass, pulling her closer. Samantha whimpered as Lucinda focused on her pulse point, nipping the tissue playfully as she toyed with the skirt's zipper.

"As much as I love your ass in this skirt, I'm ready to see it off," Lucinda growled low into the heated flesh of Samantha's neck, her statement met with a quick nod and whimper. Her fingers made short work of the skirt, sliding down the zipper and pushing it past Samantha's hips.

Samantha pulled the hem of Lucinda's shirt up higher, dragging it over her head and tossing it to the side, her gaze focused on Lucinda's near-naked torso. Lucinda felt herself flush under the scrutiny, bringing her lips to Samantha's to distract her from staring as she unbuttoned the silk shirt snuggly fit to Samantha's heaving chest. It was her turn to stare as she pushed the last of the fabric off Samantha's shoulders and to the floor, breaking the kiss to appreciate the perfect body in front of her.

"You're gorgeous," Lucinda said, reaching for Samantha so she could spin her slowly. She was absolutely perfect, all curves and soft lines, enviable abs and a pair of black lace panties that made Lucinda weak at the knees. "You are fucking gorgeous," she murmured again before pulling Samantha back in for a mind numbing kiss.

Samantha melted into the kiss, her fingers tracing greedy lines over Lucinda's own defined abs and up to her perky breasts in soft blue lace. She moved her lips along the curve of Lucinda's smile, nipping at her chin as she stepped out of her heels and forgotten skirt and began sucking on Lucinda's ivory-skinned collarbone. She felt Lucinda's fingers pull her closer as she worshipped the full curve of Lucinda's breast, licking along the lace cup while her fingers teased the nipple pebbling under her palm.

"I love the way you taste, I love the way your skin feels in my mouth." Samantha unhooked Lucinda's bra and pulled it slowly down her shoulders, revealing flushed skin. She circled her tongue around an erect nipple before sucking it into her mouth. Samantha increased the force of her suction and dragged her teeth lightly over the area as she rolled her hips against Lucinda's muscled thigh.

Lucinda pushed off the door, pulling Samantha's lips up to her own as she swept a hand down along her leg, hooking Samantha's knee up to her waist, encouraging her to meet the movement. Samantha moaned and wrapped her legs around Lucinda's waist, locking her arms behind Lucinda's neck as she opened her mouth even wider for the kiss.

Lucinda gripped Samantha's ass, holding her in place as she stepped away, breaking the kiss to glance around for a place they could lie down. Samantha pulled back, eyes wild, as she nodded toward an open door down the hall, her fingers pulling Lucinda's hair loose from the tie as she kissed along her neck. Lucinda smiled and shuddered as she felt Samantha's hot, wet center roll against her abs while Samantha sucked on the skin of her neck, still rocking gently against her.

They were in the bedroom in a moment's time, Lucinda slowly lowering Samantha onto the plush duvet cover, tossing pillows to the side as Samantha crawled up the bed, her stomach flexing lightly as her pink tongue swept over red lips. Lucinda let herself take in Samantha's black lace push-up and matching bottoms, soaked, hanging low on narrow hips. Lucinda moaned as she crawled over Samantha, licking up her stomach as her hands slipped the bra off her shoulders and tossed it to the floor.

Samantha dug her nails into Lucinda's shoulders and palmed her breasts as Lucinda licked a slow, agonizing line up Samantha's sternum before peppering light kisses over her heaving breasts. Samantha let out a quick breath as Lucinda sucked a stiff nipple into her mouth, grating it with her teeth as she smoothed her hands over Samantha's toned stomach. She hooked her thumbs under the black lace that was barely sitting on Samantha's hips and pushed down gently while she settled her gaze on hungry dark brown eyes above her, nodding in approval.

Samantha pulled her face up so their lips reconnected as Lucinda tossed aside her soaked panties and teased her fingers in a jagged line from hipbone to hipbone. Samantha moaned, her hand gripping behind Lucinda's head, holding their foreheads together as she lifted her hips, desperately searching for contact. Lucinda chuckled and pressed a firm kiss to her as she walked her fingers lower, slow and taunting. Samantha panted against Lucinda's mouth, her other hand dancing along Lucinda's front before plucking at a pert nipple and pulling urgently. Lucinda moaned and licked Samantha's lips as she pressed two firm fingers against Samantha's clit, circling slowly.

"Shit..." Samantha whimpered as she hooked one leg over Lucinda's waist, pulling them closer, skin on hot naked skin, as Lucinda slid her fingers lower, teasing Samantha's entrance. "Lucy, please..." Samantha begged, rolling her hips again as Lucinda smiled against her mouth, dragging her lips to suck on Samantha's jaw. She pressed two fingers inside Samantha, slowly. Samantha took in a sharp breath and held it as she clenched around Lucinda's fingers, her hips encouraging the build of a slow, rhythmic movement.

Lucinda felt her own sex throb at the warmth around her fingers, pulling her in tighter and deeper. Samantha had abandoned her breast and was scratching her nails along Lucinda's stomach, pushing desperately at the low-slung yoga pants before slipping her hand under the band. Samantha's breathing grew more and more erratic as Lucinda thrust deeper and faster into her. Samantha's own fingers slid under the lace barrier covering the soft curls over Lucinda's sex, moving in time with Lucinda's rolling hips to catch her up.

"I need to touch you," she commanded as she pulled up Lucinda's head to make eye contact. Wild, dilated pupils stared back at her before pink lips encased her own again. She moved her hand lower, running her fingers through the wetness, gliding up and down Lucinda's slit as she felt her own stomach winding tighter and tighter.

Lucinda gasped when Samantha pressed warm fingers against her clit making tight circles when Lucinda thrust her fingers inside Samantha. Samantha cried out, her back arching off the bed and her toes curling in the dark comforter as she tumbled over the edge.

Samantha caught a few desperate, panting breaths as she kissed Lucinda fiercely, pressing her fingers more forcibly against Lucinda's clit and gripping her ass, encouraging her to move. When Samantha sucked Lucinda's bottom lip into her mouth and bit down gently, she felt Lucinda cross into that blinding white flash of pleasure.

She froze above Samantha, eyes clenched shut, her mouth agape millimeters from Samantha's lips as the waves of pleasure washed over her. Samantha smiled and kissed the corner of Lucinda's mouth as she slowly brought her back down, making slow, easy circles on her clit while rubbing her hand over the muscles of Lucinda's back. Lucinda lowered herself, gently pushing Samantha's hand off her oversensitive sex and kissing swollen, red lips sweetly as she caught her breath.

Samantha hummed softly into the kiss. Lucinda pulled back and looked down at the gorgeous woman below her, a satiated grin on her face. "You're beautiful," she whispered as she brushed a damp strand of hair off Samantha's forehead. "And so naughty."

A blush crept up Samantha's face as she scrunched her nose in laughter. "And you are trouble," she supplied with a smile, her hands tracing lazy patterns on Lucinda's back before settling just above her ass. She snapped the elastic of Lucinda's forgotten pants playfully. "Take these off, I want to feel your skin on mine."

"You are so demanding," Lucinda teased, kissing Samantha quickly before peeling off the rest of her clothes and discarding them.

Samantha took the opportunity to fold back the comforter, exposing dark silk sheets. She shuffled under them, pulling Lucinda with her, her hands kneading gently on the skin of Lucinda's hip. Lucinda smiled and intertwined her fingers with Samantha's as they faced each other on their sides, legs woven together, lips close.

"Hi."

"Hi," Lucinda responded with a playful nibble along Samantha's jaw.

Samantha took in a contented breath, closing her eyes and appreciating the warm lips on her skin as she melted into Lucinda's gentle embrace. "I like the way you look in my bed." It was true. Lucinda's gorgeous pale skin and golden hair were perfectly framed by the dark sheets of Samantha's bed.

"I like the way I look in your bed, with you." Lucinda kissed her way back to Samantha's mouth before pressing a soft, featherlight peck to her lips.

Samantha tucked her chin to rest her head under Lucinda's and snuggled closer under the covers. "Good," she murmured.

CHAPTER ELEVEN

Samantha awakened the following morning to a gentle stirring under her. She lay draped across a very naked Lucinda Moss. Samantha glanced at the clock on the bedside table; it was very early still, but the sun would be rising soon enough. They had been up late. She smiled at the memory, a gentle throbbing between her legs serving as a physical reminder of their play. She nuzzled the underside of Lucinda's chin, kissing her softly. Lucinda smiled and blinked open sleepy eyes, dipping her head to connect their lips, gently sucking.

Samantha snuggled close as Lucinda wrapped her in a tight hug, savoring the moment and the contact. After a few minutes, Lucinda yawned and stretched before she glanced at the clock.

Samantha felt Lucinda tense under her. She knew that Lucinda had an important meeting that she definitely hadn't prepared for last night.

"You have to go." It was more of a statement than a question.

Lucinda nodded. "When do you have to be in today?" Her voice was groggy with sleep.

"I have a photo shoot for the website today," Samantha answered, her voice vibrating against Lucinda's chest. "I don't have to be in until ten."

"You should go back to sleep then. I'll call you later." She pressed a kiss to Samantha's hair as she shuffled out from under her.

Samantha yawned, stretching and scooting into the warm space left by Lucinda. She focused on the soft curve of Lucinda's spine as she bent forward at the edge of her bed, retrieving articles of clothing tossed aside haphazardly. Samantha walked her fingers across the sheets and up over the bones of Lucinda's spine, appreciating the way she stopped moving and pressed back into her touch. Lucinda glanced over her shoulder and winked before leaving the bed in search of the rest of her clothes. When she returned to the room, she was fully dressed with her hair pulled into a sloppy bun. She knelt on the edge of the bed and cupped Samantha's face before pressing a lingering kiss to her pouty lips.

"I'll talk to you soon."

Samantha smiled and settled into the bed, pulling the covers up to her chin. Lucinda turned to go but Samantha reached out and grabbed her shirt, pulling her in for one last, deep kiss. "Have a great day. Good luck with your meeting," she mumbled, already falling back to sleep.

❖

Lucinda keyed into her home with a tired sigh. A pile of work waited for her. The meeting with Richard was in a few hours and she was just crawling home now like some teenager sneaking in after curfew. She had to shower, change, prep the meeting material, go to work, take a conference call, and look like she was focused. She was most definitely going to struggle with that last part the most. How could she possibly focus when all she could think about was Samantha Monteiro?

As she dropped her keys into the dish by the front door she was reminded of a conversation she had had with Dominic after she made a similar early morning entrance. He had come over one night after work and fallen asleep on her couch, waiting for her to come home. She had been scared near to death when his head popped over the back of her couch with an annoyed sigh as she walked in. It was a sigh of judgment and she had cringed, waiting for the onslaught. He asked why he never ran into any of her love interests when he came by uninvited and pressed her about it.

At first she had avoided direct eye contact and shrugged but eventually he pulled the truth out of her. Dominic never did put up with her bullshit. She begrudgingly admitted that she didn't like having women in her personal space; the break-up with Grace had been particularly difficult, and her home was her safe haven. His stern look had faded in that moment and he consoled her, telling her that she would get everything she wanted, eventually.

Lucinda shrugged off her jacket and stretched her arms over her head as the early morning sunrise started to filter through her kitchen windows. She poured herself a glass of water and sipped it slowly as she thought of the gentle concern in Dominic's eyes. He would be disappointed to know that she hadn't woken up with another woman in quite some time. She usually slipped out, leaving a quick note or text. In fact, Samantha seemed to be the only exception to that particular rule. The idea of leaving her bed without saying good-bye almost offended her.

As she walked toward the stairs to get ready for her day, she mulled that over a bit. Would Dominic have liked Samantha? Undoubtedly. She let out a sad sigh. She missed her little pep talks with him; she could use one now as she felt herself wading into murky waters again.

❖

"Good morning, Andrew, coffee?" Samantha smiled and extended a large cup toward him.

He paused and looked around before accepting it, sliding his glasses up onto his head. "You're chipper today," he commented, eyebrow raised.

Samantha shrugged and sipped her coffee, handing the bag of doughnuts to one of the assistants bustling by. Every few months, she and Andrew had a photo shoot and publicity day to freshen up their market presence for Perfect Match, Inc. It was a tightly scheduled affair. Andrew picked out their outfits beforehand, purchasing new dresses and suits if need be, incorporating some signature pieces for continuity. This business was about presentation—clean lines, clear script, and branding. Samantha and Andrew were experts at brand representation; it was their entire business.

This year had been particularly profitable to them and they were being featured on the front page of the *Improper Bostonian* as most eligible man and woman of the dating scene. This was the first time Samantha was back in the public eye since her breakup with Eric. It was inevitable with the amount of good press she had been getting lately—the Lundstein wedding had been a front-page spread a few weeks back. Business was booming and they needed to show their pretty faces to support its success.

"So here is the list of questions that are approved," Andrew said, handing her some papers. "We're meeting with the magazine, a columnist from the paper, and a blogger today." He pointed to the last page before adding, "I did my best to refuse comment on Eric"—he lowered his voice so only she could hear—"but they're going to want to talk about your eligibility as a bachelorette for the feature. I will be there every step of the way, I promise—we'll answer everything together."

"Okay, thanks, Andrew, this looks great." She sipped her coffee and settled onto the bench behind them.

"That's it?" he asked incredulously.

"Hmm, what's it?"

"That's all you have to say? No complaints, comments, recommendations, rebuttals. Nothing? Just okay, thanks, Andrew?"

"Yes, everything looks good. Thank you." Samantha smiled and adjusted her sunglasses, leaning back on the bench and soaking up the warm sun overhead.

Andrew stood in front of her, blocking some of her light, and tapped his foot. He was staring at her; she could feel it even with her eyes closed.

"There's something different about you. You're way too calm. Are you hungover?"

"No, Andrew, it's the middle of the week. I'm just enjoying this beautiful day."

"Samantha!" Andrew barked suddenly, jarring her out of her reverie. He had his hand over his mouth, his eyes nearly bugging out, as he sat next to her and whispered harshly, "You fucked her. I can't believe it. You fucking fucked her."

Samantha averted her eyes, sipping her coffee to keep from spilling secrets she wasn't yet ready to share.

"Oh my God! Tell me everything, you filthy hussy!"

She swatted at him and crossed her legs. She was definitely not telling him anything.

"Oh, please. You couldn't shut your trap about your piece of scum ex, but you clam up about the clam? I'm offended."

Samantha choked out a laugh and covered her mouth, trying to gain her composure. "Could you please not make a spectacle of yourself?" she whispered through a forced smile. "People are staring."

"Well then, admit it. You slept with her and that's why you're so calm—because you got some." He flashed a wicked grin and sipped his coffee, turning to face her more fully on the bench.

"Andrew, we are not discussing this here," she warned again.

"I told you! I knew it! I knew you liked her. Oh, tell me, those legs that go on for days, what's it like? She's a dancer, her stamina must be amazing."

Samantha smiled slyly and wet her lips before replying quietly, "It was pretty awesome."

"Good for you, Sam!" He pulled her into a sideways hug and smiled broadly and pointed to the papers. "Okay, now learn your lines."

❖

Lucinda got ready for work in record time, feeling surprisingly awake on less than five hours' sleep. She made it in before Amanda, settling at her desk and turning on her tablet while she flipped through the file of Richard's performance evaluations and peer reviews. She reached into the top drawer of her desk and pulled out her headset, plugging the wireless adapter into the phone base. She clicked the tablet into the keyboard and turned on the monitor next to her. She wanted to utilize both screens during her teleconference so she could pull up the client's specs while she worked.

Amanda poked her head in shortly before the call. "Good morning, Lucinda. I brought your coffee and a yogurt."

"Thank you, Amanda." Lucinda smiled and waved her in, motioning that the call had yet to start. "How was your weekend?"

"Busy. Crazy," Amanda said. "We bought some new furniture, and you would not believe how bad the assembly directions were."

"Next time, let me know, and maybe I can come over and help," Lucinda offered. A soft ping signaled the client had joined the open line and was ready for the call. "Thanks again for breakfast, Amanda. Please be sure to close the door behind you."

The conference call went flawlessly. The clients liked the portfolio Lucinda's team had put together and were moving on to the next stage of project completion. There would be a follow-up call in about ten days to finalize the proposal and put into practice their crisis communications plan.

Next up was Lucinda's meeting with Richard. She had reviewed the group evaluation reports from his past five projects over her morning coffee. Her suspicions about his participation were confirmed: he was consistently inconsistent when he was a cochair or supporting staff. She found an alarming trend in his peer reviews demonstrating poorly rated performances when Claire Moseley or the other female executive were in the point position. Simple mistakes marred his reports: typos, spacing errors, one report had a coffee stain on the bottom right of the second to last page—glaring, foolish errors. A knock at Lucinda's door drew her attention to the shadowed figure on the other side.

"Come in," she called.

Richard opened the door slowly. He swallowed as he walked in, closing the door behind him. "Hi, Lucinda." He gulped nervously and sat on the edge of the chair Lucinda offered.

"Richard." She offered him a tight smile, appreciating his nervousness. "I want to talk to you about some of your recent projects. Did you have a chance to review the email I sent you yesterday?"

He nodded and tapped his fingers on the portfolio balancing on his lap.

"Good. Listen, I'm going to get right to it—your projects have been successful but I have some serious concerns about your performance. I have notes here pointing out late submissions, missed meetings, typographical errors—simple mistakes, Richard. Mistakes that are sloppy, mistakes from inattention, mistakes that don't represent the high caliber of executive performance that you are expected to exhibit. Is there something I should know? Do you feel like you're being overworked?"

"No, I'm not overworked." He loosened his tie and cracked his neck before squaring his shoulders and looking at Lucinda directly. "I can handle it. Everything is fine."

Lucinda leaned back and crossed her legs. Richard looked rattled despite the cockiness that radiated off his fake smile. She despised that smug grin. She kept eye contact with him as she reached for her tablet and pulled up his performance reports, opening windows and moving documents into a clearly presented collage.

Her face was blank as she spun the monitor toward him. "Consider this your quarterly review," she said. "These mistakes cannot continue. I expect you to cooperate fully in all groups you are a part of, turn in your portion of the work on time, and never, ever submit your final projections with coffee stains." She dragged the curser over the enlarged image before adding, "This type of oversight is positively unacceptable."

Richard narrowed his eyes and snarled at her, letting his typically cool façade falter. "I understand, Ms. Moss."

"We'll be meeting again in two weeks. I have a project I want you to complete in the meantime. I expect an email update in two days." She held out a folder to him. Richard reached for the folder as he stood, a sour expression on his face. "Your final submissions will be coming directly to me until I see significant improvement in your work." Lucinda held the folder for a moment longer, not releasing it to him until she added, "Have a good day, Richard."

He exited her office without a single word. She let out a weary sigh as he closed the door. This was the part of her job she disliked. Not the firing of insubordinates, no; it was the managerial duties that drained her. Although sometimes she missed the days when the completion of a project was her only task, she really enjoyed guiding the execs under her to success. She did not, however, enjoy dealing with people like Richard who weren't interested in getting with her program. She was proud of the strides Clear View had made under her meticulous management. This was just one of those annoying little bumps along the road to success she told herself. Three deep breaths and a sip of coffee later, she reached for her phone and texted Samantha.

❖

"Miss Monteiro?" the young, dark-haired PA called out. "Can we have you over here for the last shot?"

She let the makeup artist add some final touches before stepping toward Andrew and standing on her marked spot. She placed her hand on his back and flashed a perfect smile to the camera. *Click, click, click* and they were done for the day. Lucinda had texted her a few times over the past hour and Samantha grew more giddy with every new vibrating notification.

Andrew crowded around the monitor with the photographer to go over the last of the images and pick the best ones for the publication. They had completed all their interviews without incident and would review the final screens again tomorrow once Andrew narrowed them down a bit.

Samantha thanked the support staff and technicians as she excused herself from the main staging area to a bench off to the right. She scrolled over the past texts just as a new one from Lucinda buzzed through: *Done? How'd it go?* ☺

Samantha smiled and chewed her lip before typing back: *Yeah, it was great.*

I bet it was, you're very easy to want to photograph...

"So, giggles," Andrew interrupted her flirtation, "what's Lucinda doing later—is she coming to celebrate with us?"

Samantha turned her phone over, hiding the conversation from view. "Celebrating, huh? What did you have in mind?"

"Since we're going to be the most eligible bachelor and bachelorette of matchmaking in Boston, we should toast our success in style." He winked playfully. "You, me, cocktails, and a view of our urban playground." He bowed forward and made a grand sweeping motion with his arm.

"Well, when you put it like that, how could I say no?" Samantha stood and pulled Andrew into a tight hug, panicking slightly about the stigma of being a matchmaker who couldn't find a match. Maybe this article wasn't such a good idea after all.

He pecked her on the cheek and rubbed her arms before flashing a mischievous smile. "Good. I figured you'd say that, so I made a reservation at Top of the Hub. For three."

Samantha scrunched her forehead in confusion, then, almost if on cue, her phone buzzed and her eyes widened comically. "No, Andrew. No way."

"Sam! C'mon. It'll be fun. Plus, I'll have the opportunity to actually spend some time with your new favorite plaything." He batted his eyelashes flirtatiously and stuck out his bottom lip. "I'm feeling awfully neglected lately—it'd be nice to see why firsthand."

"I don't know about this," Samantha said. "Something tells me this is a bad idea. We're just getting to know each other."

Her phone buzzed again. Andrew snatched it from her hands and hopped out of reach. Before Samantha could get ahold of him he had pulled up Lucinda's number, put the phone on speaker, and dialed. She listened in mortified paralysis.

"Is this my favorite brunette?" Lucinda purred.

Andrew replied with a sly smile, "No, darling, it's your other favorite brunette…tell me, are you free tonight?"

Chapter Twelve

Lucinda smiled as she recalled her earlier conversation with Andrew. She was glad she hadn't answered the phone with anything *too* provocative. She had left work early to take a conference call on the ride home and decompress before dinner tonight. Two particularly body-flattering outfits were on her bed, one a black and white dress, the other a soft shirt with a pair of slacks. In the end she chose the dress.

Top of the Hub was a beautiful restaurant encased in glass at the top of the second tallest building in the city. Every table offered an unobstructed view of the city below from high atop the Prudential Tower in the center of Boston. Even Jamaica Plain, the suburban part of the city where Lucinda lived, could be identified from such a high height.

She lived close to an old clock tower in JP that served as a beautiful landmark; it was visible from the southeast corner of the restaurant. She remembered the first time Dominic had pointed it out to her after a dance win they were celebrating at the posh restaurant. She had placed a bid on an old house and had been nervously anticipating the bid's acceptance. He had been so reassuring to her, as he always was. He had a way of making everything seem much easier and less daunting. All the big milestones and important moments in her life featured Dominic Andiamo. Tonight, meeting up with Samantha and Andrew felt bittersweet without him.

As she stepped onto the elevator and opened her coat, she was reminded about her thoughts this morning, keying into her empty house, her body still buzzing from her night with Samantha. She could feel herself falling for her. It was more than just the physical attraction; Samantha had consumed her thoughts all day. The idea of creating new memories at this restaurant with Samantha was both exciting and terrifying. She wasn't quite sure where this relationship was headed, but there was a part of her that really wanted to find out. Now if only she could quiet the other parts, everything would be fine.

❖

Lucinda stepped off the elevator on the fifty-second floor and headed toward the hostess table. She checked in at the podium and was informed that the remaining members of her party had not arrived, so she headed for the bar. She ordered a martini and stood at the edge of the bar, looking out at the view of the north side of the city. The night was clear and the view was perfect, shimmering lights and the warm glow of the city street lamps illuminating the bustle of the streets below.

A warm hand rested at her hip, and she smiled, setting her drink on the bar. She had felt Samantha approaching, her senses in tune with Samantha's arrival. She pulled the hand from her hip to her front, lacing her fingers with Samantha's over her abdomen.

"Hey, there." Samantha's voice was velvety soft behind her as she gently hugged Lucinda from behind.

Lucinda let her free hand gently knead the flesh of Samantha's hip in response. Her heart rate picked up when she noticed the absence of panty lines. "Hi." She squeezed the fingers interlaced with her own before she turned fully and settled her gaze on the woman in front of her. Samantha looked amazing. Perfect hair and makeup, just stunning. "I'm happy to see you."

Samantha smiled, her cheek pressed to Lucinda's. "Me too."

Lucinda placed a delicate, lingering kiss below Samantha's ear, murmuring, "You look great."

Samantha shuddered and danced her fingers up and down Lucinda's back before stepping away. "Thanks for coming."

Lucinda flashed a bright smile and glanced over Samantha's shoulder at Andrew who was standing idly by, watching quietly with a smug look on his face. "Hey, Andrew, how are you?"

"Oh, me? I'm good, just giving you ladies a little time to catch up."

Samantha rolled her eyes. "Where's our table? I'm starved."

"Mm-hmm." Andrew quipped, "Maybe they have a fish special tonight…"

Lucinda choked out a laugh behind her martini and paid the bartender, closing her tab. "Oh, Andrew, I do adore your commentary. Thanks for inviting me tonight."

"Of course! We have *so* much to catch up about."

Samantha snorted. Lucinda laughed by her side and looped their arms together on the way to the dining room. She leaned in and whispered, "Relax, this is gonna be fun." Samantha nodded before taking a swig of Lucinda's martini.

Their table was against the window, Andrew and Lucinda opposite each other with Samantha at the head, facing the view. Andrew ordered a bottle of champagne and a few appetizers as they caught up on the day's activities. Lucinda smiled easily in their company. Andrew was hilarious—she wished she could have been a fly on the wall of the photo shoot today; she could only imagine the type of diva he was in wardrobe. They made short work of the first round of food, wiping out a bottle of champagne in the meantime. At some point during the meal, Samantha's right hand made its way to Lucinda's thigh.

Lucinda liked how physically affectionate Samantha was with her. When they first met, she had initiated all contact, tentative and slow. She couldn't help but smile when Samantha did it now; it felt very natural while still giving her a warm buzzing feeling. She dropped her hand below the table to press against the fingers idly playing with the hem of her dress. Andrew waved toward the waiter, giving Lucinda the chance to lock eyes with Samantha, who winked before licking her lips, squeezing Lucinda's thigh and pulling her hand up to the table. Samantha folded the napkin that was on her lap and excused herself, leaving Lucinda a little breathless.

She watched Samantha cross the room, her eyes lingering on the curves accentuated by the form-flattering fabric of her dress. Samantha stopped to talk to the maître d', and brushed her hair over her shoulder before settling her gaze on Lucinda. She flashed a bright smile as she ended her conversation and walked toward the restroom. Lucinda didn't bother to hide her appreciative leering; Samantha was positively gorgeous in everything and nothing. A small smile settled on her lips as she leaned back a bit into her chair.

"She likes you, you know." Andrew interrupted her trance.

"Mm. The feeling is very mutual." Lucinda laughed and glanced at him as he sipped his drink. "She's stunning, isn't she?"

He nodded and replied quietly, "She is. Be good to her—she deserves the best."

"Of course." Lucinda watched his face closely. She wasn't looking for anything in particular, just looking. She liked that he was so protective of Samantha. "You'll tell me if I fuck anything up, right?"

He placed his drink on the table before shooting her a fake menacing glance. "I have you on speed dial."

❖

When Samantha returned to the table, she took a moment to appreciate the way Lucinda and Andrew were interacting. Lucinda was laughing so hard she was wiping away tears and Andrew was waving his arms around, describing something that looked vaguely vulgar. She liked that they got along so well. It was something her past relationships lacked, particularly with Eric. He and Andrew never seemed to mesh well; it was always like oil and water between them. Lucinda held up her hand to stop Andrew as she gasped for air and sipped some water.

"What in the name of Versace are you flailing around about?" Samantha asked as she took her seat.

"How dare you take his name in vain," Andrew scolded, as he too wiped away tears.

"Andrew was telling me about his distaste of tucking up," Lucinda choked out between giggles and sips of her water.

Samantha scrunched her brow in confusion. "What? What the hell is tucking up?"

Andrew rolled his eyes and let out an exaggerated sigh. "Samantha, I expect better from you. We have discussed this before, it drives me crazy. It makes me feel so deceived!" He clucked in annoyance and sipped his drink.

"In all honesty, sometimes I check out when you ramble." Samantha looked back to Lucinda for help.

"It's common in male dancers and some gay men," Lucinda answered, resting a hand on Samantha's. "They wear underpants that are a bit tighter than necessary and tuck their penis up into the band so it doesn't hang down their leg and show through their pants."

"It's fraud! Do you know how many guys tuck up to hide how small they are?" Andrew scoffed. "That's like stuffing your pants with socks and me getting a handful of lint when we're fooling around. Equally unacceptable."

Lucinda almost spit out her drink. The tables around them shot them irritated looks as the three of them continued to laugh like hyenas.

"All I'm saying is, I appreciate clean lines as much as the next fashionable gay male, but let's not appear like we have a man-gina because your junk is up in your waistband." Andrew flashed an appalled look as he swirled the contents of his champagne glass before finishing it off. "I mean, how is that even comfortable?"

Lucinda clutched her chest again before asking, "Well, have you tried it? How do you know it's uncomfortable?"

Andrew pondered the question for a moment before replying in a hushed tone, "Of course I tried it. I needed to test the theory, make sure I wasn't missing out on anything."

"How did you even get into this conversation?" Samantha asked.

"Well," Lucinda answered, "Andrew was telling me about this new Underwear of the Month Club he joined."

"You joined a what?" Samantha interlaced her fingers with Lucinda's on the tabletop.

"Underwear of the Month Club. They send you designer underwear once a month in the fit that you like. It's fun." Andrew winked.

"You think they have a thong of the month club?" Samantha ran her thumb along Lucinda's knuckles.

Andrew quirked an eyebrow at her and laughed. "Why? You gonna join, Sam? I happen to have on good authority that you're not even wearing underwear right now."

Samantha tried to suppress her own smile. "You two are ridiculous."

Andrew's phone buzzed in his pocket and he dug it out, staring at the screen before glancing back up at his dinner companions.

"I have to take this," he apologized. "Be right back."

Samantha was looking out at the view, in her own little world. Lucinda pulled their interlocked hands from the table and onto her lap. "I want to show you something. Come with me?"

"Of course, I'd go anywhere with you." That last part came out without any thought. She internally cringed and looked up at Lucinda to see if it had creeped her out.

"Good to know," Lucinda stood, seemingly unfazed, and pulled Samantha with her. She released their hands as she walked through the dining room, pausing her stride when Samantha repositioning her hand on the inside of Lucinda's elbow, stepping close.

Samantha knew why Lucinda had dropped her hand. Just like she knew why she was greeted with a hidden kiss along her jaw during the hug. It was refreshing to be in charge of her own destiny, empowered to reach out and touch her new friend in a more than friendly way when she wanted to. It felt very natural to be close to Lucinda, touching her arm, holding her hand, brushing back her hair. It was still so new and fresh. She didn't want to rush anything or jump to conclusions. Samantha felt a little insecure all of a sudden and her face must have reflected her self-doubt.

"Hey," Lucinda asked, "are you all right?"

"Yeah, yeah. I was just thinking too much, it's nothing," Samantha mumbled shyly and put her head against Lucinda's shoulder.

"This is my favorite view from inside the restaurant at night." She pointed toward the horizon and identified landmarks for Samantha. "That's the Museum of Fine Arts, and those dimmer lights line the Fens over there."

Samantha leaned into Lucinda, listening attentively and watching the excitement as she shared her secrets.

"Over there, see that bright blue light?"

Samantha nodded and looked intently into the distance at the tiny blue orb.

"To the left of that light is a big white clock tower, and just a few streets away is my house, tucked back on top of a large hill overlooking the city. I love this view because I feel like even though I'm a little out of the city, I'm still a part of it." Lucinda kept her eyes on the blue light as she spoke, her voice soft and reverent. "And I can find my way home whenever I may feel lost."

Samantha's eyes left the view and scanned Lucinda's face. They were so close she could feel Lucinda's breath on her cheek. She was so beautiful, beautiful in feature and in heart. Lucinda Moss was beautiful.

"Will you take me there sometime? To see your place?"

"Of course, whenever you'd like."

Before she could second-guess herself, Samantha was rocking forward and placing a slow, chaste kiss to her lips. "Take me there, tonight."

Lucinda sealed her affirmation with a kiss. "Let's find Andrew and slip out of here." She cupped Samantha's cheek and rubbed her thumb slowly along her cheekbone before smiling and stepping back.

Samantha tucked her head, suddenly bashful after her bold request. She smiled when Lucinda laced their fingers together and nodded toward their table.

Andrew glanced up from busily scrolling through his phone and smiled. "Welcome back, ladies."

Lucinda pushed in Samantha's chair as she sat, her fingers grazing over a bare shoulder before she sat down and sipped her water. Samantha turned to Andrew. "Everything okay?"

"Yeah, nothing I can't handle." He shrugged before flashing a devious grin. "I'm going to assume that you'll be having your dessert elsewhere and I should get the check now, yes?"

Lucinda laughed into her water while Samantha gaped, neither confirming nor denying his insinuation.

Andrew raised his glass in a toast. "To new friends and new adventures. Lucinda, thank you for the delicious champagne on our girls' day and for making my best friend smile for the first time in a long time. Cheers!"

As Lucinda clinked glasses with her two new friends, she slipped her hand under the table and rested her palm on Samantha's thigh. "Call me Lucy."

They rode down the elevator laughing and joking about their night and promising to make this a more regular occurrence. Andrew hugged them both and hopped in a cab, telling Samantha he would talk to her later and winking at Lucinda.

Lucinda nodded toward the valet approaching with her classic car. "C'mon baby," she teased.

Samantha blushed and settled into her seat, still chuckling over the night's events.

Chapter Thirteen

The ride to Lucinda's was quick; she lived just on the outskirts of the city, fifteen minutes from Boston proper. The area was mostly populated by young professionals with an eclectic mix of food and local harvest grocers. There were restaurants, old-time barber shops, and old Irish bars with meticulous storefronts and lots of trees.

"I bought this place for its proximity to all the open space of the Arboretum," Lucinda explained to Samantha. "I take sunset hikes and early morning runs. You wouldn't believe the sunsets, and the sunrises."

"That must be wonderful." Samantha sighed.

"It is. I love to be outdoors, even in the heart of the city," Lucinda said. Lucinda lived in a medium-sized single-family home set off the street on a hill. It was two-stories high with a double porch and perfectly groomed garden. Light blue with dark blue shutters and white accents, the house was gorgeous. Lucinda pulled into the driveway and glanced over to Samantha a little timidly. "Home sweet home."

"Luce, it's beautiful." Samantha flashed a broad grin, her expression sincere.

Lucinda stepped out of the car and moved to the passenger side to help Samantha and her skintight dress out of the leather bucket seat. She placed a soft hand on Samantha's lower back and guided her up the stone steps onto the porch. The large antique oak door with blue paneled stained glass and intricate carvings displayed an attention to detail not found in modern architecture. Lucinda unlocked the door and stepped inside, turning on the light in the front foyer and watching Samantha's gaze trace over the wide-board wood floors and ornate door casings, before she danced her fingers lightly on the original wainscoting that ran the length of the entryway. Lucinda was proud of her home. She loved the history of the wood and the luster of the banister to the second floor. This place was beautiful and she had worked hard to preserve its charm.

She deposited her keys and purse on the table in the foyer before nodding toward the kitchen. "Can I get you something to drink? Some wine? Water? Coffee? Tea?"

Samantha smiled. "Wine, please."

Lucinda walked through the living room to a massive open kitchen and pulled out a bottle each of red and white wine. She felt Samantha's eyes on her as she reached into the cabinet and pulled down two glasses, flicking on a few lights along the way. Samantha nodded toward the red and smiled as Lucinda procured an opener from one of the dozens of drawers that lined the marble countertop.

"Your kitchen is stunning, Luce. Do you cook?" Samantha seated herself at the island on a stool.

Lucinda uncorked the bottle and poured the wine with care, appreciating the settling of the sediment before handing the glass to her. Samantha swirled the glass lightly to aerate the wine and appreciate the aroma before toasting Lucinda with a smile.

"I do cook, actually. This kitchen was one of the major selling points of the house. Well, this and the master bedroom." She winked and sipped her wine, leaning against the counter.

Samantha laughed into her wine, putting it down on the kitchen island and standing before purring, "When do I get the formal tour?"

Lucinda raised an eyebrow and uncrossed her ankles. She placed her glass down and walked slowly toward Samantha. She reached out and ran her palm up Samantha's side before leaning in to kiss her.

Samantha reciprocated immediately, opening her mouth and teasing her tongue along Lucinda's lip. Lucinda responded with a low moan and kissed Samantha deeply before trailing her lips along her jaw, settling below her ear.

"Let's go upstairs," she murmured before sucking the skin into her mouth and releasing it. She pulled back and laced her fingers with Samantha's, leading her toward the staircase. Samantha Monteiro would be the first woman Lucinda had in her bedroom in years. She let that thought marinate a bit and realized she was glad she made the bed this morning.

As they ascended the final steps, Lucinda started to second-guess herself. There was a reason she never brought women back here. But before she could process that thought any further, Samantha's free hand roamed up her hip from behind and pulled her close at the top step. Lucinda's concerns melted when Samantha pressed a soft kiss to her shoulder, sweet and affectionate. Lucinda turned on the spot and cupped Samantha's face, kissing her lips tenderly before pulling back to look at her face.

She watched Samantha closely, seeing the gentle blush on her cheeks, and the way her collarbone rose and fell. Lucinda kissed her softly once more before walking them into the master bedroom to the right of the stairs.

Lucinda left Samantha to survey the new environment as she clicked on the bedside lamps and drew the blinds. The room was large; a four-poster bed against the far wall was adorned with sheer curtains and fluffy pillows—she liked it because it looked like a welcoming cloud. The fabrics were lighter than Samantha's, hues of white and cream, light blues and teals, a contrast to Samantha's dark comforter and sheets. Her bed was flanked by two bedside tables in matching cherry oak that complemented a large dresser at the end of the bed. The dresser's center held a grand mirror with accents of gold in the framed wood. Tucked into the corners of the frame were a few pictures, familiar smiling faces, Lucinda in full dance regalia.

Lucinda moved about, plumping pillows, arranging things just so, busying herself as she let Samantha explore. She watched Samantha slowly caress the wood carvings along the dresser as she looked at the images Lucinda had stubbornly refused to put in frames: pictures of Connie as a child, pictures of her teaching a dance class, a snapshot of a picnic with Massimo and his dog Duke, a faded image of her stuffed bear from when she was tossed from foster home to foster home, a heart shape made out of trees naturally formed in the area behind her house...little memories that kept her grounded. She felt naked with Samantha studying them so closely.

Lucinda stepped into the master bath and ran the water, rinsing off her hands and watching in the mirrored reflection as Samantha finally reached for the one picture that haunted Lucinda the most, the one of her and Dominic dancing. It was the last competition they were ever in together, and they had swept all three events, as usual, but it had felt different the whole time. Like something was off. She'd had no idea it would be their last recorded performance together. She might have done something differently. She might have said something more. She didn't want to do this, not now, not with Samantha here. She didn't want to mourn, she refused to. She stuffed the feeling down and admired Samantha's perfect curves. What Lucinda wanted, tonight, was to touch her, taste her skin, love her body. And she could.

She stepped up behind Samantha, gliding her hands up Samantha's sides and brushing her hair off to one side. She lowered her lips to the naked skin, kissing along the crest of Samantha's shoulder, licking the flesh as she went. She kept her eyes on Samantha's reflection, slowly nipping and soothing, watching her reaction closely.

Samantha closed her eyes and breathed out deeply when Lucinda's lips met her skin. She gripped the edge of the bureau as Lucinda kissed up her neck, nuzzling at her ear. Samantha reached up and slowly took out her earrings, one at a time, with her eyes open now, watching Lucinda intently.

Lucinda's hands pressed Samantha's hips against the dresser, staying close as she slowly unzipped Samantha's dress, letting it fall to the floor before slipping off Samantha's bra and tossing it aside. Her lips never left Samantha's skin and her hands were constantly in contact, manipulating her position, guiding her into place. Samantha stepped out of the discarded dress and moved to take off her shoes, but Lucinda placed a steady hand at her hip to stop her. "Leave them on," Lucinda husked into her ear before biting down on her earlobe. Samantha shuddered and nodded, straightening out and looking through hooded brown eyes at Lucinda's reflection.

Lucinda rid herself of her own dress and pressed flat against Samantha, her hands running up a tight abdomen to perky breasts, palming them softly at first before increasing her pressure and rolling her fingers over pert nipples.

Samantha moaned and arched into the touch, her back bowing naturally. Lucinda continued lavishing attention on the skin of Samantha's neck and upper back as she turned her chin toward her. She kissed Samantha once, slowly and softly, whispering, "Let me lead."

Samantha nodded and began kissing Lucinda with a fierceness that caught her breath.

Lucinda broke the kiss and bent Samantha forward so she was leaning on her hands, watching in the mirror. With one hand, Lucinda continued to toy with Samantha's chest as the other slid down to her hip and over her ass, nudging her legs apart as Lucinda resumed kissing her upper back. Samantha's legs parted slowly. Lucinda traced her fingers up the slick skin on the inside of Samantha's thighs, teasing the flesh as she continued to give attention to swollen nipples. She bit down gently on Samantha's shoulder as she moved her hand up to cup her center, then teased her fingers up and down slowly over Samantha's sex.

Samantha moaned and let out soft, fast breaths at all the stimulation.

Lucinda watched Samantha struggle to maintain eye contact as she slipped lower, pressing two fingers against her tight entrance before entering slowly. Samantha whimpered and pressed back farther into Lucinda's hand, rolling her hips to take the new addition fully. Lucinda moved in and out of her with a steady rhythm increasing as she went and added a third finger. Samantha bucked back, eyes widening momentarily before resuming their hooded gaze, so wet against Lucinda's hand that she almost slipped out of place.

Lucinda pressed against Samantha to anchor her control as she brought her lips up to Samantha's ear again. "Did you like it when I called you baby?"

Samantha groaned and her mouth gaped. She sucked in a deep breath as Lucinda continued to thrust and nodded her head. Lucinda rewarded her with a bright smile and tender kiss to her neck as she bent her forward a tiny bit more and whispered, "Touch yourself for me."

Lucinda barely got the gentle command out before Samantha complied with enthusiasm. Her eyes fluttered shut momentarily as she clenched tightly around Lucinda's fingers, the pulsing of her sex becoming more erratic against Lucinda's hand.

"Slow," Lucinda demanded as she sucked on the skin under her ear. Samantha calmed her frantic movements as Lucinda released her breast and slid her hand up her chest so it was resting under her collarbone. Lucinda increased her pace slightly before pressing her thumb lightly over the puckered flesh of Samantha's asshole. Samantha gasped and bit down on her bottom lip.

"Come for me, baby," Lucinda said as she licked the shell of Samantha's ear.

Samantha cried out and she increased the frantic circles on her clit. Lucinda continued thrusting in and out in controlled strokes as she felt Samantha start to tumble over the edge. Just as Samantha trembled against her, Lucinda slipped the tip of her thumb inside and curled her fingers, sending Samantha into a second, more aggressive orgasm.

She crumpled forward, panting and gasping. Lucinda pulled her flush against her body, slipping her hand out and wrapping it around her abdomen. She held Samantha tightly, kissing softly along her neck and jaw while Samantha tried to catch her breath. Lucinda turned her slowly, nudging Samantha's nose with her own as she pressed a gentle kiss to her lips between jagged breaths before scooping her up and carrying her over to the bed.

She placed Samantha down with care, slipping off her heels and pulling the covers over them as she gathered Samantha to her, kissing her head lightly. "You are so beautiful when you let go," she said softly into dark hair.

Samantha wrapped her arms around Lucinda and raised her head long enough to kiss Lucinda sweetly on the lips. She smiled sleepily and cuddled closer before falling fast asleep.

❖

Lucinda woke up thirsty a few hours later. She had been spooning up behind Samantha when she awoke and slid back silently, trying not to disturb her. She padded downstairs to the kitchen in nothing but lace panties. The glasses of wine sat abandoned on the counter, the bottle neglected by the sink. She tidied up the glasses and resealed the wine before pouring herself some water. She leaned against the cool slab of the countertop by the sink, looking out into the night, surprised at how calm she felt in this moment. The quietness of the house was soothing to her. Upstairs, a very naked Samantha Monteiro was sleeping in her bed and Lucinda didn't feel nervous or anxious at all. In fact, she was very happy and relaxed.

She felt warm arms wrap around her waist as she sipped her water and smiled. "Awake, sleeping beauty?" she asked.

Samantha kissed her shoulder and took the glass, stealing a sip for herself. Lucinda turned around and looped her arms loosely around Samantha's hips. "Hey, you." She smiled warmly.

"Mm, you're so soft," Samantha purred as she sidled up closer, placing the glass on the counter behind Lucinda. She ran her hands up Lucinda's sides and clasped them behind her neck, pulling her down into a kiss. Lucinda smiled as Samantha sucked her bottom lip into her mouth, running her tongue over it slowly. Samantha sensed the change as Lucinda's libido kicked in, and grinned, increasing the aggressiveness of her kissing, pulling her lips back just enough to force Lucinda forward to meet them. She nipped and sucked at the lips in front of her, teasing as she pulled Lucinda toward the island. She pushed Lucinda's hips back, pressing her ass against the edge as she dragged her lips along the pale skin of Lucinda's neck.

Lucinda groaned and tilted her head back, exposing her neck to Samantha's hungry mouth. Her hands grabbed at Samantha's ass and hips, no doubt still keyed up from before.

Samantha slapped Lucinda's hands away, putting them on the countertop behind her as she peppered kisses along a naked collarbone, hands roughly cupping Lucinda's breasts. Lucinda arched her back as Samantha ducked lower, swirling her tongue around a pale pink nipple as she scratched slowly down Lucinda's perfect abs. She sucked the nipple into her mouth as she pressed confident fingers against Lucinda's clit through light blue panties. Lucinda's hips bucked forward at the contact and one hand moved to cradle Samantha's head. Samantha sucked harder and gently bit down on the rosy bud in her mouth. She removed her mouth with a slow lick before moving to the other breast and resuming her activities. Lucinda's eyes were clenched shut and her hips rolled slowly, seeking out more friction from Samantha's fingers.

Samantha continued to tease until a low grunt from Lucinda brought her back to the moment. She chuckled against swollen flesh as she pulled her tongue back into her mouth and looked up at Lucinda. "Hands on the counter," she commanded and Lucinda's fingers pulled out of her hair quickly. Samantha kissed lower, sucking on each defined abdominal muscle while her fingers hooked the band of Lucinda's low slung panties. She nudged long, muscular legs apart and knelt down in front of her lover, teeth pulling the undergarment down the rest of the way to be discarded on the kitchen floor.

She kissed the inside of Lucinda's right knee, teasing her tongue along the defined lines of a dancer's leg while her hands rubbed up and down toned thighs. Lucinda kept her hands clamped to the counter as she watched Samantha look up at her and move her lips closer and closer to her center. Samantha placed two very wet kisses just to the right of Lucinda's sex, causing her to whimper pathetically, her hands leaving the counter and hovering nearby, but not touching Samantha's head.

Samantha was reminded of earlier: the hungry look in Lucinda's eyes as she bit down on Samantha's shoulder, the confident hand on her breasts, the agonizing taunt moving to her clit and back, swirling and dipping. She had wanted to close her eyes and let her head fall back, but she didn't want to miss that paralyzing look even for a moment. It was her turn to dominate now.

"Tsk, tsk," Samantha clucked against flushed pink flesh, "hands on the counter, Luce."

Lucinda shuddered as hot breath swept over her throbbing clit, not touching, just teasing. She pulled her hands back and clamped down again, knuckles white with frustration. "Good girl," Samantha cooed before closing the distance and dragging a slow, wet tongue over a very wet Lucinda.

Lucinda moaned at the contact, her chest flushed with color. Samantha could see her struggling to keep her hands at her sides while she kept her eyes on Samantha doing terrible things to her below.

Samantha swirled and dipped her tongue, focusing on the swollen nub at Lucinda's apex before sliding lower. She sucked gently on the lips in front of her as her hands continued to drag blunt nails up and down toned thighs. Lucinda's legs started to quake as her breathing picked up even faster. Samantha took this as a cue to switch things up a bit. She pulled her mouth back and stood slowly, replacing her tongue with two fingers as she motioned for Lucinda to get up on the counter. Lucinda clambered up onto the surface, sitting close to the edge. Samantha continued to stroke her lightly as she kissed the soft flesh at the top of Lucinda's breast. "I like you like this," Samantha murmured. "Lay back, baby."

Samantha distracted Lucinda from the cold surface of the counter by pressing her palm flat against Lucinda's heaving abs as she lowered her mouth over her clit again, licking and sucking gently, dragging her fingers lower. Every time Lucinda would get close and whimper a warning, Samantha pulled back and slowed down, changing directions or positions slightly, keeping Lucinda at the precipice, taunting her. Lucinda wrapped her legs tightly around Samantha's shoulders, and Samantha reached up and pressed Lucinda's hands to her own breasts, encouraging her to massage and squeeze as she refocused her attention lower.

"Baby, please…" Lucinda begged as she rocked her hips into Samantha's mouth.

Samantha nodded and smiled before wrapping her lips around Lucinda's clit and sucking gently while she thrust two fingers into Lucinda's soaked center, curling and twisting until Lucinda cried out.

Lucinda's breathing halted and her body froze, trembling a bit before it relaxed under the soothing sucking of Samantha's ministrations. Samantha withdrew her fingers and kissed each hip bone tenderly before climbing up onto the counter and kissing along Lucinda's neck. "I like the way you taste."

Lucinda laughed and wrapped her arms around Samantha, holding her close as she kissed the top of her head. "You are something else."

"So which is it—is the selling point of the house the kitchen or the master bedroom?" Samantha teased as she kissed up Lucinda's chin to her lips.

"Verdict's still out, I may need to see the bedroom again to decide." Lucinda kissed Samantha quickly before sitting up, pulling her off the counter and chasing her upstairs.

CHAPTER FOURTEEN

Dark eyes and even darker hair encased Lucinda's face as plump lips descended upon her own, pulling her focus back to her mouth. Samantha was straddling her thigh, one hand clasped tightly with her own with the other holding her face close. This had started a few minutes ago, soft murmurings that came at the end of sleep and the start of waking. They had gravitated toward each other, bodies intertwined. The gentle rocking and kissing was getting away from them.

Lucinda didn't care—she loved it. In fact, she gripped her hand on Samantha's ass, guiding her harder and faster against her own thigh, pushing her further and further. Samantha gripped Lucinda's hand tighter, her rhythm getting frantic. Lucinda slid her hand up, caressing Samantha's chest as she kissed her more deeply, encouraging her to let go. Samantha shuddered and pulled her hand from Lucinda's jaw, pressing it between them and into an unsuspecting Lucinda, her gasp of surprise propelling them both to climax. Samantha melted onto Lucinda's chest, tucking her head against her neck, kissing the skin softly between staggered breaths.

"All mornings should begin that way," Samantha said quietly, nuzzling closer.

Lucinda chuckled and nodded as she wrapped her long limbs around Samantha, rolling them so she was on top. She danced her fingers along Samantha's hairline, brushing stray hairs aside to give her a better view of the perfect face below her. "Hmm, yeah, sounds good." She traced her eyes along the soft features of Samantha's face: her naturally pouty lips, perfectly plucked eyebrows, high cheekbones, and those damn dimples. She could look at Samantha all day and never get bored.

"What're you thinking there, blue eyes?"

"Nothing much, just, you know, about you."

"Nothing much, eh?" Samantha teased. "I'm nothing much, am I?"

Lucinda raised an eyebrow. "You are many, many things, but nothing much isn't one of them." She punctuated the statement with a soft kiss to the corner of Samantha's mouth.

Samantha smiled into the kiss and pulled back, settling her eyes on the tousled blond mess in front of her, over her, on her. She wanted more of these moments. These imperfect, quiet moments with Lucinda felt stolen. The exhilaration from it was almost wrong or dangerous. She felt as though she was taking little pieces of Lucinda and putting them into this folder that she kept referring to throughout her waking minutes. She wanted more pieces. She was starting to realize with a little anxiety that she wanted all the pieces. She didn't want fragments, she wanted the entire picture. It surprised her to feel so strongly about something or someone. She wanted more than great sex and occasional dates with Lucinda. She wanted imperfect, quiet moments. Lots of them.

She thought back to the photos on Lucinda's mirror from last night; she had stepped toward it instinctively, wanting to see more of Lucinda's life. She wanted to know all Lucinda's secrets. She was so mysterious and quiet—her past was locked up tight. Lucinda was better at deflecting than anyone Samantha had ever known, disarming her curiosity with distractions, be they physical or otherwise. Samantha realized she didn't know much about Lucinda at all. A worm of doubt wiggled its way into her chest. Was she really ready to get involved with someone again? Someone she knew next to nothing about? What was she doing?

"Are you seeing anyone else?" The question sort of blurted from her subconscious.

Lucinda blinked, pulling back her lips from Samantha's skin. The question seemed to have caught her off guard. She looked down into Samantha's eyes but didn't say anything, her expression unreadable.

Samantha shifted under her, uncomfortable with the silence. She wanted to retract the question, but her pride flared. She wanted an answer as to why she wasn't good enough more than she wanted to flee from the question.

"No. I'm not." Lucinda supported herself on her elbows. The pause in her reply was for no other reason than she was in her own little blissful world of breathing in the smell of Samantha's skin and recording it to memory. No, she wasn't seeing anyone else. In fact, she wasn't even remotely interested in anyone else. The subtle mask that had settled on Samantha's face started to fade; she blinked once, twice, three times before breathing out slowly. It was as if she was clicking back her emotions, scaling them down to a more manageable level. This amused Lucinda, to think that Samantha was concerned about her answer. "Are you?" she asked, already knowing the answer.

Samantha's eyes narrowed in mock defiance. "No." Her expression relaxed as she appeared to consider her next question. "Do you want to?"

Lucinda smiled. "Do I want to what? See anyone else?" Although she was enjoying this back and forth, she realized that Samantha was perhaps unwittingly giving her an out. Lucinda had long come to accept that she couldn't trust the permanence of anything in her life; she had learned that anything that matters got taken away. She had already ventured into new territory with Samantha. Was she ready to open herself up to the chance to lose something again? She thought maybe this time things could be different. This already felt different.

Samantha scrunched her nose and averted her eyes as she blushed.

"Samantha Monteiro, are you asking me to go steady?" She tickled her fingers along Samantha's side, deciding to take a chance and see where this might lead.

She choked back a laugh as she unsuccessfully glared at Lucinda. "Fuck you, Lucy."

"Did that, multiple times now." Lucinda giggled as she continued to torture a squirming Samantha before pressing their lips together, quieting the moment. "I'd like to date you, exclusively, if that's what you're asking."

Samantha sighed and held her lips against Lucinda's for a while before speaking. "Okay. Good. I want that too."

Lucinda laughed and pecked her lips quickly before settling down on top of Samantha, intertwining their fingers again, and making sheet angels in the bed. Samantha laughed and wriggled under her, enjoying the pressure of Lucinda's lean body on top of her and the playfulness that she brought to the moment. A soft buzzing beside them, somewhere deep in the linens, interrupted their play.

Lucinda frowned and rolled to her side, reaching blindly toward the noise as Samantha captured her lips once again, cradling her head between her hands. The buzzing stopped and was quickly forgotten, until it buzzed again, louder this time, more insistent.

"Ugh. Is that mine or yours?" Lucinda asked.

"Probably yours. Mine is in my purse, which I think is in the kitchen, with your underwear." She nipped at Lucinda's bottom lip with a laugh.

Lucinda groaned and reached around for the intrusive object. She found it on the floor under a displaced pillow, next to a gorgeous high-heeled shoe that belonged to the damsel currently sucking on her neck. She pressed the screen, silencing the alarm and displaying the time. She groaned again, this time because reality was settling in. She had to get ready for work—their playtime was ending much too soon. "Hey, babe"—she gently nudged Samantha off her neck—"it's late."

A warm hum vibrated against her neck as Samantha relinquished her kissing duties and sighed, rolling onto her back and staring up at the ceiling. She chewed her bottom lip softly as she seemed to mull something over. Lucinda felt her gaze as she scrolled through emails on her phone, assessing the day's responsibilities.

"Call out today."

"What?" Lucinda glanced over at her, confused, thumb still idly scrolling the touch screen.

"Call out today. Spend the day with me."

Lucinda ran through the day's schedule in her mind, ticking off the to-do list as she went. There was a conference call at noon she couldn't really get out of, but everything else could be moved. The prospect of taking a day off hadn't even crossed her mind. The last day she called in was… "You've been my girlfriend less than fifteen minutes and you're already asking me to play hooky from work?" she teased.

"Well, girlfriend"—Samantha laughed—"we didn't get a ton of sleep last night and I can't honestly tell you I have any ambition to leave this bed for any reason other than food or a house fire."

"Well let's hope it's not the latter." Lucinda looked around with wide eyes, surveying her room. "I'm fond of this place."

"So will you play hooky with me?"

Lucinda pretended to mull it over. "Well…sure. I'd love to." She was immediately wrapped up in warm limbs. She tossed the phone to the side and refocused on the best thing that had wandered into her life in a long time.

❖

Lucinda asked Amanda to reschedule her day and have her conference call forwarded to her cell phone. Samantha escaped the bed long enough to call Andrew and reschedule her own meetings to later in the week. She was pleased to find that Andrew was not surprised in the least and fully endorsed Samantha's absence and demanded a blow-by-blow of the night's activities at lunch the next day.

They emerged from the bedroom a few hours later, well-rested and playful. It was late morning by the time Lucinda and Samantha sat at the kitchen island fighting over fruit salad and sipping coffee. Samantha found herself grinning as she adjusted her borrowed shirt.

"What are you smiling about?" Lucinda asked, stealing the last blueberry from the fruit salad before leaning in to peck Samantha on the lips.

"I was just thinking that this feels so terribly normal—like we eat fruit out of the same bowl for breakfast all the time. And how odd that is."

"Odd because of the other things we did on this surface or…" Lucinda teased with a wink.

Samantha scoffed and nudged Lucinda's hand away from the last piece of pineapple. "No. Odd because it feels like déjà vu. Like we've done this before." That was true. This felt deceptively easy. Almost too easy. And yet, foreign to her at the same time.

"Well, I can't ever recall anyone looking so good in my shirt and shorts before this morning, so that seems doubtful." Lucinda laughed and poked Samantha in the ribs before reaching for her phone. "I have to step into my office and make this work call. It won't be too long. You gonna be okay by your lonesome?"

"I intend to snoop around and find out what weird quirks you're hiding from me." Samantha stole the last melon. "So as long as we both know that's what's happening, I won't feel bad about it."

Lucinda reached for her work bag and pulled out her tablet, headset, and some folders. "Have fun snooping. I plead the fifth on all things that may appear self-incriminating."

Samantha narrowed her eyes in a playful taunt. "I have my ways of uncovering the truth, don't you worry."

"Oh, that sounds delightful. Let me know how it all goes." Lucinda winked and walked toward the office off the kitchen. Ornate French doors led into a room full of natural light with a view of Lucinda's small but private backyard. The oak desk Lucinda settled into after shutting the door was large but appropriate for the space. Samantha watched as Lucinda sat quietly, powering up her tablet and plugging in her headset. She pulled some papers from a drawer over here, moved her folders there. A keypad emerged at some point and a soft bell rang, indicating she was connected to the call.

Lucinda wore a loose fitting yoga shirt and soft black pants, one knee brought up to her chest while the other swung comfortably from the chair. Although Samantha couldn't hear what Lucinda was saying, she could tell her tone was very different from the one she engaged Samantha with. It was businesslike and assertive. She moved the mouse over the desktop quickly and shifted her position, sitting up straighter as she responded to something. Samantha wasn't sure how long she had been staring, lost in her own thoughts, when a familiar ring drew her attention to her purse. She fumbled around for it while keeping her eyes on Lucinda behind the glass in the other room. On her third attempt to free it from the confines of her purse, she touched the screen tentatively; this wasn't a ring she often answered purposely.

"Hello?" She tried to swallow the anxiety that bubbled up as she answered.

"*Mija*, I called work and was told you were out today, is everything okay?"

Samantha stifled a sigh. "Yeah, Ma, I just took a day off."

"Oh, good. You know, a business won't run itself, *mija*." Samantha could hear the disgruntled cluck through the phone as if her mother were chastising her in person. "I hope you aren't making this a habit."

"Is that really why you called, Ma? To make sure I was successfully running my business?"

Her mother was quiet for a moment, no doubt contemplating whether to attack or let it slide. Samantha's relationship with her parents wasn't exactly what she would describe as smooth.

"Samantha. Honestly. I was hoping you'd outgrow your attitude after we sent you to that expensive prep school—"

"Guess not," she bit back. "What can I do for you on this lovely afternoon, Mother?"

❖

Lucinda wrapped up her call and cracked her neck. She was happy to be done with work for the day. She finished off a quick email and packed up her work supplies, organizing her desk before stepping out of the office. She heard the soft murmurings of a conversation coming from the couch. She assumed Samantha was on a call. As she stepped closer to her bag to put away her supplies she caught a mix of English and Spanish hurriedly tumbling from her favorite pouty lips.

Lucinda shuffled around the kitchen, pouring a glass of water and trying not to eavesdrop. Really, she couldn't. Half of the conversation was foreign to her, although from the bits she could hear, it sounded like Samantha was going to get some unwanted visitors at some point. She grabbed the glass and walked into the living room, poking her head over the couch to offer the water to Samantha.

Samantha was stretched out on the sofa, her eyes shut and her hand pinching the bridge of her nose. Lucinda lightly touched her leg to alert her of her presence; Samantha opened weary eyes and frowned, mouthing an apology as she pulled the phone from her ear. Lucinda chuckled at the sound of angry Spanish flying through the speaker.

Samantha took a sip of the offered drink before handing it back and motioning for Lucinda to sit on the couch. Lucinda smiled, placing the glass down and lifting Samantha's legs onto her lap. She absentmindedly started to massage the toned legs in front of her as Samantha responded to the female voice on the phone. Lucinda smiled when she noticed that the conversation started to slow as her hands moved farther up Samantha's thigh. A quick glance at her face revealed that Samantha had checked out of the conversation and was attentively watching Lucinda's hands.

"*Mija!*" An angry bark echoed from the phone.

"What?" Samantha replied distractedly as Lucinda shuffled her legs to the side so she could crawl up her body, naughty intentions abounding.

Lucinda slowly pushed up the fabric of Samantha's borrowed shirt, kissing the exposed flesh of her stomach, teasing it with her tongue as she slid her hands up and down Samantha's side.

An angry growl erupted from the phone, drawing Samantha's now hooded eyes back to focus before narrowing slightly. She ran her fingers through Lucinda's hair before turning her head to the side and responding, fast and agitated. "God. Fine. Relax. I'm busy…I'll talk to you later. *Adiós.*" She tossed the phone to the side and pulled Lucinda's face up to hers. "I'm sorry," she murmured against soft lips, kissing her apologies into an eager mouth.

Lucinda continued to nudge the soft cotton shirt up, exposing the underside of Samantha's breasts to warm hands gently kneading the skin. She kissed away from her lips and worked her way to Samantha's neck. "Everything all right?"

Samantha moaned at the sensation of Lucinda's hands and mouth on her skin. She was resisting the urge to gently rock up into the body over her. "Yeah, fine. Just my mother terrorizing me on my day off. Nothing new." She breathed out slowly, willing her heartbeat to slow down a bit.

Lucinda continued to tease her mouth along Samantha's neck, kneading her hands where they were, not advancing them any higher, much to Samantha's frustration. "Tell me about her."

"Oh, um, she's sort of the typical overbearing mother. Always sticking her nose where it doesn't belong, insulting me casually, you know..." Her eyes were closed as she continued to talk. Her honest reply was rewarded with tender kisses along her collarbone and warm palms on her breasts. She sighed contentedly.

"What else? Do you have a big family?" Lucinda hands continuing their slow teasing.

"I have an older brother. He's the golden child, has two point five kids, wife, successful doctor, blah-blah-blah..." Lucinda pulled Samantha's shirt up over her breasts, leaving it balled under her neck as she dragged her lips lower.

"Your father? What's he like?" Lucinda's soft lips made their way to Samantha's nipple.

A steady vibration wound its way through Samantha's center as she slowed her breathing as best she could. "He's a doctor, like my brother. A surgeon. Works a lot. Absent most of the time. Agrees with my mother always, even if she's dead wrong." She paused as Lucinda swirled her tongue around the sensitive flesh.

Lucinda stopped and looked up. Samantha cleared her throat and continued, immediately rewarded with lips on skin.

"They live in New York, outside of the city. They don't approve of my life choices, so we only speak when necessary. My career path is sort of a—" She gasped as Lucinda gently bit down before moving to her other breast. "They think what I do is foolish and don't understand it. My father thinks he wasted money on an education for me, my mother thinks I'll die alone with fifty cats..."

Her voice trailed off as she let herself enjoy the gentle sucking. The sudden rush of cold on her nipple refocused her thought process.

"Things have gotten progressively worse over the past year." Lucinda returned her lips to Samantha's skin, slowly kissing up the length of her sternum, her body pressing against Samantha's naked torso. Samantha gasped, this time not from the warm flesh on her own, but from a shameful admission she couldn't stop from spilling from her lips. "They liked Eric, they thought he was perfect. They blame me for it ending. My mother thinks I'm a failure."

Lucinda stopped her hands, her mouth, her breathing. She stopped and just looked at Samantha, her eyes open now and sad, staring vacantly up at the ceiling. Lucinda knew that Samantha had stumbled upon something during their play. It pained her to see the self-doubt spread across Samantha's perfect features. She pressed a soft kiss to Samantha's lips. She wanted to know everything about this woman, even the painful things. But she would be patient. She wouldn't pry.

It sort of terrified her—a recent ex, who was so important as to plan marriage with, a man no less. She broke the kiss, pulling down Samantha's shirt before she pressed her head to Samantha's chest, settling her body on top of her. "Do you want to talk about him? About what happened?"

Samantha settled her hands at Lucinda's nape, gently stroking. "Not particularly."

Lucinda nodded and hugged her arms the best she could around Samantha. She lay there silent, letting the slowing beats of Samantha's heart soothe her sudden anxiety over the moment. She felt surprisingly vulnerable.

After a few minutes, Samantha whispered, "How much do you know?"

Lucinda considered her answer carefully. After the wedding she had pulled the file at work and scanned the final outcome. The details regarding the indiscretion were very limited; the less people knew the better. Curiosity might have tempted her, but her own morals and high regard for privacy made her close the folder before she got the answers she was looking for.

"I don't know anything, truthfully. Nor do I need to." Lucinda picked her head up and looked into Samantha's sad eyes. "I don't need to know anything you don't want to share."

Samantha swallowed. Lucinda realized she had just given her a pass, much like the one Samantha had extended to her earlier that morning. She wanted to know the whole truth, but she wasn't quite sure if their roles had been reversed she would share her own pain.

"I was with him for six years. I met him shortly after college one night at some silly auction I was doing for my best friend." Her tone was flat, but she kept Lucinda's gaze. "It was sort of heavenly to start, all giggles and romance. He swept me off my feet in every sense of the word, everything was grandiose and perfect. We moved in together about a year and half afterward and were happy. I thought we were happy."

Lucinda swept a dark hair off Samantha's forehead as she listened, doing her best to remain calm and patient.

"We were in no rush to get married. I had started the business with Andrew and was working long hours getting it off the ground. Eric was a pharmaceutical rep and spent a good deal of time traveling along the East Coast for work. After the company launched and we had a few big clients under our belt, Eric proposed." She sighed before adding, "The months to the wedding were winding down and I was getting a little nervous, admittedly. Things had been a little rocky for me and Eric. It seemed that the wedding was pushing us apart instead of bringing us closer together. Business had blossomed for Perfect Match, all the little pieces we had set in motion were falling into place, all at once. It was overwhelming and gratifying at the same time." Her eyes shone brightly for a moment as she remembered. She spared a small smile to Lucinda before continuing, her hands gently caressing Lucinda's shoulders as she went, as if she was trying to calm herself through touching Lucinda.

"I had been sort of harried one day leaving the house. In my rush I left my laptop on the counter." She paused, stilling her hands and blinking slowly up at Lucinda before pressing their lips together. She held the contact, before sighing and finishing. "I came home at lunchtime to retrieve it and caught Eric in bed with someone else. Needless to say it wasn't received well by any of the parties involved. I tossed him out on the spot and Andrew came by to help me pick up the pieces." She shook her head sadly. "It was like a bad made-for-TV movie. New up and coming matchmaker's fiancé cheats, ending fairy-tale romance.

"Andrew and I silenced it for as long as we could but it was sort of like a ticking time bomb. We had to make sure Eric didn't breathe a word of the indiscretion for fear that it would ruin the business. That's where your company came in, crisis management and public relations megastars to sweep this whole ordeal under the rug and secure my freedom from him. He agreed to silence, for money of course, and also to stay as far away from me as possible. Eric and I released a statement to the press amicably splitting and wishing each other great love and health. Andrew worked some kind of fairy gaymother magic and canceled the wedding and handled the press without any real waves. It was so embarrassing. I was ashamed and felt so terribly guilty. A failure at love when that's all I do—how could people trust me to find them happiness when I couldn't even find my own?" She sort of sighed the last statement before studying Lucinda's face for a moment. "My mother jumped on the breakup like a lion on injured prey. She's been relentless in her verbal assaults and unplanned visits of late. It's like this was the exact type of justice she had secretly been hoping would come my way for disobeying their wishes. My successes mean nothing to them if I'm not married with children. A point they like to remind me of regularly."

Lucinda frowned at the resignation in Samantha's voice. It was as if all her insecurities had been cemented into truth over the course of one bad breakup. People did terrible things to one another, Lucinda knew that firsthand. But her heart hurt for Samantha. She cupped her cheek softly.

"You are not a failure. What you do is brave and heartwarming and wonderful. You make people's dreams come true—dreams they may not even know they have. You have an eye for detail that is uncanny. You read people with a fluency that is unbelievable. You see hope in dark places and defend true love. You're saving happy endings and giving them out because you believe in love, even if it's a hard road. You will not die alone, and you'll have fifty cats if you damn well please because you can, and no one has the right to tell you otherwise."

She brushed away the silent tears escaping Samantha's eyes. "You are not at fault for the actions of others. You are not anyone's plaything or trophy. You have every right to the same happiness you find for others, and you should not settle for less." She rubbed her thumb lightly over Samantha's cheek before continuing so quietly it was almost a whisper.

"You are smart and funny and beautiful and special and you deserve to be reminded of that every day."

Samantha's eyes welled with tears. "Thank you."

The words were heavy with sincerity and meaning. Lucinda got the impression that she was thanking her for more than her words.

"Thank you," she repeated and pressed a chaste kiss to Lucinda's hovering lips. Samantha shuddered and sobbed softly, as if unable to stifle the sudden rush of feelings.

Lucinda felt them too. It hurt to feel the sobs rake through Samantha and reverberate against her own chest. She pulled Samantha into her lap, adjusting her clothing and rubbing her hands along her back as she slowly rocked Samantha back and forth, letting her know she was not alone. She pressed kiss after kiss to her tear-soaked cheeks, willing the hurt away.

"Sh, baby girl, come here," she cooed as she cradled Samantha against her chest. She pressed a firm kiss to the top of her head as she tossed the blanket draped over the back of the couch over them, tucking them in. Samantha's sobbing slowed over the next few minutes, her hands balled into fists around Lucinda's shirt, pressing against her chest between them. She continued to sniffle and shudder periodically as Lucinda rubbed up and down her back under the warm blanket, soothing her as best she could.

"It's all right. Everything is going to be fine." She breathed out as she hugged Samantha close. She wasn't sure who she was saying that to, Samantha or herself.

Chapter Fifteen

I'm surprised you answered, Sam. I thought for sure you would bounce me to voice mail." Andrew's voice echoed a little over his Bluetooth.

"I will always answer for you, darling," Samantha replied, "anytime, anyplace."

"Eww, did you answer during sex? Please tell me no," he scoffed, the sound of his blinker clicking in the background.

"What? No, Lucinda's making dinner. I was just moving away from the sink."

"Are you at home or…?"

"We're at her place."

"Still?"

"Yes, Andrew, still." Lucinda laughed behind her.

"Wow, Sam," he teased, "are you going to be able to walk tomorrow?"

"You're an ass," she bit back with a laugh. "How was work today?"

"Oh, fine, the usual. We have a few meetings tomorrow. Are you planning on coming in?"

"I don't see why not. What time is the first one?"

"I think nine fifteen. Hey—your mother called the office, just a warning."

"I know. She already got to me. But I appreciate you telling me."

"Everything okay? You wanna talk about it?"

"I'm good, actually. It went as usual, name calling, rudeness, et cetera. She sort of threatened to visit sometime soon, date still pending approval. Make sure we save our out-of-state meetings in case that happens, okay?"

"You got it, babe. Listen, I need to get inside before my trainer breaks my ass for being late. Not that I would really mind, I guess— he's got such nice abs."

"Have fun at the gym, thanks for calling, see you tomorrow." As Samantha ended the call she admired the shapely form in front of her, moving between the stove and the counter.

Lucinda shut off the burner and deposited the contents of the pan into the dishes in front of her, carefully mixing the brown rice with the stir-fry and setting aside the remainder onto the unused burner. She turned around to catch Samantha's gaze lingering on her body. "Hey." She smiled.

"Hi."

"Ready to eat?" Lucinda quirked an eyebrow, teasing a bit.

"Um, yeah."

Lucinda placed the dishes on the table and retrieved the wine from the night before, pouring two fresh glasses and lighting the candle in front of them. Samantha smiled at Lucinda's attention to detail, reaching her hand out to lightly touch Lucinda's knuckles affectionately. The contact was rewarded with an open palm and interlaced fingers. Lucinda raised her glass. "Thank you for being my dinner guest, and having a wonderful day with me."

Samantha touched her glass to Lucinda's and smiled, sipping the wine and squeezing the hand in her own. "Anytime." She winked.

Lucinda scrunched her nose and giggled, poking at the contents of her plate before asking, "How's Andrew?"

"He's good." Samantha raised a forkful to her mouth and chewed slowly. "Oh my God, this is delicious." She closed her eyes and let the multiple flavors and textures cross over her palette. "Where did you learn to cook like this?"

Lucinda laughed. "You must be easily impressed. It's really no big deal, just vegetables, rice, and shrimp. The whole thing took fifteen minutes."

Samantha bit into a shrimp and mumbled, "Yeah, but it's so good."

"Thanks. I like cooking."

"Do you always cook? Or do you take out more?" Samantha envisioned Lucinda curled up on her couch, sifting through takeout menus in her bra and panties.

"I cook pretty often. I find it soothing. There's something rewarding about making a meal from scratch."

"Have you always been that way?"

Lucinda considered this for a moment. "I used to cook when Connie and I were younger—just small meals and snacks here and there. I didn't really embrace food and its many flavors until college when I had to be more aware of the fuel I consumed while dancing competitively. Eventually, I progressed to more intricate meals. My ex, Grace, was a culinary wiz. Her father was a restaurant owner in the city, so I learned a little along the way. My greatest food exposure came from my years with Grace—I suppose that was one good thing I got from that train wreck." She shrugged and sipped her wine.

Samantha got the feeling she was walking on uncomfortable ground as she watched Lucinda start to retreat into herself a bit. Yet she felt compelled to know more about her. She wanted to feel like they were sharing equally, even if it was messy or uncomfortable. "At the wedding, when you said you stayed with Connie when you were younger, what did you mean?"

Lucinda swallowed her bite and looked up. She pursed her lips and sighed before answering. "I was placed there as a foster child when I was eleven, until I was seventeen." She scratched her nose and reached for her wineglass, averting her eyes from Samantha.

Samantha's brow furrowed as she took in this information. Eleven was young. As much as she couldn't stand her family, she couldn't imagine not having one either. When she didn't say anything right away, Lucinda looked up at her, almost nervous.

"I never knew my father. My mother had a drug problem. I had been in the system for a while before I met the O'Malleys."

Samantha frowned, her thumb gently rubbing over Lucinda's knuckles. "How long is a while?" she whispered.

"Since I was four."

Samantha had to fight back a gasp. She couldn't help but think of all the little things in her own past that served as milestones from her youth: her first princess-themed birthday party, the first time she rode a bike, presents and cakes, security. She had always had security. That was something she had taken for granted.

"Babe, I'm so sorry." She frowned deeper as she felt guilt wash over her; she had been very well-off as a child and into adulthood. Life had been easy for her, comparatively.

Lucinda just shrugged, eyes on her food again. "It's not your fault. It's just how it was." She was quiet for a minute before adding softly, "Before the O'Malleys, I had been in five homes. Connie was my first real family. Her mother was a saint—she nearly worked herself to death to make sure I wasn't shuttled back into the system. She probably saved my life."

Samantha considered what she knew of Constance O'Malley Lundstein: she had two older brothers, her mother died of cancer when she was young, and her father was an alcoholic with a mean streak. Somewhere along the line she had been removed from the home to live with an aunt. Samantha worried about Lucinda in that moment. Where had she gone? Who took her in? She pushed her now empty plate away and slid her chair closer, Lucinda eyeing her warily.

"Constance is a great girl. You must have done something right with her, she adores you." She let a small smile cross her face as she pulled their conjoined hands to her lap.

Lucinda made no attempt to pull her hand away, but the warmth of their usual interactions was missing. She knew she was visibly uncomfortable with this topic. After all this time she still felt a little shameful admitting she had no one to claim her. She wanted to try, but the truth was the only person she had ever talked with about this was Dominic. Even Grace had gotten a quick summary version for the sake of discussing their pasts, but she never shared how truly awful it had been. How many times she had been returned. How hard it was to trust anyone. In the beginning of her time at the O'Malleys, Lucinda had struggled to connect with Connie, afraid she would get attached only to be discarded again. It got harder and harder to get placed as she got older and even harder to get over the rejection. She'd had a lifetime of good-byes.

She answered Samantha with a sad smile. "Connie is great because she had a great mother and she's a smart girl. I'm just glad to have met her and kept her in my life."

Samantha's grip on her hand tightened. "You've never told me about dancing. What happened?"

Lucinda felt like the wind got knocked out of her. She had successfully deflected any and all questions about her dancing and her dance partner. She knew she was on borrowed time when Samantha saw those photos on her bedroom mirror. She couldn't keep avoiding this topic.

"Connie's mother put me in a dance class one afternoon to help me open up a bit and find other kids my age. It was one of those selfless things she did so frequently. When I said Catherine O'Malley saved my life, I meant it—had she not supported me and given me a chance, I never would have known what a family could be and I never would have met Dominic." She sipped her glass. "Dominic was in that first class with me. We hit it off in a competitive kind of way, but eventually we became inseparable. He was a very gifted dancer, but he came from a world apart from me. He had a loving family with plenty of wealth. They were so generous, still are. When they saw how well we danced together, they paid for every class for me moving forward. They covered every competition entrance fee and equipment cost, all of it. And Dominic became the brother I never had."

She sighed and leaned back. "I moved in with his family when my fostering ended with the O'Malleys. I danced day and night, trying to forget all the bad things that had happened to me. Dominic always told me that what I lacked in training, I made up for in natural talent, but it took a lot of work to polish and sculpt my dancing to match the caliber of his. He was always so patient though—he never doubted me. So we trained and danced and practiced until my feet bled. One day, before I knew it, we were the best. We quickly flew up the ranks in the professional circuit, sweeping competition after competition, but I took a bad spill in practice one night and nearly ruined my dance career. I was on crutches for weeks, and the weekend I was going to resume dance practice, I got a panicked phone call from Massimo, Dominic's brother."

Samantha breathed out in recognition. "He said you danced into his life at the aquarium. He meant that literally."

Lucinda nodded, then slouched. "Massimo was calling to tell me that Dominic had collapsed in the Commons during his run. He kept saying something about an undiagnosed heart condition. It took me forever to get him to tell me that Dominic had died. It's like he couldn't believe it. Some days I still don't believe it."

"Oh, Luce." Samantha's expression was pained, silent tears rolled down her face. Lucinda knew her face mirrored Samantha's. She struggled to finish.

"I didn't dance after that. Not for a long time. Part of me blamed myself for what happened—I should have been training with him. Had I not been distracted during that practice and injured myself, I would have been beside him. Maybe that would have made the difference—maybe time would have been on our side." She shrugged. "No matter how many times I tried to partner up again, the connection was always missing. No one could replace Dominic. Eventually I stopped trying to compete altogether. I finished school, found a career that I loved almost as much as dance, and tried to move on. I couldn't fully give it up though—I opened that dance studio in his honor and try to give the gift of dance to everyone I meet." She wiped her face, exhausted.

Samantha was silent for a few moments before she murmured quietly, "I'm glad I met you." She smiled and added, almost inaudibly, "I'm not going anywhere either, okay?"

Lucinda felt some of her pain lessen as she tugged Samantha onto her lap, wrapping her into a loose hug. "I'm glad I met you too. I'm quite fond of you, you know?" She nuzzled Samantha's neck and kissed the skin softly.

Samantha nodded and pressed her lips to Lucinda's. "Me too."

CHAPTER SIXTEEN

Samantha sat at her desk, admiring the large bouquet Lucinda had sent her yesterday. As silly as it seemed to be celebrating a one-month anniversary, Samantha couldn't be happier. Things had been going so well that she wondered if by the time the *Improper Bostonian* article ran that she might no longer be one of Boston's most eligible bachelorettes. The thought warmed her; Lucinda entering her life had been exactly the change of pace she had needed.

Her first appointment of the day was with Logan Carter. When her clientele had become more and more affluent, she found herself having to do more background work than originally anticipated. She had commissioned Logan as a private investigator to check up on both her clients and the potential admirers. He was a retired police officer in his midforties who had left the force after an injury rendered him unable to work the beat.

She met with him about once a month, though with the way things were buzzing since their relaunch she had already seen him twice in two weeks. When the article was published later this month, she expected another influx of calls. Last week alone they had six new clients for whom she had to organize dates and run background checks on the potential ladies and men. Logan would be by any minute to give her an update on the list she'd sent him.

A soft knocking at her door drew her attention to Logan's smiling face.

"Come on in," Samantha called from her desk, closing the window on the screen in front of her.

"Hey, Samantha, happy Friday. How's it going?" An attractive man with an athletic build and slightly graying hair, he had a smooth timbre to his voice.

"Oh, you know, desperate people looking for love, me trying to filter out the wack-jobs." She gestured for him to sit. "What do you have for me today?"

"I have to say, I was surprised to get another list from you. You guys must be crazy here."

"You have no idea. Anything interesting?"

Logan pulled a folder from his bag and started reading down the list: a few women with shady credit history were after Shelly; Alec Frost had gotten into an altercation with an ex-boyfriend of some waitress he was harassing at a restaurant over the weekend; a new client had two children she'd failed to mention on the application; two people applying for the position of Samantha's new assistant had lied on their resumes; and someone named Lucinda Moss had an assault charge filed against her a few years ago.

Samantha hoped her voice was steady as she said, "Who told you to look up Lucinda Moss?"

"I did." Andrew appeared in the doorway, shuffling head shots. "I want to know more about that, Logan," he pressed. "What else do you know about the assault charge?"

Samantha found herself holding her breath in fury and nervous anticipation.

Logan cleared his throat. "It happened a few years ago, between Ms. Moss, a Grace Richter, and someone identified only as Suspect Two. It looks like some sort of lovers' quarrel with a third party involved. It only went as far as paperwork in the station, and it was eventually dropped."

"Who filed the grievance?" Andrew arched an eyebrow as he sat on Samantha's office couch.

"Grace Richter. I figured you might be curious about her too, since this Moss person was bolded in the email." Samantha shot Andrew a death glare. Logan continued. "She's the daughter of some well-known chef in the area. It seems as though she was heavily encouraged by her father to file the complaint. She didn't pursue it long—there's evidence that her statement was recanted later on. All in all, Lucinda Moss came back clean. She does have a spotty back history though. She was in foster care for most of her life with multiple residences associated with her name. She danced professionally for a short stint, went to college locally, and works at a marketing firm downtown now." He shrugged and closed his folder.

Samantha was seething. Andrew had a guarded look with his hands clasped in his lap but said nothing.

Logan looked between them briefly before he asked, "Someone want to fill me in on this?"

Samantha spoke first. "Andrew and I obviously have different ideas about how your services should be utilized. Thank you again for your work, we really appreciate it. I called you in today because I have another list for you. I think it's going to be a little busy the next few weeks—is that going to be a problem?"

"No, that's fine, I'm around. I'll get this back to you in a few days." Logan took the list from her hand and excused himself, closing the office door as he left.

Andrew stood, dropping the head shots onto the couch and crossing his arms. "I put a call in to Logan when I realized you and Lucinda were getting more serious. I thought I would intercept him before he got to you."

Samantha didn't say anything at first. Maybe because she was shaking. Maybe because she felt as though she had violated Lucinda's trust through Andrew's actions. She did not want to hear about anything pertaining to Lucinda's life unless it came from Lucinda herself.

Andrew shifted uncomfortably under her stare. She let out a slow breath, her lip curling with disgust as she hissed out, "What were you thinking?"

"I was thinking that if you're going to get in a relationship with someone, I'd like to know a little bit about them first," he bit back defensively. "And that maybe you should know a little bit about them first, as well."

"Andrew, what the fuck?" She stood and shoved her chair back with more force than necessary. Tears welled in her eyes before she could stop them. She ducked her head, slamming closed the open folders in front of her and reaching blindly for her purse.

"Samantha." Andrew's voice softened. He took a step forward and raised his hand to slow her frantic movements. "I just wanted to make sure you weren't getting involved with the wrong person. I can see how much you like her, I just wanted to be sure."

"Be sure of what, Andrew? Be sure she wasn't some fucking serial killer? Seriously?" Samantha couldn't believe Andrew would go behind her back like this, another betrayal by someone she cared about. "Did you ever think that maybe I could be responsible for my own actions? My own choices?"

Andrew recoiled, hurt. "I don't want to go down that same road with you again. Deceptions happen."

"Oh, please tell me you are not comparing this situation to Eric." She was livid. She felt nauseous. She couldn't unlearn the things she just heard. Assault? A domestic dispute? "What were you thinking?"

Andrew gaped. "Samantha, I'm sorry, I was just trying to protect you. I saw how badly you were hurt before—it almost ruined you, it almost ruined this business." His tone changed. "Someone has to be proactive here. We didn't work this hard to be knocked down by another liar. I just wanted to make sure she was good enough for you."

"Good enough? This isn't some client, Andrew, this is me here. You don't get to screen my girlfriend without my permission. You don't have that right."

"Samantha, please, wait." Andrew stepped toward her as she moved to leave her office. "I didn't mean to upset you, I just—"

Samantha stopped him by holding up her hand. "Don't, Andrew, just don't. It's done. You can't take it back."

❖

Sweat poured down Lucinda's face. She hadn't had this much physical exertion in a while, and she missed it. She missed the physicality of it, the way her skin flushed and her muscles burned, begging for rest. She loved it. She spit the water out of her mouth and pulled herself back up. She had been distracted, thinking about Samantha, and she had gotten clocked in the side of the head. That just wouldn't do. She adjusted her mouth guard, repositioned her hands in her gloves, and stepped back into the ring.

She had taken up boxing a few years ago to help burn off a little steam. Dominic called it her rage workout. Years of foster care and bullying proved to make Lucinda a decent fighter; she could take a hit and throw one like a champ.

Toni brought his gloves up and bounced in front of her before jabbing with his left and swinging low with his right. She ducked and swerved to avoid the hits and countered hard against his ribs twice with her right while she blocked with her left. He coughed out a laugh and pressed forward, shoving her by the chest before swinging high with his left, narrowly missing her chin as she hit him with a hard uppercut, knocking him back. A bell rang behind her signaling the end of the sparring practice—just in time for both of them, who were breathing heavy and already sore.

"It's been a while, Lucy, you are getting sloppy," Toni teased between gasping breaths.

"Not too sloppy to miss hitting you in that enormous chin of yours," she countered as she leaned against the ropes, rolling her shoulders.

He chuckled and pulled off his gloves, removing his headgear and cracking his neck. "When will I see you again?" he asked as he helped her tug off her gloves.

"I was thinking, maybe next week?"

"Sure, let me check the schedule, I'll be right back." He tossed her a bottle of water as he ducked out of the ring and jogged to the office off to the right.

"Hey, Luce," Toni called out five seconds later, "you got an admirer."

Lucinda looked up from unwrapping her hands and saw Samantha across the gym. She flashed a wide smile before ducking under the ropes and climbing down the stairs. Samantha walked toward her slowly, her heels echoing in the large room, a matching grin on her face. "I see you found the place. Welcome to my workout."

Samantha's eyes settled on Lucinda's sweat-covered stomach, pulsing with her still ragged breathing. She had wandered into the gym about ten minutes earlier and caught the end of Lucinda's sparring match. After her fight with Andrew that morning, she'd texted Lucinda to ask to see her before their scheduled dinner plans, telling her she needed to talk. Lucinda had called her immediately to make sure everything was okay. She lied and said she was fine, just busy at work, and Lucinda had suggested they meet at her gym. For the rest of the day, Samantha had avoided any of Lucinda's attempts at communication. She didn't want to believe any of it. She didn't want to believe she could be so wrong about someone again. So she curled into herself and avoided it. Until right now.

"Hey, Casanova!" Toni hit Lucinda in the chest with a rolled-up gym towel. "Dry off, you stink." He chuckled when she shot him an annoyed scowl. "I'm available on Wednesday or Thursday night around this time," Toni said. "Or we can do a midmorning Saturday thing. What's your pleasure, blondie?"

Lucinda dried herself off but not before Samantha noticed she spent some extra time making slow circles over her abs. "Wednesday works. Maybe Saturday too, I'll confirm on Wednesday. Sound good?"

Toni faked a jab to Lucinda's jaw before nodding. "Yeah, you might need both days, Luce, you're a little rusty. Or is it just a little distracted?" He winked and waved over a young kid gawking nearby. "Julio, get in the ring, you're late."

He turned back to the women. "Nice to meet you,...?"

"Samantha."

"Nice to meet you, Samantha. Watch this one, she's trouble." He jerked a thumb toward Lucinda, who rolled her eyes. "See ya, Luce." He touched her shoulder before jogging back to the ring.

Lucinda looked a little bashful as she stepped up, lightly tracing her fingers along Samantha's arm. "So, how long have you been here?"

"Long enough to see you get nailed in that pretty blond head of yours." Samantha grimaced as she stepped forward, brushing back a stray lock off Lucinda's forehead. "Are you okay?"

Lucinda turned her head and kissed Samantha's palm. "Yeah. This box of rocks is stronger than it looks." She stepped a little closer before hesitating and stepping back. "I really want to scoop you into a hug, but I'm kinda gross."

"I love being close to you when you're all wet and sweaty." Samantha smiled. "But I prefer when it's because of me and not some hairy guy that got you there."

"Oh, ouch." Lucinda grimaced playfully. Her face turned serious for a moment before she asked, "Are you sure everything is all right? You sounded a little flustered before."

Samantha shrugged. She didn't really want to lie, but she was already feeling better. "I just had a long day. We can talk about it later."

"Listen, give me like ten minutes to rinse off quick and we can head out. Do you mind waiting in here? I know it's not the warmest of environments."

Half a dozen men were lifting, using the heavy bags, jumping rope, all casting Samantha the occasional once over. "I'll be fine here, don't worry. If I need anything, I'll just call out to Toni, okay?" She smiled reassuringly, part of her loving the predatory glare Lucinda was shooting the guys.

Lucinda nodded quickly, looking around once more. "All right, fine. I'll be super quick, I promise."

"Don't be too quick—I'd like you not smelling like a jock strap when I finally kiss you." Samantha winked, her smile disguising the anxiety she felt in her chest.

Lucinda grabbed her bag from the ring steps before trotting toward the women's locker room.

Samantha watched Lucinda walk off as she tried to force away the thoughts circling in her head. Her purse vibrated again, causing her to frown. It was either Andrew or her mother—she was almost positive of that. And she didn't care if that was Andrew calling, or if it was her mother trying to track her down. She had nothing to say to either of them.

She stood there for a few minutes, trying to ward off the feelings of uneasiness before she wandered toward a corkboard in the corner by the office Toni had retreated to earlier. There were sign-up sheets for sparring partners, posted matches with ticket markers attached, some ads for new and used boxing equipment, and photos of Toni with a few younger adults holding trophies or wearing medals. There was a framed picture of Muhammad Ali with a gleaming silver autograph next to the board, and above it were Rocky Marciano's signed gloves in a glass frame with a plaque that read, *Rocky Marciano, signed September 25, 1954.* Over the door to the office was a black-and-white photo of someone named Tony DeMarco, and the inscription next to it stated he was a famous Boston boxer.

"That's Toni's great-grandfather." Warm hands settled on her hips as Lucinda breathed against her ear. "He was a notorious heavy slugger, real hard worker. They named a street after him in the North End."

Samantha smiled as she covered one hand with her own. "I love it when you spout random Boston facts so seductively in my ear. It's fascinating how much you know." As unsure as she felt in this moment, Lucinda's touch soothed her and she welcomed it.

Lucinda placed a quick peck to her cheek before spinning her around. "So, darling, you ready to go? I have to get you out of here before one of these guys tries to pick you up and steal you from me."

"Oh, please," Samantha said, laughing, "I don't think anyone here has the stamina I've gotten used to."

Lucinda flashed a lopsided grin as she laced her fingers with Samantha's and tugged her to the door. As they hit the front door she paused. "I wasn't anticipating seeing you until later and I sort of jogged here from work. I took the train in today fully expecting to have time to go home and change before our date."

Samantha smiled. Lucinda was adorable, even when she was beating the crap out of someone thirty pounds heavier than her. "I drove, babe, it's okay. So, your place?"

Lucinda nodded as she walked with Samantha to her car. The sleek black Audi had a matching black interior with soft red dash lighting and heated seats. It was as sexy on the inside as the outside. Lucinda settled into the seat and rested her head back, her still damp hair hanging limply on her shoulders. She closed her eyes and took in a few deep, calming breaths, appreciating the smell of new leather paired with Samantha's perfume. Her eyes still closed, she reached out and gently squeezed the exposed skin on Samantha's thigh, resting her palm there before quietly asking, "So, you want to tell me what's going on? Or should I pretend I didn't notice?"

She heard Samantha exhale nervously and squeeze both hands tightly on the leather-covered steering wheel, making a rubbing sound in the pin-drop quiet car. When she didn't respond right away, Lucinda opened her eyes and took in a nervous and oddly guilty looking Samantha Monteiro.

"I…" Samantha clamped her mouth shut, as if not sure how to start.

Lucinda remained quiet, giving Samantha time to figure out what she wanted to say. She pulled out and began to drive along the road in silence. Lucinda was careful to leave her palm resting softly on Samantha's thigh while Samantha had a death grip on the steering wheel, obviously at war with herself. After about ten minutes Lucinda cleared her throat. "Take this next left."

"What?" Nervous eyes darted to hers.

"Turn up here on the left."

Samantha nodded and flicked on her blinker, following Lucinda's directions until they were driving up a small hill to an open parking lot. She pulled into a spot and looked over anxiously at Lucinda who gave her a small smile before pulling back her hand and stepping out of the car. Samantha shut off the engine when Lucinda got out, waiting in the car until Lucinda opened her door, reaching down and extending her hand to pull her out.

Lucinda led Samantha from the car, walking the short distance on this warm night to a break in the clearing in front of them. She stood at the top of a large, sloping hill with Samantha holding her hand by her side. A paved path weaved its way down to two illuminated softball fields below. She could see that both fields were occupied with teams and fans sitting in the short-stacked bleachers kitty-cornered on each side. Lucinda motioned for them to head over to a large flat stone a few feet from the clearing.

Lucinda sat down and patted the space beside her as Samantha slowly lowered herself and crossed her legs, eyes directed to the ground.

"Do you know where we are?" Lucinda asked softly, her eyes on the perfect profile to her right. Samantha shook her head, finally making eye contact.

"We are at the back of Franklin Park." She pointed off to the right. "Behind those trees, down the road, is the Franklin Park Zoo. And over there, that's a golf course behind that small hill. And right down there? That's where I first played after-school softball on an intramural team in junior high. And if you squint and look real hard, through those trees on the horizon are a few tall buildings of the city skyline."

Samantha's gaze followed Lucinda's gestures, taking in everything.

"We used to call this Lovers' Rock, because from here you have a great view of all the wonderful things that make up the largest park in Boston. And it's tucked far enough off to the side that you can mack it with your girl without too many onlookers," Lucinda added with a smile that Samantha matched with a blush.

Lucinda put her hand over the nervously clasped hands in Samantha's lap and leaned in, pressing a sweet, soft kiss to Samantha's lips. "I missed you today." She pressed her forehead to Samantha's.

Samantha nodded and closed her eyes, leaning forward to kiss Lucinda earnestly, teasing her tongue until Lucinda deepened the kiss. She pulled a heavy sigh from Samantha as she broke away a few moments later.

"Now tell me, what's up, beautiful?" Lucinda asked.

Samantha nodded and looked out at the field of players below. "Andrew and I got into a fight this morning." She was quiet for a moment before looking up at Lucinda. "It was about you."

Lucinda felt her eyes widen in surprise. This was unexpected.

"I have a private investigator do background checks on all my clients and prospective suitors. It's just part of the business, keeping honest people honest." She shrugged, her frown deepening as she breathed out heavily. "Andrew took it upon himself to run your name in the list without telling me."

Lucinda quirked an eyebrow, her face tensing as she moved her jaw slowly, clenching and unclenching her teeth. She left her hand on Samantha's, but it was a struggle. Her natural reaction was to recoil and scoot away. She was silent for a moment before she asked coolly, "What did he find?"

Samantha fidgeted on the rock. She unclasped her hands and pulled Lucinda's in between them. "There was information about your time in foster care and an assault charge from a few years ago."

Lucinda breathed in through her nose sharply, directing her eyes out at the horizon as she braced herself. "What do you want to know?"

"Truthfully?" Samantha whispered. "Everything."

Lucinda nodded slightly, her eyes focused down at the softball games below them. It wasn't necessarily that she had many secrets; quite the contrary really, she was just a private person. With private pains and memories she would rather forget. She had grown accustomed to walling herself in from the real world after she was continually disappointed by its inhabitants. Samantha Monteiro had a way of pushing past her boundaries or scaling them with ease.

"You know about the foster care stuff." Lucinda blinked a few times, her jaw clenched in stress as she turned to face Samantha. This time she pulled her hand back into her own lap. She needed to ground herself. She could see the hurt and strain etched on Samantha's face. Lucinda hated this.

"The assault charge is from a few years ago. I had been dating Grace for a couple of years before we split up. But I was foolish and had been casually seeing her on the side, being a doormat of sorts, I guess." She kicked at the dirt with her toe, admitting this made her feel weak and stupid. "I put up with the drama of it all because I was in love with her. I thought she was the one, you know? Then her new boyfriend caught us out together. He was furious and making a scene, spewing all kinds of shit at me while she just looked on and did nothing. I think I was so hurt by the fact that she just let him verbally assault me that I was distracted when he shoved me backward into a wall. Instinct took over and I belted him in the mouth. He was surprised but he wound back to hit me and I kicked him, knocking him and his fist into Grace. She ended up with a black eye and a hairline fracture of her cheek. I escaped with a few bloody knuckles and a stern talking to from the bouncer at the bar. I didn't know about the assault complaint until the next day when a few cops showed up at my dance studio after a class. They took my statement and assessed my injuries, informing me that I had to come down to the station with them." It felt like the night around them had grown quiet.

"I sat there for hours while they tried to track down Grace. Eventually, they let me go and told me they would be in touch. I found out a few days later that she recanted her statement and called it an accident instead. But the damage was already done. We were over."

Lucinda relaxed her jaw a little, willing herself to be patient. Samantha had recently had a world of hurt put on her; Andrew was probably just looking out for her best interests. Not that that made any of this less infuriating for Lucinda, to be researched like a criminal for no reason. But she was trying.

"Not my finest hour, but I never hit her. It was an accident. I guess she just came to her senses. It wouldn't have gone anywhere anyway, there were plenty of witnesses at the bar that would have supported my story."

Samantha held Lucinda's gaze before reaching out to touch her hands. Lucinda was rigid at first, not pulling away, but not exactly welcoming the touch. Samantha pulled Lucinda's hands up to her chest and pressed them over her fast-beating heart.

"I am so, so sorry that these things have happened to you and around you. Andrew and I fought because I didn't want to hear anything about your life unless it came from you directly. I was a little distant earlier because a part of me felt really wounded that you hadn't told me yourself. I realize you probably had a reason for that—I just felt really overwhelmed by the way I feel about you. It's scary. All I want is you and everything you will share with me, when you are ready, because you want to. I let you in when everyone else has been locked out for so long that it feels new and raw with you, like it's the first time. Andrew went behind my back and made a decision about my relationship with you that was absolutely wrong. I was nervous to tell you because I didn't want you to think I didn't trust you, because that is so far from the truth, Lucy. I am so, so sorry."

Lucinda felt the ice encasing her chest start to melt as Samantha begged for understanding. She could see the sincerity written all over Samantha's face, a face she realized she loved. She wriggled free of Samantha's grasp and pulled her forward into a firm kiss, accepting her apology with soft lips moving together, breathing unspoken truths to tender flesh.

Samantha smiled into the kiss, pressing farther into Lucinda's body, her hand sliding to Lucinda's hip, gripping it tightly. She pulled back, her eyes wet with tears. "Just make sure you tell me, okay? All the important things and the mundane stuff. Whatever it is, I just want to know you, all of you. At your pace, but all of you."

Lucinda's heart fluttered at the simple honesty of Samantha's words. She nodded and reached over to Samantha, pulling her from the rock and walking them back to the car before they slipped into the seats and locked the doors in amicable silence.

"So, I know you had this romantic dinner thing planned tonight," Samantha said with a shy smile, "but what do you think about staying in with some takeout and a movie?"

Lucinda laughed and nodded her head. "Sounds good, baby, whatever you want."

"I love it when you say that." Samantha leaned across the console to kiss Lucinda sweetly. "There's a new Mediterranean place by my house that I've been dying to try, sound okay?"

"Your place it is."

Chapter Seventeen

Lucinda canceled their dinner reservations while Samantha placed the order on the ride to Samantha's high-rise. When they got to the apartment, Samantha hopped in the shower to wash away the grime of the boxing gym. By the time she was out and in pajamas, Lucinda had the movie loaded and the food set up in the living room. Within a few minutes they were settled into the couch, lounging lazily across each other and sampling their small mountain of food. About halfway through the movie Lucinda realized she had lost interest in the content and was only focusing on Samantha. It started out innocent enough, but when Samantha crawled across the couch and straddled Lucinda's lap, tossing her arms behind her neck, her mind went blank.

"What's this movie about?" she teased, kissing along the column of Lucinda's neck.

"I have no idea," Lucinda mumbled, her head thrown back.

"Okay, good. We'll finish it later…" Samantha's kissing turned to licking and Lucinda wondered if it was possible to literally combust on this couch.

Lucinda murmured a thoughtless reply, her hands slipping under Samantha's soft T-shirt. She settled her hands at the narrow hips in front of her, pressing her thumbs lightly into the natural indentations Samantha's hip bones made under the cotton waistband of the flannel pants. Although they had talked daily, the last time she and Samantha had any legitimate physical affection was over a week ago. She could feel her eagerness threatening to dissolve her attempts at controlled teasing.

Samantha moaned softly and rolled her hips forward against Lucinda's firm stomach. "I really missed your touch," she husked into Lucinda's ear, taking her earlobe into her mouth and sucking on it lightly. "You feel so good." She pressed greedy open-mouthed kisses along Lucinda's jaw, distracting Lucinda from her mission of freeing Samantha from her pants.

Lucinda practically growled into Samantha's mouth as Samantha rolled her hips again and again into Lucinda's abs, her hands threading tightly into Lucinda's hair. She felt drunk off the hungry lips caressing her own, the warm tongue fighting hers for dominance. She loved when Samantha was aggressive; she opened her mouth wider to deepen the kiss. Lucinda pulled Samantha closer on the next roll of her hips, guiding her ass in small circles before sliding her hands up and under the cotton shirt to cup satin-covered breasts.

Her actions were rewarded with a whimper as Samantha broke their kissing long enough to suck in some quick breaths. Lucinda took the opportunity to pull the shirt up and off Samantha's body, tossing it on the loveseat to her left. Samantha was gorgeous, all lean torso and perfectly smooth skin encased in a hot pink lace push-up bra that was killing Lucinda to look at. She wrapped one hand around Samantha's waist, encouraging her to continue her gentle ministrations, while the other kneaded the full cups in front of her. She peppered soft kisses along Samantha's upper abs and over her breasts, licking the fabric over a budding nipple and sucking it into her mouth through the satin.

Samantha shivered, her fingers scratching at Lucinda's scalp, pulling her closer as she rolled her hips a little more aggressively. "I love the way your mouth feels on my skin." She shuddered as Lucinda bit down on her nipple, tugging it forward slightly. Lucinda palmed her breast firmly before she slid to the back, unclasping her bra and pulling it down her arms. She pressed wet kisses along the inside of each breast, working her way up to Samantha's mouth as she continued to guide Samantha's hips against her, harder and harder.

"Take these off." She licked across Samantha's mouth, her breathing coming in short gasps as Lucinda snapped the elastic on her pants.

Samantha nodded frantically, rising off Lucinda's lap just long enough to pull down the soft flannel pajamas and expose hot pink and black lace boy shorts just as quickly discarded. She yanked at Lucinda's shirt in between desperate kisses.

"Please," she begged against Lucinda's mouth, "I want to rub against you." Her hand slid between them and she scratched at Lucinda's firm abs, bringing her hips down again slowly.

Lucinda smiled into the kiss, leaning back to remove her top and bra as fast as she could before she pulled Samantha close again. She could feel how wet Samantha was as she was pinned to the couch by Samantha's arms and legs, as Samantha rolled her sex against the defined muscles of Lucinda's stomach, over and over, coating her with her essence.

"God," Samantha purred, nipping at Lucinda's lip and kissing her roughly. "Watching you at the gym tonight…you're so hot." She pressed their lips together again, groaning in protest when Lucinda pulled back slightly.

"We need to go to the bed now—there's just not enough room here." Her hands slipped down Samantha's sides, abandoning her breasts to grip her hips, slowing Samantha's movements. Lucinda pulled one hand back, dragging her fingers up her own stomach, gathering Samantha's wetness on her fingertips and placing two into her mouth. "I need to taste you, but I want to lay you out. I need you, all of you."

Samantha's eyes were hooded and her cheeks flushed. Lucinda tapped Samantha's bottom lip lightly, pulling it from her teeth and slipping her other two fingers into Samantha's mouth, letting Samantha taste herself. Samantha rolled her tongue over the long pale fingers slowly before releasing them.

When they got to the bedroom, things slowed a bit. It wasn't the frantic, desperate need to fuck from the living room. It was different. Samantha pulled back the covers and turned to help Lucinda out of the rest of her clothes, pulling the fabric down and away slowly, pressing kisses to hip bones and along the inside of her knee. She ran her hands over Lucinda's thighs and massaged the skin gently before standing. Lucinda grasped her close, letting their flushed skin press together, hands roaming over backs, caressing slowly.

Lucinda kissed Samantha like it was the last time she ever would, pulling her along as she sank onto the bed, never breaking the kiss. She rolled them so Samantha was underneath and pressed a bruising kiss to Samantha's lips, trying to share all her secrets. She was lost in the feel and taste of Samantha's mouth, gently rocking her body down against her lover, her hand gripping tightly at Samantha's hip.

"You're just…it's so…"

Samantha smiled. "I know. It's so much."

Lucinda nodded, feeling understood before she kissed a path along Samantha's jaw, down her neck. She pressed shaking lips to her collarbone before weaving lower over firm breasts, her hands scratching along Samantha's sides. She licked sloppy lines over Samantha's flat stomach, encouraged by small hands gently kneading her scalp. Lucinda nudged Samantha's legs apart before sliding between them, nuzzling a hipbone before kissing lower, slowly, painfully slow.

"You are so soft," she whispered reverently between kisses. "I love your skin."

Lucinda kept her eyes on Samantha's. She kissed the soft, wet flesh just to the right of Samantha's sex. "I love your taste." A soft exhale. "I love your smell." She moved that last little bit and pressed a featherlight kiss to Samantha's clit before whispering, "I love your everything."

Samantha sucked in a sharp gasp as she dragged the flat of her tongue along Samantha's slit, pulling a loud moan from her lips. Lucinda smiled against the blood-flushed skin, exploring Samantha intimately with her tongue. Lucinda basked in the wetness. Samantha was practically dripping from all the foreplay. Samantha's hands continued to gently scratch and tug at her hair as narrow hips rolled against her face, begging for more, always begging. She dipped and swirled her tongue, moving slowly before speeding up, her nose periodically nudging Samantha's clit.

Samantha cried out after a particularly firm nudge to her clit, her body starting to convulse. She could feel Lucinda's tongue everywhere: in her fingers, pulsing through her chest, swirling in her gut, deep inside her—pulling, pulling, pulling her closer, faster, toward the brink of her pleasure.

Lucinda thrust her tongue deep into Samantha, pulling her hips lower, filling every ounce of space before curling her tongue and bringing Samantha to climax.

Samantha's eyes widened before fluttering closed as she halted her staggered breaths, staying there paralyzed, floating, at the whim of Lucinda's mouth and firm hands. She panted as Lucinda slowly brought her back, cradling her skin, licking and kissing her softly, easing her down with all the care in the world. Her body continued to tremble, little aftershocks rolling through her as Lucinda moved up, wrapping soft lips around Samantha's clit and gently sucking, pulling her into a second orgasm, just as strong as the first. She cried out, screaming Lucinda's name as her hands clutched at the bedsheets. She shook and shivered as she rode out the end of her orgasm; Lucinda's warm hands were on her abdomen, helping her settle back into the bed, soothing her.

Lucinda overwhelmed Samantha, taking all of her and winding her up, but she never let her fall. She always guided her back down with care. Always. Samantha savored the feeling of being so completely cared for. She had writhed under the heat from Lucinda's mouth as she spoke of all the things she loved about Samantha. It had felt like Lucinda was burning the words into her flesh, like every word would be there forever, reminding her. She couldn't stop the shiver that ran through her as Lucinda kissed her abdomen softly, her hands soothing up and down her sides, massaging the skin. Samantha reached down and traced still shaky fingers along Lucinda's jaw, hooking under her chin.

"Come here."

Lucinda raised herself along Samantha's body, a broad smile on her face as she settled over Samantha.

Samantha grabbed either side of her face, pulling her close, watching her eyes intently before firmly kissing her, tasting herself and moaning. Lucinda deepened the kiss, seeming to enjoy every bit of Samantha's mouth.

Samantha pulled back, still cradling Lucinda's face before asking, "Do you…" She paused. "Did you mean it?"

"Every word."

Samantha let a timid smile cross her lips before feathering a soft kiss to Lucinda's lips. "Tell me."

"I love you."

The deep, velvety laugh that spilled from Samantha's lips was automatic as she kissed Lucinda again, this time rolling them so Lucinda was on her back, laughing. Samantha kissed along her mouth, moving to her jaw before sucking on her pulse point. Her hands traced the defined lines of Lucinda's shoulders, down to her hands, intertwining their fingers above her head as she slipped her thigh between her legs, pressing against her. Lucinda moaned, rocking against her immediately.

"Tell me again," she implored against Lucinda's skin.

"I love you."

"I love you too," Samantha whispered.

Samantha woke up smiling; long limbs were wrapped around her chest and legs. Lucinda was spooned up behind her, one leg draped across hers, her left arm hooked under Samantha's and her hand gently closed against her chest. It was the warmest most comfortable position Samantha had ever woken up in. She could feel the slow, rhythmic breathing against her bare shoulder as Lucinda remained peaceful, lost in sleep. She pressed herself back farther into the crook of Lucinda's hips, enjoying the sensation of being completely enveloped by another human being. Last night had been magical. It was intense and passionate and tranquil all at the same time. Seeing the park, hearing her story, sharing their secrets, loving her, being loved, it just felt unreal. But it was real—there was a very real, very naked Lucinda Moss pressed up against her and Samantha wouldn't have it any other way.

"You're awake?" Lucinda kissed her shoulder.

"I thought you were sleeping," she purred as she turned her head to kiss Lucinda.

"Nope, just enjoying how good it feels to have you all wrapped up in me." She pecked Samantha's lips before nuzzling her cheek.

Samantha slid her arm up and over Lucinda's, entwining their fingers at her chest and encouraging Lucinda to hug her more tightly. "Mm, this may be my new favorite position." She shifted back infinitesimally into Lucinda.

"Oh, that sounds like a challenge." Lucinda nipped at the skin of Samantha's shoulder. She pulled her hand from Samantha's and walked her fingers down a flat abdomen before Samantha stopped her.

"Baby, as much as I want to, I have to pee…and probably shower." She frowned and wiggled her hips forward a bit.

"Okay, that's a good enough reason I guess." Lucinda placed one last kiss to Samantha's shoulder before releasing her and stretching out on the bed.

"Oh, by the way"—Samantha sat up with a stretch and a yawn before turning back to look at her very relaxed girlfriend—"I love you." Lucinda gave her one last quick kiss before she stumbled out of the room to the bathroom.

Lucinda couldn't help the goofy grin plastered on her face. The last thing she had ever expected when she went to Connie's wedding was to meet someone, anyone, let alone a woman as charming and complex as Samantha Monteiro. Sometimes she wished she had given herself more opportunities to be vulnerable in the past. But life had taken her on quite a ride so far, and she was grateful for the maturity she had acquired at this time in her life, the time when Samantha entered her world all dimples and bright smiles. She wouldn't fight her feelings this time; she wouldn't shy away from any intimacy. She wanted to be a better person—she wanted to use her past experiences to make the right decisions for her future. A future she hoped would include the beautiful woman she could hear humming happily from the bathroom next to her.

A moment later, Samantha stood in the doorway of the bathroom, a silk robe tied loosely around her waist. "Hey beautiful," she said, "care to join me in the shower? You know, to save water." She flashed a devilish smile.

Lucinda beamed. "Massimo would be so proud." She gave one final stretch before hopping out of bed on her quest to save the environment.

CHAPTER EIGHTEEN

Samantha knew some people found mundane tasks like ironing or doing the dishes to be relaxing, the kind of mindless activity that required minimal attention but had a steady rhythm that lulled you into a peacefulness you didn't know you needed. Samantha felt that way about primping. She sat at her makeup table, blowing her damp hair dry, but letting it settle as it would naturally, in loose, easy curls. As a child, she had hated her hair, but she had learned to appreciate it as she grew up, eventually becoming the envy of most men and women she met, beautiful, long hair, dark as night and full of natural body.

She had let it mostly air dry after her play with Lucinda in the shower; she was in no rush to iron out its nature. She closed her eyes and smiled at the memory of their shower together. It had been sweet and innocent, mostly. Or at least, it had started that way. And most importantly, it had ended that way. Samantha loved the feminine strength that Lucinda brought to their relationship. Strong hands and shoulders, long, lean muscle paired with soft curves. Lucinda possessed a natural confidence and security that seamlessly transitioned between her work life and their bedroom play. She was effortlessly perfect all the time.

"What're you thinking about?" Soft words and a gentle squeeze of her shoulder brought Samantha back to the present. She smiled.

"You."

Lucinda kissed Samantha's shoulder before gently running her fingers through Samantha's hair, taking the dryer in her own hand and helping with the back. "I love when you let your natural curls come out to play."

Samantha closed her eyes, leaning her head back into Lucinda's touch. "I know. That's why I didn't straighten it."

Lucinda smoothed her hair a bit before pulling on a curl, letting it spring back. "You're too good to me."

Samantha rolled her shoulders and cracked her neck as Lucinda shut off the blow dryer and set it aside. She finished applying her mascara and watched Lucinda pull her own hair into a loose braid before applying a sheer pink lip gloss. Their eyes met briefly in the mirrored glass, each of them caught staring at the other before the doorbell broke their trance.

"Ugh," Samantha complained, "who could that be?"

"Your place not mine, babe, you tell me."

Samantha's eyes flickered around the room as she stood. Her landline was slightly askew; it must have been knocked off the cradle during the night. Maybe it was the concierge knocking. She wasn't expecting any deliveries and no one would be looking for her, well, except maybe Andrew. Who she imagined at this point might be frantically searching for her. "Maybe Andrew called the cops…it's just dramatic enough to be plausible for him."

Lucinda walked to the phone and repositioned the receiver. "I'm sure he's worried. You should probably call him."

"Let him worry! Who fucking has their best friend's girlfriend investigated?" Samantha pulled on some pants and looked for a shirt.

"Although I can't disagree with your…irritation"—Lucinda seemed to choose her words carefully—"I'm sure he had your best interests in the forefront of his mind."

The doorbell rang again, this time a moment longer than before. Samantha buttoned her jeans and pulled on a soft jersey T-shirt from the drawer. "You are much nicer than I am. Maybe I ought to let you get the door." At that she padded out of the room.

Samantha opened the door and was greeted by an enormous chocolate-dipped fruit bouquet and a nervous looking doorman from the lobby. "Oh, hey"—she leaned forward and read his name tag—"Jasper. Thanks."

He nodded and looked left and right. "Sorry Ms. Monteiro, we tried to call up but the phone was busy." He shifted nervously on his feet as she turned from him, motioning him in.

"Sorry about that. Just set it over there, Jasper, thanks." She hurriedly cleared off the table behind the sofa to make room.

"Um…" he mumbled as he placed the basket down, his gaze flickering around her foyer, eyes everywhere but her face.

Samantha turned slowly. "Yes?"

"I think what the poor boy is trying to spit out," a crisp voice chimed from the doorframe, immediately sending ice down Samantha's spine, "is you have a visitor."

Jasper nodded apologetically before retreating and bringing two suitcases through the door. "Put them in the guest room would you, dear?" Her mother directed the panicked doorman as he glanced back up at Samantha for her consent. "It's the second door on the right past the kitchen."

Samantha shook her head and held out her hand. "Jasper, you can go. Thank you." She flashed him a bright smile as he closed the door with a nod.

"They are not lackeys for you to order around, *Madre*," she hissed before scooping up the fruit basket and moving it into the kitchen.

Marisol Monteiro crossed her arms and let out a heavy sigh as she followed her daughter into the kitchen. "I tried to call your phone multiple times to let you know I was coming. Why didn't you answer?"

Samantha glanced into the living room; Lucinda must have cleaned up while she was drying her hair. The dishes were in the dishwasher and the leftovers were in the fridge. All the couch cushions had been fluffed and put back with care, and even her discarded clothing was neatly folded off to the side. She didn't think she could love that woman any more than she did in this moment—

because had her mother seen the remnants of their night, there would have been hell to pay. And a lot of explaining to do.

Marisol did not tolerate untidiness well. Forget about the prospect of her daughter's underwear thrown across the room during a heated moment with her lover, who happened to be female. Her mother had never really approved of her dating women in the past. She had happily supplied that she was glad the phase was over when Samantha brought Eric home.

"Well it didn't stop you from popping by, did it?"

Marisol tapped her foot. "Well?"

Samantha's forehead creased with irritation, "Well, what?"

"*Mija*, don't you think you ought to greet your mother with a hug?"

Samantha plucked the card from the fruit bouquet and tapped the envelope on the countertop. "*Madre*, it's always a pleasure when you are around. Where are my manners? I'm sorry." She slipped an arm around her mother. The exchange appeared to appease her for the moment.

"Who sent you such a beautiful bouquet?" Marisol asked, eyeing the envelope. "Eric?"

Samantha chose to ignore her mother's obvious baiting and directed her attention to the envelope.

Samantha, I am sorry for questioning your judgment. You deserve to be happy, and I'm glad that you are. Call me. Please enjoy some fruit from your favorite fruit, Andrew XOXO

❖

Lucinda hadn't planned on spending the night at Samantha's and definitely was not about to crawl back into her work clothes from yesterday. She shuffled through her gym bag, pulling out mascara and perfume as she heard Samantha engaging in a conversation with someone in the other room. Her cell phone chimed in the kitchen, and she heard a woman say, "So your phone does work! You were just avoiding me then?"

Answering it in her underwear was probably not the wisest idea. The clothing she had let Samantha borrow lay neatly folded on the edge of her dresser, waiting for her. She laughed and pulled them on before ducking out of the bedroom.

"Actually, that's my phone." Lucinda walked in slowly, holding Samantha's cell in her hand. "Your phone died." She held it up toward Samantha with a frown before scooping up her cell phone and silencing it.

"Samantha, why didn't you tell me you had a guest?" the woman chided before turning toward Lucinda. "I'm Marisol, Samantha's mother." She extended her hand with a small smile.

Lucinda matched the smile and shook her hand. "Lucinda Moss. It's a pleasure to meet you."

Samantha's nostrils flared slightly as she plugged in her cell and glanced down at the screen. Lucinda could see that she had six missed calls, five from Andrew, one from her mother. "Hey, Luce, look—breakfast." Samantha smiled apologetically and motioned toward the fruit before handing Lucinda Andrew's card.

"Breakfast?" Marisol eyed her daughter suspiciously. "It's nearly noon, dear."

"It's also a weekend." Samantha sighed, leaning against the counter and crossing her arms. "But thanks for the update."

"Well, I'm going to use the ladies' room. It was a long ride."

Lucinda watched her adjust her hair before stepping out of the kitchen and into the guest bathroom. "So, she seems...nice," she quipped with a smile.

Samantha let her head tip back against the cabinet and groaned. "All I want to do is spend my entire weekend with you, naked, and christening every available surface. Not entertaining my mother."

Lucinda plucked a chocolate-covered strawberry from the bouquet, stepping in front of Samantha and biting into the fruit. Samantha smiled into the kiss as Lucinda pressed the fruit and chocolate into her open mouth before pulling back with a wink. "Christening every available surface, huh?"

"Mm-hmm. Naked."

"Sounds delicious," Lucinda purred, as the sound of the bathroom door opening alerted her to step back.

Lucinda wiped the excess chocolate off the corner of Samantha's lips, sucking her thumb into her own mouth and stepping to the other side of the counter.

"Lucinda," Marisol said to her directly, "my daughter seemed against the idea of me letting that nice boy put my things in the guest room, is that because you're staying?"

Samantha visibly cringed and turned to make coffee, except Lucinda had already made coffee, so she just shuffled nervously to find some cups. Lucinda tried her best not to laugh.

She popped a grape into her mouth and swallowed. "No, just stopped by for a little brunch. We have a standing date. I didn't know you would be stopping by, otherwise we could have rescheduled."

Samantha returned with three cups, quickly making hers and Lucinda's to their liking before turning to her mother. "What brings you to town?"

Marisol took the third cup and walked over to the coffeemaker, serving herself and reaching for the milk, her back to Lucinda. "Well, I thought it might be nice to spend some quality time with my daughter. Also, I hoped I might see a few sights while I was here."

Lucinda pulled a pineapple-and-melon flower from the bouquet and bit into the fruit, her eyes on Samantha's reaction as she dragged her tongue along the remaining piece.

Samantha threw a grape at Lucinda and hid her smile behind her coffee mug. The bite of her prior interactions was gone now that Lucinda was doing everything in her power to make Samantha laugh or melt. She was totally winning. She asked her mother, "How long were you planning on staying?"

Marisol turned back in time to see Lucinda pop the rest of the fruit into her mouth and settle into the stool at the island. "A few days. Your father is traveling for business this week, so I won't be missed."

"Oh, I doubt that." Lucinda grinned. "If you're as charming as your daughter here, I'm sure you will be missed immensely."

Samantha coughed into her coffee.

"At least your friends have a sense of humor, *mija*." Marisol picked up Andrew's card and frowned. "Speaking of which, where is Andrew?"

"I don't know, call him." Samantha took the card back before her mother could read its contents, filing it away in a drawer behind her. Her mother's purse vibrated on the counter and Marisol answered the call, replying animatedly in Spanish and wandering into the living room.

"Ugh, it's the firstborn son…" Samantha nodded toward her mother who was talking on the phone, her back to them.

"I feel like I should learn Spanish," Lucinda quipped. "Think of all the things I could glean from you both." She paused before adding, "Think of all the things you scream out in bed that I could finally understand…"

"You're going to make this as difficult for me as you can, aren't you?" Samantha looked both amused and turned-on.

"That all depends," Lucinda teased as she stalked over to Samantha, and ran her fingers along the inside of Samantha's arm. "Will I be punished for it later?"

Lucinda stepped closer, her eyes directed toward Marisol's back while her hand stroked higher up the inside of Samantha's right arm, brushing against her breast. Samantha gripped her coffee mug harder, forcing out a slow breath as Lucinda's movements grew bolder, her thumb grazing dangerously close to an erect nipple.

"Because if you can guarantee I'll get my just deserts"— Lucinda flattened her hand against the curve of Samantha's breast before squeezing lightly—"then yes, I plan on making this positively unbearable for you."

Samantha's eyes fluttered when Lucinda pulled her hand back and reached behind her for the coffeepot to refill her mug. She stayed close enough to whisper, "No reason that your mother arriving should ruin all the fun I planned to have with you this weekend, don't you agree?"

She walked in front of Samantha, letting her left hand graze the front of Samantha's jeans, hesitating just long enough to press the material against her girlfriend's center.

Samantha choked back a whimper, her hips rolling forward as Lucinda stepped away, reaching for the milk and increasing the space between them as Marisol concluded the conversation and walked back into the kitchen. Lucinda made sure to increase the sway of her hips as she retreated to the safety of the other side of the kitchen island, doing everything in her power to make Samantha aware that she was entirely serious. If the look on Samantha's face was any indication, she was succeeding with flying colors.

Chapter Nineteen

Later that week, Lucinda sat in her office, ostensibly working on client notes, but in truth, daydreaming about Samantha. Lucinda had called in a favor with some of the girls she used to dance with and got them a private box at the ballet for tonight. Marisol was bringing Andrew as her date; he had smoothed things over with Samantha by promising to entertain the older Monteiro woman with a late lunch before the show. Evidently Marisol adored Andrew, found him charming and handsome. It was perfect—she would have someone to go to lunch with and chat with during the performance and Samantha would have the opportunity to escape. Lucinda was glad things were better between Andrew and Samantha, but they were still working on it. This was an olive branch; it was progress.

She was still considering her own feelings about the Andrew thing when her intercom chimed with Amanda's voice. "Lucinda?"

"Yes, Amanda?" she continued typing before dragging her finger across the tablet screen to change the window in front of her.

"Brian is here, should I send him in?"

"Yes, thanks."

Brian knocked before opening her door and stepping in quietly. "How are you today?"

"Good, good, what's up?" She wasn't intentionally being dismissive, but she wanted to finish this email. She closed the file and looked up at him expectantly.

"I wanted to follow up with the Richard issue. The intern has been relocated to another department so as to limit her interactions with him. He was called in to HR and given a strong warning. Documentation was signed agreeing to their terms. Mostly, I wanted to know how he was doing with you."

Lucinda considered her answer before replying. "He's been submitting his work to me directly. It's improved, but not markedly. No typos, no late submissions, but it's just so-so work." She tapped her fingers on her desk. "I gave him his own project so I could evaluate his competence. I'm not impressed thus far."

Brian mulled this over. "Our priority is the best interest of the company. I'm sure you'll figure out what's best—you've been doing a great job so far."

"Lucinda?" Amanda chimed again over the intercom.

Lucinda smiled apologetically to Brian. "Yes?"

"Sorry to interrupt, Samantha Monteiro is here."

"Send her in, please. And hold my calls," Lucinda replied. She stood and walked to the front of her desk, leaning against it, her ankles crossed.

"I'll see you again later in the week, thanks for the update," Brian said, before excusing himself and heading toward the door. He opened the door as Samantha was reaching for it. He introduced himself, before waving back to Lucinda and closing the door behind him.

Samantha paused inside the door, reaching behind herself to lock it. She turned with a smile. "You look radiant." She eyed Lucinda's frame and settled her gaze at Lucinda's chest before flickering up to her eyes.

Lucinda licked her lips, taking in Samantha's skintight dress, eyes lingering on the slit on her right thigh. She quirked an eyebrow. "Do you always dress like that for work? Maybe I ought to swing by the office a little more."

"Mm, maybe you should." Samantha pursed her lips as she stalked toward Lucinda. She tossed her purse onto an office chair before stepping close and gently running her fingers along Lucinda's arm.

"I missed you." Lucinda inhaled the scent of Samantha's shampoo and perfume before pressing a soft kiss to her jaw.

Samantha tilted her head, exposing her neck as she closed her hands over the ones Lucinda had leaning on the desk, holding her up. She took in a slow breath as Lucinda placed soft, wet kisses along her jaw to her lips, pausing just short of her mouth.

"Tell me," Lucinda teased, kissing the edge of her lips.

Samantha closed her eyes at the taunting, sucking her bottom lip between her teeth as Lucinda continued to pepper soft kisses everywhere but on her lips. "I love you."

Lucinda rewarded the response with a hard kiss to her mouth, her hands leaving the desk to pull her closer, deepening the kiss. Samantha moaned into her mouth, parting her lips and pressing her hips against Lucinda's. Lucinda let one hand slide down Samantha's body before settling at her hip and holding her close. She kissed soft lips with a smile. "Hi."

"Hi."

"How was your day?" Lucinda gently rubbed her thumb along Samantha's earlobe.

"Mm, fine. Better now. You?"

"Same." Lucinda purred before kissing Samantha softly again, her left hand slipping from Samantha's hip and toying with the slit on her thigh. "I like this dress...is it new?" She kept her mouth close, breathing the words across plump lips.

"We went shopping yesterday...I bought all kinds of nice new things to show you." She pulled back and gave Lucinda a sly smile.

"Like what?"

Lucinda felt Samantha's hand close over hers and slip her fingers under the slit of the dress, pushing the hem up until her fingertips danced over silky fabric.

"Like these," Samantha replied as she licked into Lucinda's mouth, pulling a moan from Lucinda before stepping back and letting Lucinda take in the new article of clothing.

"Hmm." Lucinda leaned back and edged Samantha's dress up higher, exposing the silk and lace underneath. She took a moment to turn Samantha so she could see the back and how they hugged her ass in just the right way to make them look painted on. She traced her fingers along the curve of the fabric. "What do they look like off?"

Samantha feigned innocence as she pushed her dress back down and stepped back to sit in the leather chair positioned before Lucinda. She smiled politely and clasped her hands in her lap as she crossed her legs seductively. "Why don't you close the blinds and find out?"

Lucinda's heart skipped a beat as she leaned back over her desk and reached for the remote to close the shades, tapping the button lightly before sitting up straight to look at Samantha. She cocked her head to the side before adding, "I've been thinking about you all day."

"Oh?"

"About how tonight was going to be near impossible to get through without touching you."

"I can see why you would be concerned." Samantha uncrossed her legs and spread her knees a bit. She tapped her finger over her lip in thought as her dark eyes settled on Lucinda's lips. "We should probably figure out a way to make tonight more bearable."

Lucinda stepped forward and placed her hands on the arms of the chair, her body hovering over Samantha's as she nudged her knee between Samantha's legs and pushed them farther apart. She looked into the dark eyes in front of her before nodding and chewing on her bottom lip. The urge to ravish Samantha made her stomach wind tighter and tighter.

Samantha knew it too; the little smile on her lips as she pulled her dress up again, exposing her panties, was a blatant taunt. Lucinda was getting payback for the other day.

Samantha's hands touched the thigh between her own, her fingers tracing up and down, squeezing the muscle of Lucinda's leg and releasing it. She moved her hand higher and gently cupped Lucinda through her pants, slightly curling and uncurling her fingers. Lucinda let out a groan, pressing forward and closing her eyes as Samantha continued her ministrations, teasing and pressing in before pulling back. She whispered into Lucinda's ear, "I've been thinking about what it would be like to feel your hands on my hips and your lips on my skin, pressing into me, sucking on me gently, licking me, and teasing me. I've been thinking about the way you make me feel like I can't take any more and I may die from the pleasure, only to push me further and pull me tighter."

She licked Lucinda's ear before sucking the lobe into her mouth. "I've been thinking about the way your mouth on my sex makes me want to spend my whole life in bed with you just so I can feel every way you could fuck me into unconsciousness."

Lucinda was panting now, her hips moving, and pressing herself more firmly into Samantha's hands, her knuckles white as she gripped the arms of the chair tighter. Samantha pressed her fingers hard against Lucinda before reaching out to palm her breast aggressively through her shirt, strumming her fingers over the swollen nipple.

"I've been thinking about watching you squirm and beg for me to touch you ever since you teased me in my kitchen." She kissed along Lucinda's jaw before biting her chin lightly. "Are we at that point yet?"

Lucinda moaned as Samantha pulled harder on her nipple while pressing her palm flat against her and thrusting up.

"Come on, Luce," Samantha growled with her lips just millimeters from Lucinda's mouth. "Are we there yet?"

A soft whimper spilled from Lucinda's lips as she finally submitted with a nod, unable to resist the game any longer.

"Good girl." Samantha kissed Lucinda hard on the lips and pressed her back against the desk as she stood. Her hands worked fast, unbuttoning Lucinda's tailored pants and pushing them down her legs as she slipped beneath Lucinda's soaked panties and slid two firm fingers into her. Lucinda curled forward, her head pressed into Samantha's neck as she thrust in and out at a practiced pace, dragging her thumb against Lucinda's throbbing clit. She used her body to press Lucinda against her desk, one hand gripping her hair and tugging her head back far enough to kiss her mouth and silence her whimpers.

All the teasing and talking caught up with Lucinda quickly; she came undone after a particularly well-placed thrust and curl of Samantha's fingers, beckoning her over the edge. Samantha swallowed her moan and cradled Lucinda's head against her neck as she slowed her hand and pulled out with care. Lucinda's legs trembled as she slouched back against the desk, catching her breath, still unbelieving of what just transpired. After a minute or two of Samantha speaking softly between featherlight kisses, Lucinda was finally able to exhale fully and recover.

Samantha pressed a soft kiss to Lucinda's lips before bending forward to help her redress. Then she guided Lucinda's hands to her hips, pulling her dress up the rest of the way before she whispered against kiss-bruised lips, "I've also been thinking about what it would be like to be fucked on that enormous desk since the first day I walked in here and caught you staring at my ass." She paused before asking, "You got stamina for that, champ?"

Lucinda swept all the papers off the desk and onto the floor. She lifted Samantha up and placed her gently onto the surface before pulling down the panties that started this whole exchange. "Have I told you how much I love you?" She kissed Samantha and enthusiastically fulfilled her request.

❖

The Opera House was a gorgeous place, its architecture positively stunning: gold-leaf finishes, chandeliers, rich tapestries, grand staircases, silk wall panels, and painted murals. It was spectacular. Lucinda smiled at the familiarity of this environment; it reminded her of many good times. Walking into the theater was like stepping back in time, old-world charm paired with the most state-of-the-art staging. Their box was to the right of the stage with a perfect view of the dancers and the orchestra.

Andrew and Marisol were already seated when Samantha walked in with Lucinda. Samantha looked over at Lucinda and released her hand with a heavy sigh before she hugged the other two occupants of the balcony, talking to her mother while Andrew shuffled out of his seat.

He stood, fastening the button on his designer suit and smoothing it before stepping toward Lucinda with his shoulders squared. Lucinda smiled, appreciating the way he was attempting to appear confident. Samantha had already clued her in that he was nervous she might bite his head off, since this was the first time they were seeing each other again after the private investigator incident.

"Lucinda, it's good to see you again." He stepped toward her, his eyes nervously tracing her.

"Hey." She smiled, reaching for his hand and squeezing it gently as she kissed him on the cheek.

"Look, I really screwed up and I'm sorry, I—"

Lucinda held up her hand. She had told Samantha she understood why Andrew had done it, but it didn't really make her feel any less violated; it just made her feel a little sad. "Andrew, I get it, really I do. I don't like the way you went about it and I don't like the way it made me feel, but I can appreciate that your heart was in the right place." She paused. "Don't do it again. If you want to know something, just ask. I'm serious about Samantha and I want to get along with you because you are very important in her life, and she is very important in mine. Okay? Agreed?"

He swallowed and nodded. "Okay, yeah, I'm sorry." He pulled her into a hug and kissed her cheek before whispering into her ear, "She's great, huh?"

She looked over at Samantha and breathed out quietly. "The best."

Andrew looked thoughtful at her response. He narrowed his eyes and looked at her intensely for a moment before he made the shape of a heart with his fingers and pointed to Samantha with a kissy face, causing Lucinda to blush. They shared a private smile before Lucinda shoved Andrew playfully and walked over to greet Samantha's mother.

"Marisol, how was your lunch?" She cleared her throat and tried to act like she wasn't on fire. Samantha was out of her chair and playfully slapping Andrew out of earshot, murmuring something to him quietly as he laughed.

"Oh, Lucinda! It's so nice to see you again, these seats are wonderful." Marisol beamed as she looked back at the stage, the overhead lights dimming to alert the audience that the show was about to start.

"I'm glad you like them. I have a few friends that dance with the company. Maybe afterward I can introduce you to some of them." The lights dimmed again and Lucinda glanced back toward her seat. "Enjoy the show—let's catch up at the break."

Marisol placed her hand on Lucinda's forearm and squeezed gently before turning to face the stage. Samantha shoved a laughing Andrew toward the seat next to her mother and looked up at Lucinda with an apologetic smile. Lucinda returned it and nodded to her seat, choosing to position herself on the end with a space between her and Andrew for Samantha.

Samantha sat beside her as the lights fully dimmed and the orchestra began. She leaned close to Lucinda and said quietly, "He knows."

Lucinda kept her eyes on the stage as she feigned ignorance. "Knows what, baby?" The velvety chuckle beside her made her heart melt.

"That I love you." Samantha pressed a quick kiss under her jaw, their exchange hidden in the shadows. She laced their fingers together between the seats, covering them with a program of the night's performance. "I love you and I'm doing a shit job of hiding it."

Lucinda gently squeezed Samantha's hand and rubbed her thumb along Samantha's knuckle as the first round of dancers took the stage, the coolness of the program burning against her skin. She looked at the beautiful woman to her right and smiled sadly. She knew this was still new and fresh and scary, but she felt so strongly already, she wanted everyone to know how important Samantha was to her. But she didn't want to rush her into any grand announcement either, particularly to her mother who was just two seats away. So she just smiled and breathed out slowly, appreciating the memory of this afternoon and the ride here and the hand in her own.

"I love you too."

Samantha glanced over and saw the fading sadness in Lucinda's eyes reflected in the light of the stage. She hadn't realized that what she had said might have struck a nerve in Lucinda. She wasn't quite sure what to do with all these new feelings. She loved Lucinda. She made her feel appreciated and respected, loved and cared for. She was attentive and patient. God, was she patient. Even now, even here, Lucinda was patient. The program draped across their hands felt like a thousand-pound anchor pulling them down. Samantha was tired of fighting all the feelings her mother stirred up in her. She looked once more at the woman who made her heart sing with a silly text or some flowers, or a hand on her lower back as she walked through a door, or that perfect smile. She loved her and she didn't want to hide that.

"Hey." Lucinda smiled reassuringly, undoubtedly trying to convey her understanding because she was a perfect human. "It's okay. I get it. I'm here."

Samantha shoved the program off their hands and brought them onto her lap. She squeezed Lucinda's hand in her own as the orchestra rose in volume. She shook her head once more and leaned in to press a quick kiss to the lips of a shocked-looking Lucinda.

"I love you and I'm not afraid of that." She settled back into her seat and bit her bottom lip, feeling a little embarrassed but, at the same time, better.

"Good. Me too," Lucinda whispered into Samantha's ear. "You lead and I'll follow this time, okay?" She punctuated her words with a soft kiss to the shell of Samantha's ear.

Samantha knew she was blushing. Lucinda Moss was everything she had ever wanted and never knew existed. She let the warmth of that realization settle in her chest as she redirected her attention to the ballet unfolding in front of her.

Chapter Twenty

Intermission came faster than Samantha had anticipated. Lucinda had slipped away before the house lights came on to grab them some refreshments before the lines got too long. Samantha had watched her leave with a flutter in her chest. Lucinda was stunning tonight in all black and low heels. she could watch her walk away all the time, as long as she knew she was coming back.

Andrew cleared his throat, startling her. "You ought to cut back on the leering, dear, people will notice...and by people I mean Mommy Dearest over here."

Samantha turned back to face him. "It's dark, shut up."

The lights came on and the audience stood to stretch, chatting idly in the rows and gushing about the performance. Marisol turned to them with a smile. "This is positively lovely. These seats are unbelievable. What a pleasure to see the arts in such luxury."

Samantha couldn't help but grin and feel proud that her girlfriend had not only suggested this delightful little diversion but also worked her magic to score such amazing seats. She had to admit, it was a beautiful view from here.

Andrew stood and cracked his neck, stifling a yawn as he loosened his shoulders.

"Up late last night, Andrew?" Samantha teased, stretching in her seat.

Andrew shot her a look. "I went out with Ben again, the guy from the wedding."

"Oh yeah? How'd that go?"

"Oh, you know," he jabbed back with a smug grin, "about as well as I imagine your lunch meeting went today."

Samantha kicked him in the shin as her mother zoned in on their conversation.

"What's that? Andrew, are you seeing someone?" Her curiosity overcame any sort of socially appropriate feigned ignorance of the private conversation unfolding nearby.

"Well, I'm always seeing someone," he joked as he looked around. "But, sort of, yeah, he's cute."

"Tell me about him. What does he do?"

"Ma, seriously," Samantha interrupted, "who asks that?"

"Samantha, it's perfectly acceptable to ask what he may be doing, I don't want Andrew getting involved with some gold digger."

"No, it's okay," Andrew interjected. "He's an actor. He does formal event work on the side. That's how we met, at a wedding."

"Oh, I love weddings." Marisol smiled and clasped her hands together. "Who was getting married?"

Samantha was suddenly very interested in her manicure.

"One of our clients actually," Andrew answered. "It was another one of those perfect matches we work so hard at."

Marisol's smile remained, albeit significantly smaller. She made no attempt to hide her contempt of Samantha's *work*, as she liked to call it, air quotes and all. Although she had more manners than to insult Andrew directly, Samantha had no doubt that would come later in barbs she would trade with her daughter if they got into it.

"That's also where we met Lucinda, isn't it, Sam?"

Samantha looked up, alarmed. "Uh, yeah."

"Use your vocabulary, *mija*," Marisol clucked.

"Yes, we met her at the wedding, she was at our table."

"The misfit table, if I remember correctly," Andrew added, laughing.

Marisol watched the interaction between them curiously. "Hmm. What does she do? And how is it she is so friendly with the dancers here?"

"She's a marketing director now, but she used to dance professionally. She teaches at a studio not far from here," Andrew supplied casually. Samantha wondered if he could see her breathing pick up a bit. She felt very tense all of a sudden.

"Well, that's marvelous. Dancing is a lost art. It takes such discipline." Marisol nodded to herself. She cocked her head to the side and looked at Samantha, suddenly curious. "Is she a client of yours?"

Samantha kept her cool. "No. Why?"

"It's just that she is so lovely, quite beautiful really. I imagine she would have brought a date to such an event like this." Marisol gestured toward the stage. "Is she single?"

"I don't really think that's any of your business," Samantha said, a little harsher than she intended to.

"If you and Andrew here are in the business of hooking people up or whatever it is you call it, you might extend the services to your friends as well. Don't you agree, *mija?*"

Samantha gritted her teeth and rolled her shoulders as she leaned against the balcony. "Ma," she whispered, her tone sharp, "stop."

Samantha could tell that her mother did not appreciate being scolded. Before she had a chance to reply, Lucinda emerged at the opening of the box, precariously juggling four very full glasses of champagne.

"Am I interrupting something?" she asked warily, looking between the serious expressions on the Monteiro women and Andrew doing his best to fade into the background.

Samantha broke the glaring contest and smiled at Lucinda, rushing forward to assist with the glasses. "No, sorry, I would have come with you had I known you were so ambitious." Her fingers grazed over Lucinda's as she took two glasses, handing one to Andrew and avoiding her mother.

Lucinda handed a glass to Marisol and offered a toast. "To great friends and family."

Marisol sipped from her flute quietly before she faced Lucinda. "Andrew tells me you used to dance professionally, is that true?"

"Yes, for a short time."

"Why did you stop?"

"I suffered a pretty significant injury a while back and my partner passed away before I healed. So I finished school, got into PR, and I teach instead."

Marisol looked perplexed for a moment. "Why not just find another partner?"

Lucinda nodded. This was always the question. "In dance, as in life, there are perfect pairings. When you find your perfect fit, anything else just doesn't quite feel right. That's what happened with me. I tried, but I was unsuccessful." She frowned as she uttered the heavy truth. Dominic was the water to her fire, the calming influence to her chaos. He was irreplaceable.

Marisol considered this, sipping her champagne. Seemingly appeased by her response she moved on. "So Andrew is dating an actor and Samantha is stubbornly single…Lucinda, are you seeing anyone?"

Samantha took a step toward her mother, her eyes dark with anger. Andrew coughed into his glass almost choking on his drink. Lucinda just stood there, silent, observing the defiant looks being exchanged between her girlfriend and her girlfriend's mother.

"Yes." Lucinda's tone was clipped but soft. "I am."

"Is he a dancer?" Marisol mused, finishing off her drink. "Perhaps he can help Samantha find someone—"

A low growl rolled out of Samantha's throat as her grip on the champagne flute got dangerously tighter.

Lucinda stepped forward, taking the glass before it became a weapon, giving Samantha's hands a gentle squeeze before she stepped between the women. She eyed Marisol carefully. "No, professionally, she does not dance. But she is an excellent dancer." She paused before adding, "And as far as Samantha goes, she is plenty qualified to find someone for herself, arguably better than anyone else I know."

Marisol listened to her answer, her eyebrow arched slightly. She was clearly perturbed by the assertive response, perhaps also the female pronoun. "Hmph. I like you. You are quiet but steady. Your partner is very lucky to have you."

Lucinda replied with a slightly bowed head in acknowledgment. "She's perfect. I'm the lucky one. And thank you." She nodded toward Andrew and Marisol's glasses. "I'll grab us refills—enjoy the start of the second act. Samantha, would you mind helping me?"

Samantha grabbed the empty glasses and exited the box as the house lights dimmed again. Once they turned the corner, Lucinda paused, handing Samantha her partially full glass and taking the empties while motioning for her to finish them off. Samantha gave her an appreciative nod, downing the glasses' contents and letting out a slow sigh. Lucinda waited a moment, looking left and right before pressing a soft kiss to Samantha's lips. "You don't really have to come with me. You just looked like you needed some air... and more liquor."

Samantha pinched the bridge of her nose and closed her eyes for a moment, breathing out slowly before looking back at Lucinda. "I don't know what I did to deserve you—"

Lucinda cut her off with another kiss, this one longer. Samantha leaned into it, easily guided closer by Lucinda. "C'mon, let's get some bubbly."

Lucinda held Samantha's hand as they walked down the lush red-carpeted stairs, along the marbled halls, and toward the center of the lobby. She guided them through the stands selling liquor, champagne, and snacks to the ballet attendees. A few stands offered T-shirts and other merchandise benefiting the arts; these were Lucinda's favorite stalls. She dropped off the glasses, ordering four more and paying before Samantha could argue. She squeezed Samantha's elbow and told her she'd be right back.

Samantha watched Lucinda slink away and get lost in the crowd as she waited patiently for the bartender to fill the glasses. She resisted the urge to order a shot of Patrón, just to make it through the rest of the evening with her mother. But there had been rare instances in her life when tequila made things better, so she decided against it.

The bustle of the crowd started to lessen as the orchestra began indicating the start of the second act. Everyone was dressed beautifully, men in designer suits, women in long dresses, little girls and their mothers holding hands and laughing. Samantha couldn't remember the last time she had been carefree with her mother that way—it must have been a lifetime ago. The sight made her sad, but in a way she wasn't expecting; she felt terrible because Lucinda never had that with anyone while she was younger. The little blond-haired girl in pigtails getting Twizzlers and a water with her mother at the bar overwhelmed her. How could such a wonderful woman emerge from such a hard life? She thought of how masterfully Lucinda had handled her mother just moments before. She was so confident in the way she described Samantha and the importance that Samantha played in their relationship together. It was moving to be the object of those affections. If she was being honest though, it was a little scary too; being with Lucinda felt so right and raw at the same time. Like she was experiencing things for the first time, every time. Sometimes those feelings overwhelmed her.

"All set?" A warm breath on her shoulder sent a shiver down Samantha's spine. Lucinda smiled and picked up two glasses, nodding toward the grand staircase in the direction of their box. "Ready?"

Samantha followed her up the stairs and through the mirrored halls accented in gold leaf and ornate crystals, letting her mind wander to the thoughts Lucinda had interrupted. As they approached the box, Lucinda slowed, pausing by a tall bar table positioned near the entrance to the platform. She placed the glasses down and turned toward Samantha with a shy smile.

"I wanted you to know," she said softly, "that I appreciate you being here with me, you being with me around your mother, as impossible as she makes enjoying anything—*you* are making my night very enjoyable. And I wanted to thank you for that."

Samantha felt like she might cry. Here was this lovely woman, this woman who was strong and confident and patient, thanking her of all people for being with her tonight. This was the kind of thing Lucinda did that overwhelmed her, overwhelmed her with honesty and sincerity. She found herself again and again being surprised by Lucinda, if for no other reason than she seemed too good to be true. "She's right about you. You are strong." She cupped Lucinda's face with her hand and pressed a chaste kiss to her lips. "You are my light."

Lucinda smiled into the kiss, deepening it, letting their lips slide across each other's, enjoying the moment. She pulled Samantha's hand from her face and pressed a small object into it, closing her fingers around it before bringing Samantha's closed hand to her lips, kissing her knuckles tenderly.

Samantha opened her palm to find a small snow globe with a blond prima ballerina inside, dancing in the soft snow falling around her. The base was bright red with a gold banner inscribed *Boston Opera House*. The bottom had the date and name of the performance in Lucinda's script with a small heart drawn in the corner.

Lucinda traced her fingers along Samantha's open palm and whispered, "The first time to the ballet is supposed to be special. Tonight's performance is about love lost and found again by a young girl in wartime. It's our first ballet together. You're a beautiful young woman, and I would consider time spent with your mother as battle. So it seemed appropriate to remember it."

Samantha laughed and kissed her quickly. "Thank you, Luce. For everything."

"Let's get back before they think we ditched 'em."

The rest of the show was beautiful and surprisingly moving. Samantha found herself unexpectedly emotional at the final scene when the young girl is reunited with her lost love. At some point in the final moments of the show Samantha found her hand on Lucinda's thigh, clutching like she needed to be grounded. She must have been holding hard enough to bruise, but Lucinda didn't even flinch. She just covered Samantha's hand with her own and soothingly stroked the skin.

Lucinda introduced them to a few old dance friends by the orchestra pit after the show. She swapped war stories with them about the company and playfully remembered her favorite shows, and shows she would rather forget. Samantha's favorites included one hilarious performance of *The Nutcracker* when a pair of tights on the lead male split at the crotch midleap. Andrew found this particularly exciting and was extremely disappointed to have missed the performance, though he vowed to search the Web for it later. As the evening wound down and they exited the theater into the cool night air, they parted ways.

"Lucinda, thank you again, I had a wonderful evening," Marisol said. "I hope to see you again sometime."

"Of course, I'm glad you liked it. Have a safe trip if I don't see you before you leave."

Andrew kissed Lucinda good-bye and started walking with Marisol toward the cabstand, leaving Lucinda and Samantha alone. Samantha let herself be wrapped in Lucinda's arms and held close, hating the fact that she was going home with her mother and not with her girlfriend.

"Call me later, okay?"

"Always." Samantha relaxed further into the hug. She glanced over Lucinda's shoulder at their companions and saw Andrew pointing out some building in the theater district so she took the chance and planted a firm kiss to Lucinda's lips, right under the marquee lights.

"Thank you for tonight and for the snow globe and for having the most kissable lips ever." She spoke quickly, pressing another kiss to Lucinda's lips. "I love you."

"I love you too." Lucinda matched Samantha's frown as she stepped back and motioned for her to go.

Samantha trudged toward the waiting cab, ducking through the throngs of people. She glanced back woefully to watch Lucinda head toward the car park to retrieve her car, their night finally coming to a close.

❖

Lucinda tapped her hands on the leather steering wheel to the beat of the music playing on the speakers. She wasn't listening to anything in particular—she just liked the background beat when she wanted to think, or drive and think, as was her habit of late. Tonight had been a lot of things: her first night with Samantha at the ballet, her mended fences agreement with Andrew, spending time with a member of Samantha's family, even if it was under the guise of friendship… It had been a good night. But it had been a hard night too.

Being around all those memories tonight—the dancers, the ballet company she was so familiar with—it was a challenge. She was blending new with old, and her old came with a lot of pain. She had been fine until they walked into the Opera House. Her anxiety flared and a part of her wanted to turn back into the night. If she was ever going to move forward, she had to open up those painful memories and allow new ones to take their place, or at least take their place beside the old ones. So she swallowed her anxiety, rested a hand on Samantha's hip to ground herself, and embraced the formation of new memories. That was a hard lesson that she had learned in her youth: when your past comes back to haunt you, you treat it with politeness and respect because it helped you become who you are today. Embrace the good with the bad, because one day there won't be anything to embrace but pain if you don't forgive and move on. Resiliency—that's what the social worker at the orphanage called it after her fourth home in as many years. She was resilient. Maybe that made her strong. Or maybe that just made her hard. Hard and strong were two very different things. She was definitely hardened, but was she more than that? Samantha and her mother seemed to think so.

She had just finished purchasing Samantha's snow globe and writing on the bottom when it hit her: maybe this could be more than something casual. Maybe this could work for the long-term, maybe she had found her match. The humor of that was not lost on her, a match with a matchmaker.

As she sat at the light a few streets from home, her phone buzzed next to her. It was Samantha, texting that she was sad to be without her. The feeling was mutual. Tonight had been good, but hard. The feelings were strong right now. Hard and strong, at war again. The thought amused Lucinda as she pulled up to her house and keyed in, flicking the lights on as she went, scaring the shadows back to their corners. If only it were that easy.

CHAPTER TWENTY-ONE

Samantha let out a sigh of relief as her mother's hired car took her back to New York. She considered throwing a bon voyage party at her office with Andrew to celebrate her departure. She had to admit that this visit had been better than most, but she had a feeling that had a lot to do with Andrew and Lucinda. Andrew had made himself unusually available to *Madre*-sit and kept offering to stop by to help make dinners more tolerable—undoubtedly in an attempt to make up for the Logan-Lucinda debacle. On the days she did work, she had intentionally logged longer days at the office to limit their alone time. Then Lucinda saved everyone's life when she scrounged up those ballet tickets last night—the perfect end to a less than perfect week: entertainment on a grand scale for her mother and a secret date with her girlfriend. Although it didn't make up for her sabotaged sex-only weekend with Lucinda, it helped to soften the blow. And that lunch meeting helped too, she remembered with a smile. It helped her twice in fact, maybe three times if you counted that she felt a little fatigued at the show and didn't have the energy to throttle her mother like she wanted to when she started asking too many damn questions.

It wasn't the questions in and of themselves that made Samantha fume, it was the self-righteousness that they were delivered with. Very few people could incite rage in her, but her mother, she had a gift for it. Samantha practically cried when her brother called the night of the ballet to ask if their mother would be home to watch the kids the following day. She would have kissed him if he weren't such a raging suck-up and all around asshat. He even set up a car service to take her mother back to his McMansion outside the city. Considering how things could have gone, it really wasn't all that bad. She'd dodged a bullet this week and she knew it.

As she walked into her office with a little extra spring in her step, she thought about how well her mother and Lucinda had gotten along. Granted, it was probably Lucinda working overtime to accommodate her mother's natural unpleasantness, but she had been pleasantly surprised that it hadn't gone up in flames. It was important to her that someone in her life could play well with her family. Maybe she would see them more. Now that would be an epic change. Eric had tolerated her family but never quite embraced them—he had made it easy for her to drift from them. That's why she found it so unbelievable that her mother and father were disappointed that her relationship had ended. Eric was not the golden boy they had hoped he'd be. Of course, it had been a disappointment to her as well. But if that disappointment led to her finding Lucinda, then maybe it was worth it. Just maybe. She allowed herself a few more moments to daydream about the woman who literally kept her up at night before she settled into her desk and began to work.

❖

Lucinda frowned as she dialed security and had Amanda send Richard in, encouraging her to take a walk for a few minutes. Lucinda sighed; this wasn't going to be very fun.

Richard walked in and adjusted his tie nervously. He had missed two days of work the past week, once not bothering to call in at all, the other not calling until well after ten in the morning.

"Sit please, Richard."

He nodded and obliged, staying perched at the edge of the chair.

"I've gone over your work and your attendance records for the last month. I noticed a small change in the beginning after our first discussion but have seen a steady decline again in the past few weeks." Lucinda stood and nodded. Two security guards holding an empty box entered the room. "This isn't working out. I'm sorry, but we're going to have to let you go."

"You arrogant bitch," Richard hissed as he stood. "You don't know what kind of mistake you're making. You are coasting by on your looks and you know it. You'll get yours. Don't worry." He punctuated his statement by pointing his finger at her.

Lucinda's blood boiled. She squared her shoulders and ran her fingers along the edge of the desk before biting back, "Now, now, Richard. Let's not make a scene. I'd hate for your flimsy Prince Charming reputation to get flushed with your career aspirations."

She looked at Al's and Franklin's angry expressions behind him. "Take him to his desk to collect his things and escort him out. Find me when it's done."

Franklin stepped forward, his deep voice echoing in the suddenly quiet room. "Let's go, Mr. Thomas." When Richard continued to glare at Lucinda and made no attempt to move, Franklin barked out sharply, "Now." Richard turned toward the irritated security guard before stalking out of the office and disappearing down the hall.

Lucinda followed them to the door, grabbing Al's arm before he could leave. "I want his badge, his laptop, his phone, everything. Make sure it all gets back to me. Don't let him touch his computer or his files. Keep it quiet if you can, but if he gets rowdy drag him out and I'll clean off his desk…into the trash. All right?" She knew he would do as she asked—she was good to them, and they were good to her.

"Yes, Lucinda."

Lucinda closed the door behind them, walked back to her desk, and let out a slow breath. She never quite got used to the feeling of being insulted. It wasn't that it happened often anymore, but in her youth, it had been a common occurrence. A hard life with a rough start brought a lot of insults her way. She gritted her teeth and rolled her shoulders before sinking into her seat and closing her eyes.

Al and Franklin returned twenty minutes later with Richard's work supplies organized in a box they placed in the corner of Lucinda's office. She would take them home later and skim through them, making sure everything was in order.

"It's all set," Franklin said, his tone much softer this time. "We alerted the building security supervisor to have the other shifts keep an eye out for him. It should be fine."

Lucinda smiled and stood to shake their hands. "Thanks, guys." She paused. "Do you think you could have one of your guys walk Amanda to her car tonight, just to be sure?"

"Of course," Al responded. "Do you want someone to walk you to your car as well?"

"Nah, I'm all set. Let him try something and see how well that goes." Al and Franklin laughed, saying good-bye and closing the door behind them.

No, Lucinda wasn't worried about handling Richard. She was only worried about who would be there to pick up the pieces afterward. She sat back down at her desk and attempted to finish her workday. This evening's dance class—a mixer with Shelly White— couldn't come fast enough; she was missing Samantha right now more than ever.

❖

Samantha spent the entire day at the office. She had appointments, conference calls, Skype meetings, and a luncheon date scheduled for a client that needed chaperoning by some staff. It was a veritable shit show. Andrew was surprisingly perky considering all the running around they had to do. Maybe it was because their magazine article was coming out that afternoon. He had wanted to host a little celebration party later, but she was hosting a meet and greet at Lucinda's dance studio for Shelly and a few women who were near-perfect matches for her, on paper, so the celebration would have to wait. She had texted Lucinda to check in on her, but none of the texts she sent had been read or replied to. She must be busy if she hadn't even checked her texts.

"Stop frowning at your phone. She's working—you're coming off as pathetic," Andrew teased from her doorway.

"Shut up, ass." She scowled, tossing her phone aside.

"So, you change your mind yet?" He waved something back and forth in front of her. "Because the courier just dropped by with the feature and the cover looks *amazing*."

"It's here?"

"Yup." A devilish smile spread over his lips. "But…"

"But, what?"

"But you can't see it until you agree to go out with me tonight—drinks, dancing the whole shebang."

She groaned. "No can do, stud. Tonight is Shelly's mixer."

"Oh yeah, right, that. Okay, this weekend, then, there will be celebrating."

"Sure, let me just double-check with Lucinda to make sure we don't have any plans."

"No, Samantha, just because you're all wifed up doesn't mean you're allowed to get old on me." He scoffed and glared at her. "She's more than welcome to join us, but it's on. We are going out."

She looked at her phone once more. "Okay. Fine. But you're paying."

"Great! Because I was planning on writing it off as a work expense anyway."

"Get over here and show me already."

He scurried across the room, perching himself on her desk as he handed her the copy of the *Improper Bostonian* magazine. The picture on the front was great. The title read, "Boston's Most Eligible Matchmakers," and it showed her and Andrew with their backs to each other, leaning against each other and smiling. They looked perfect, if she did say so herself.

"The write-up is hilarious. He did a good job catching our sarcasm and charisma." He smiled and clapped his hands together. "This is big, Sam."

She scanned the article, laughing at the dynamic between her and Andrew that the writer caught so vividly on the page. Shots from the photo shoot and little background pieces on both of them lined the pages of the interview. She loved the way he ended the article, encouraging people to let professionals find them love in this wild world, her eyes settling on the last two lines.

Andrew noticed and asked. "Yeah. Do you even remember saying that?"

"Um, sort of."

"I remember thinking, well, that's off script. But it was adorable and so honest, I'm glad he added it."

Samantha read the lines again. This was definitely going to get a few calls sent to voice mail over the weekend. She had to decide what to tell them when the inevitable questions came rolling in.

"So…before you float away on cloud nine, we need to talk about Alec Frost." Andrew took the magazine from her hands and placed it on the desk.

She closed the folders and laptop in front of her, shuffling some head shots aside. "What's to talk about? I was pretty clear before—"

"I know. I just want to make sure we're on the same page before I make the call."

It was good to reevaluate their prior discussion with clear heads, but her feelings were the same. "Cut him loose. The last incident that Logan uncovered is plenty of evidence that his temper is a liability and affecting our ability to match him. I'll take the financial loss, let's just unload the bastard and move on."

"What then?"

"Make sure legal is ready for any Claudette Frost backlash that may result and make sure we keep PR in the loop. That's all we can do."

"I'll be glad to have him off the client list, to be honest." Andrew frowned and crossed his legs. "He's always felt like a ticking time bomb."

"Yeah, I hear ya," Samantha agreed as she stood to pack up her belongings. "Oh, I forgot to ask, you're coming by the studio later, right? I want to make sure we have plenty of distractions available."

"You want someone else there to help the night run smoothly so you can gawk over your girlfriend, you mean?" Andrew winked.

She felt the blush heat her face and swept a loose hair behind her ear. "Shut up, Andrew. Just be there on time." Samantha pulled on her coat and grabbed Shelly's file. She wanted to make sure everything was all set before Shelly arrived, so she was meeting

Lucinda early to prep the space and fill her in on the protocol of the evening. She smiled as she stepped into the elevator; she had been looking forward to this all week.

❖

Samantha was greeted with a soft melody playing over the speakers when she arrived at the studio. It was pristine as always, but Samantha noted that Lucinda had strung white holiday lights around the windows and doorway, illuminating the room in a warm glow. There were a few tables set up around the edge of the studio, decorated with plain white cloths and candles. The caterer and a bartender would be by in a while to finalize the setup. Shelly only needed one successful evening, so she could realize her anxiety was manageable and she could meet someone without spilling her drink on her.

Samantha took off her jacket and pulled out Shelly's folder as she sat on the bench in the corner. Tonight there were five women coming to meet Shelly. She had also arranged for some couples to attend, along with a few of Andrew's friends, so that everyone had someone to pair off with while Shelly spent time with each of her prospective mates. Samantha had been pleased to see that Connie and Nathan Lundstein were confirmed for tonight. Lucinda had beamed when Samantha mentioned they might come. She spent a little time telling Samantha that Connie was an excellent dancer and could help facilitate an easy flow for the evening. Samantha settled back into her seat, letting the weight of the day slowly drip off, as Lucinda wandered into the room from her office. She looked tired and her mouth was in a frown as she rubbed the bridge of her nose, lost in thought.

Samantha stood and walked toward Lucinda, hoping to wipe some of that fatigue from her face.

Lucinda lit up when she saw Samantha, sweeping her into a tight hug, "Mm, I missed you, baby." She placed soft kisses along Samantha's neck as she nuzzled close.

Samantha kissed Lucinda's cheek. "Everything okay?"

Lucinda nodded and pressed a firm kiss to Samantha's lips. "I love you, you know that?"

Samantha repeated the sentiment softly as she kissed Lucinda back. Lucinda let out a long sigh and Samantha enveloped her in a tighter embrace, pressing her cheek to Samantha's shoulder.

"I had a long day." Lucinda paused. "I had to let one of my staff go and will have to pull double time at the office over the next few days to do a little damage control. Considering how busy things have been lately, investing more time at the office is the last thing I want to do."

Samantha stopped the light kisses she had been placing along the column of Lucinda's neck. So much had happened in the past few weeks, it didn't seem fair to have to lose any more time with her. She couldn't hide the disappointment if she tried.

"I know, I'm sorry. The timing literally could not be worse." Lucinda looked apologetic.

Samantha bit her lip before nodding. She got it, she really did. Being a business owner meant that more weekends than not she had to work and Lucinda's new position meant she would have to put in some extra hours to keep the ship sailing smoothly. Her career was as important to her as Samantha's was to herself. Deciding this was as good a segue as any, she proposed an idea that had come to her on the ride here.

"Hey, Luce," she said, "do you think maybe we could get away sometime soon?"

Lucinda's eyes shone as she raised an eyebrow. "Like a vacation? Together?"

Samantha looked down with a shrug. "I mean, yeah, maybe even a weekend away if you don't have the time for a trip or something, just, you know—"

Soft lips pressed against her mouth silencing her rambling as Lucinda traced her tongue lightly along Samantha's top lip, asking for admittance. Samantha sighed contentedly and opened her mouth, deepening the kiss.

Lucinda wrapped her into a tight embrace, her hands caressing Samantha's back before settling at her hips and pulling them closer together. "I would love to, let's make some plans."

And just like that the stress of the day faded between them as Lucinda swept her toward the back office to greet her more appropriately before the caterers came.

❖

Samantha was perched on Lucinda's desk with her legs wrapped around her when the studio door chimed. At the sound, Lucinda withdrew her tongue and abandoned the flushed skin of Samantha's chest, pulling Samantha's shirt back into place. Her hands settled along Samantha's ribs, her thumbs rubbing gently over the erect nipples under the silk. Samantha groaned and pulled Lucinda's mouth back to hers for a hard kiss before slapping her fingers away from her chest and pushing Lucinda back a bit.

"God. You need to be less fantastic at that, or we need fewer interruptions," Samantha said as she released Lucinda from her legs and attempted to button her shirt. A warm chuckle and a soft peck on her cheek were all she got in reply as Lucinda turned to leave the office.

"Wait."

Lucinda stopped and looked back at Samantha as she shuffled off the desk and back into her heels. Samantha came up to Lucinda and cupped her face. "Stay with me tonight. Even if you have to leave early, stay with me tonight."

Lucinda pressed a kiss to Samantha's lips. "There is nowhere else I'd rather be."

Chapter Twenty-two

A side from the unfortunate interruption, so far everything was going off without a hitch and Samantha couldn't be happier. The caterers set up the food and the bartender brought in the cases of wine as people started to arrive. Samantha and Andrew coached the women on what they expected, reminding them to be patient and polite. Lucinda reset the stereo and synced the music to the back speakers. Connie and Nathan had arrived early to help get everyone ready and were laughing and joking with Lucinda at the front when Shelly arrived. The night would begin with Samantha thanking the guests and inviting them to enjoy the refreshments, although she had forbidden Shelly's potential dates to drink until the end of the night, as per protocol of Perfect Match, Inc.

Lucinda began by pairing people into couples and instructing them on a basic waltz and a few other dances throughout the evening, offering tips along the way and facilitating the partner switch every few songs. She had a fellow dance instructor floating among the groups to help her stay on target.

Halfway through the evening, Andrew cut in with Nathan, and Connie paired off with Samantha, when Lucinda changed the track to a basic ballroom piece. Connie nodded toward Lucinda and coached the boys on their movements as she led Samantha through the steps with ease.

"So, tell me, how's married life?" Samantha asked with a smile as Connie repositioned her hand on Samantha's hip.

"It's great, he's perfect," she replied dreamily looking over at Andrew and Nathan trying not to step on each other's feet.

"Good. I'm glad." Samantha's chest swelled with pride. She loved these two together—they were adorable.

"What about you?" Connie winked at Samantha. "How are things going with you and Lucy?"

Samantha wasn't surprised that Connie knew, but the acknowledgment by someone close to Lucinda made her stomach flutter with excitement. "Um, good. Great, actually."

Connie beamed and broke position to embrace Samantha. "Good. I'm so glad. You two are such a great-looking pair." She pulled Samantha back into position before twirling her on the spot, Samantha's eyes catching Lucinda's briefly across the room. "You know, I don't think I've ever seen Lucy this happy."

Samantha smiled and looked over at Lucinda who was counting beats to Shelly and a volunteer firefighter—prospective mate number three—adjusting Shelly's hand and her date's occasionally. "You know, she talks about how much she loves you all the time." She spoke softly to Connie, a reverence in her voice. "I saw that picture of you two together when you were younger...she adores you."

Now it was Connie's turn to blush, her eyes suddenly very clear as she slowed their movements. "Wait, the one on her dresser? You've been to her house?"

"Yeah, a few times. Why? Is that weird?"

"No, no, it's good. I mean, Lucy doesn't take girls back to the house, it's like a *thing*. God, let me think, the last woman I saw there was...probably Grace. That was forever ago. I was just out of high school..." She trailed off, lost in thought.

"Really?"

"Yeah, really." Connie nodded, "Lucy must really like you for her to bring you home." She smiled genially before a hand slid along her back, interrupting her.

"I do," Lucinda supplied from behind her ear, her eyes locked on Samantha's as she spoke softly. "I love her."

Samantha blushed as Connie released her, spinning to hug Lucinda. "Luce! I'm so excited for you!"

"Sh, Connie. Focus. We have a class to run here. Go help the boys before Nathan ruins Andrew's expensive alligator shoes." Lucinda shuttled a bouncing Connie away before stepping into her spot, her hand sliding easily into Samantha's as the music continued.

"You do, huh?" Samantha smiled as Lucinda rested her hand along her lower back, guiding her into a gentle dip.

"Mm-hmm. And now Connie knows, so it's official." Lucinda held Samantha in the dip for a moment before pulling her back up and into position, their bodies closer than the other dancers on the floor as Lucinda pressed her hips into Samantha's.

"Where have you been all my life?" Samantha asked, sounding half-joking, half-serious.

"Waiting for you." Lucinda felt her chest glow as she slowed their dancing to a stop with the end of the music. She had been waiting. Waiting to meet someone she would want to spend every moment with, someone who made her feel complete. She was sure, in this moment, that Samantha Monteiro was that person.

"I really want to kiss you right now, but then it would get a little heated and I would scandalize everyone here. So I'm not going to, but know that I want to." Samantha laced her fingers into Lucinda's briefly before they both had to go back to their duties. She leaned in close before parting from Lucinda and said, "Thank you for waiting."

Lucinda thought the night had gone smoothly. Shelly managed to step on only a few feet and got over her nervous stutter halfway through the first dance. Lucinda stayed close to her, cueing her until she was more confident. She floated away but stayed near in case she needed her. She didn't. She was perfect. By the end of the night she had danced with all her potential dates, and with Samantha, Connie, and Lucinda. She even took Andrew for a quick spin. It was the most carefree and comfortable Lucinda had seen Shelly. She had really embraced the dance training. Samantha set up a couple of second dates with two of the girls Shelly seemed to connect with the best: Sasha, a firefighter, and Abby, an accountant. Now all they had to do was wait and see how she did without their supervision.

After the studio cleared, Lucinda followed Samantha to her apartment, thinking about the night's successes. Connie knew about Samantha now, and it was nice to know someone else could be happy for her. Connie was more than her sister—she was her best friend, a role previously shared with Dominic.

Oh, Dominic. God, this was awful without him. She wanted to call him and tell him all about the raven-haired beauty who kept her up at night, running through her dreams. She wanted to tell him that she finally felt complete, that Samantha made her want a million tomorrows. She wanted to introduce them, watch Dominic charm Samantha and flirt with her shamelessly just because he could. She wanted him to make his famous red sauce and speak Italian to her, introducing Samantha to the family like she had been. She wanted him to dance with her, so Samantha could experience the way he made everything feel weightless and free. She wanted him to hug her close and tell her he approved. She wanted Dominic to give her the confirmation that her heart already knew—Samantha was everything she had ever wanted. But it felt wrong to have it without him too.

❖

Samantha waited in the lobby for Lucinda to walk through the large glass doors and join her on the elevator ride to her apartment. She smiled as Lucinda joked with Mario and ran her hand affectionately along his arm. She loved how seamlessly Lucinda had fit into her life. She was perfect. Lucinda flashed her a bright smile and linked arms with her as they stepped into the elevator. Samantha rested her head on Lucinda's shoulder, watching the numbers flick by the higher they climbed.

"So, what did you think? Success?" Lucinda asked.

"Mm," she hummed happily. "Major success."

"Good." Lucinda wrapped her arms around Samantha. "I'm glad."

"Thank you."

"For what, baby?"

She shrugged and snuggled closer. "For everything."

The elevator pinged on Samantha's floor and she stepped away from Lucinda long enough to walk to her door. She was tired, but happy. It had been a long day.

Samantha opened the door, kicking off her shoes and dropping her purse. Lucinda called out that she was heading to the bathroom to wash up a bit. Samantha nodded and bit her lip, watching Lucinda's retreating form go toward the master bathroom. She poured them each a glass of wine, admiring her view of the Boston Commons and waiting.

Strong arms wrapped around her waist, pulling her into a bone-crushing hug before spinning her on the spot. She nearly dropped her glass as Lucinda lifted her up onto the counter and looked deeply into her eyes.

"You. Are. Amazing." Lucinda's eyes twinkled as she spoke. Samantha smiled, looping her arms around Lucinda and leaning down to press their lips together.

"Is that okay?" she asked against smiling lips.

Lucinda laughed and kissed her once more before leaning back. "Is it okay that you bought all of my toiletries, lotions, and hair products and stocked your master bathroom with them for me? Um, yeah, it's okay." She paused for a moment, looking at Samantha with such affection and love that Samantha was burning under the gaze, but she didn't look away. She never wanted to be outside of the adoration that was reflected in those eyes.

"I don't sleep as well without you, I miss you when you're gone," Samantha admitted quietly. "I want you to be as comfortable in my home as I am in your arms."

Lucinda reached over and took the glass gently from Samantha's hand, placing it on the counter. She wrapped Samantha's legs around her waist while sliding her hands under Samantha's ass and lifted her off the counter.

Samantha instinctively held her arms tighter around Lucinda's neck as Lucinda started kissing across her collarbone and along the column of her neck. She walked them slowly through the kitchen to the bedroom. She pressed wet kiss after wet kiss along Samantha's jaw as she held her close, cradling her ass in her hands as they approached the bed. She stopped at the edge of the bed, bringing her lips to Samantha's, holding her tightly.

"I want to spend every minute of every day with you," she whispered across Samantha's kiss-plumped lips.

Samantha whimpered softly as Lucinda lowered her gently to the bed, breaking the kiss as she knelt in front of her, rubbing her hands up and down Samantha's thighs before she began to slowly undress her. Samantha's eyes were focused on Lucinda's, as strong, steady fingers unbuttoned her shirt and slid it down her arms before moving to the fastener on her designer slacks and easing them down. Lucinda took Samantha's hand in her own, kissing her palm softly before moving to her wrist, sucking on the skin as she kissed up her forearm to the inside of her elbow, up her biceps, along her shoulder, back to her lips, her fingers caressing Samantha's back and unclasping her bra.

Samantha responded to each kiss, lips and tongue teasing, her breathing in short pants as Lucinda hooked her fingers into the band of Samantha's lace thong, guiding it off and to the floor. She pressed her mouth firmly against Samantha's lips, walking her up the bed as she crawled over her, this time never breaking the kiss.

When Samantha settled against the dark sheets, Lucinda finally pulled her mouth back, gently tugging on Samantha's bottom lip with teeth before she hastily disrobed, lowering her body to the perfect form below her. She worshipped the skin in front of her, pressing hot kiss after hot kiss to the curve of Samantha's breast, along her sternum, up her neck, sucking on the skin under her ear, lips tugging along an earlobe. Her hands skimmed soft skin, tickled along ribs, pressed an open palm over a flat stomach, dragged blunt nails along protruding hipbones. Lucinda let her lips speak every thought she had ever had of love and affection into Samantha's flesh, one syllable and one word at a time.

Samantha writhed beneath Lucinda's affections; firm pressure met with a gentle roll, her leg slid up Lucinda's hip and around her back, her fingers got lost in Lucinda's hair, scratching at her scalp, breathing in and out, murmuring *I love you* with every gasp, every lick, each touch of fingers to soft skin. Lucinda attempted to stimulate every nerve ending in Samantha's body without ever attending to her soaking wet core. If Samantha's raw reaction was any indication, she was succeeding.

Lucinda rolled her hips against Samantha's, her hand holding Samantha's leg flush to her body as she pressed down again. Samantha groaned at the sensation and her hands moved to her breasts and hardened nipples. She massaged and squeezed as Lucinda lavished her neck with kisses and gentle nips, rolling her hips over and over.

Samantha felt dizzy. She felt positively electric underneath Lucinda, safe, loved, and on fire. It was difficult to focus between the blood pooling at her core and the hot mouth working its way to hers. She moaned before sucking Lucinda's tongue into her mouth and grinding her hips upward, harder this time. She needed to feel all of Lucinda, now. She wasn't above begging. In fact, it felt inevitable.

As if reading her mind, Lucinda pulled back from the kiss. She shifted her position, lifting one leg over Samantha's and slipping the other underneath the leg wrapped around her waist until their sexes were just inches apart. Samantha's eyes widened when she realized what Lucinda was silently asking. She nodded and rose off the bed slightly, bringing their lips together as arms and legs intertwined while Lucinda ground down against her. A sound she didn't recognized spilled from her lips as Lucinda started an even rhythm, rolling their centers together, again and again. Samantha's hand fell to Lucinda's chest, adoring the soft flesh before teasing along her nipples.

Her hand gripped at Lucinda's ass, encouraging her as their wetness mixed and made it harder to maintain the friction they both needed. Lucinda embraced Samantha while littering kisses along her jaw, grinding faster and harder, her movements becoming erratic. Samantha's stomach was wound tighter and tighter as her breathing became more and more desperate. A wave washed over her as she felt herself approaching the precipice. "Mm, baby, I'm gonna come…"

Lucinda brought her mouth back to Samantha's, licking at her lips while she slipped a hand between them, caressing Samantha's breast as she lowered her mouth to the pebbled nipple, swirling her tongue around it before sucking it into her mouth, hard. Samantha cried out at the unexpected force of the suction, her hand slipping from Lucinda's breast to scratch angry lines across perfect, pulsing abs as she started to shudder with pleasure. Lucinda hissed but shortly followed Samantha over the edge. She tucked her head into Samantha's neck as Samantha repeated Lucinda's name over and over, almost trancelike, unable to stop herself.

After a few moments of continuing to move against each other gently, drawing out their orgasms, Samantha swooned when Lucinda initiated a sweet kiss between gasps for breath. The gentle contact was in such stark contrast to the intensity of their lovemaking that Samantha sighed into the kiss, rubbing noses with Lucinda's. "I'm sorry I scratched you."

"I loved it. I love you." Warm lips silenced any further apology.

Samantha melted into Lucinda, hugging her close and pressing kisses along her sweat-damp neck as she continued to catch her breath. "I love you so much, Luce." She kissed the skin below Lucinda's ear. "So much. To the moon and back."

"To the moon and back?"

Samantha nodded shyly; Lucinda had a way of pulling things out of her that she didn't know were there. Lucinda leaned back, glancing between them, admiring the four angry lines on her stomach.

"Sorry."

"Stop apologizing." Lucinda looked devious. "On second thought, maybe you can make it up to me."

"Oh yeah?" Samantha traced her fingers along Lucinda's collarbone. "What did you have in mind?"

"I want to taste you."

Samantha's heart rate and breathing picked up again. The idea of Lucinda tasting her made her faint. Lucinda slowly lowered her onto the mattress and pressed a chaste kiss to her lips, pausing there, seemingly enjoying the moment before slanting her mouth down and along the skin of Samantha's chest, over her twitching stomach muscles, until she hovered above Samantha's wet, swollen sex.

Samantha closed her eyes and arched her head back as Lucinda dragged a flat tongue over her, tasting their combined juices, moaning into the movement, and sending vibrations deep into Samantha's soul. She gave careful attention to Samantha's lips, cleaning and lapping along them before sucking gently on her clit. Samantha's hands clutched the sheets as she wound tighter and tighter again, still so sensitive from their first round of play. Lucinda dipped lower, slipping her tongue inside as she brushed her thumb over Samantha's swollen clit, pressing down hard with one final thrust. Samantha curled forward, her breathing halting in ecstasy there before slumping back with a sated sigh.

When Lucinda climbed up Samantha's body, she met her with hungry lips and tongue, tasting them both with an appreciative moan.

"Mm, so good, baby," Samantha purred as she pulled Lucinda down on top of her, reaching to their side to drape the covers over them, wrapping Lucinda up in her arms and savoring the feeling of Lucinda draped over her, warm from the afterglow of passionate lovemaking and vulnerability.

Lucinda rested her head on Samantha's chest and whispered, "I love you."

"I love you too," Samantha said as she closed her eyes and welcomed sleep.

CHAPTER TWENTY-THREE

Lucinda woke up early. It was still dark in the bedroom when she unwrapped herself from Samantha. She watched Samantha's silhouette; she was so peaceful lying there, a small smile on her lips. She looked so tranquil, like she was sleeping deeply for the first time in a long time. It killed Lucinda to see; she wanted to be there when she woke up. It occurred to her in that moment that she wanted to be there every time. But not today, today she had to leave; she had to deal with her work demons. Hopefully she could finish up early enough to take Samantha out to dinner.

Yesterday was so busy that she didn't have the opportunity to talk to Samantha about the *Improper Bostonian* article. Lucinda had called in a favor from one of her clients that worked there and got an advance copy sent over that she promptly brought to a custom framing store on Newbury Street. They assured her it would be done today, so she planned to pick it up and sweep Samantha off her feet at Del Frisco's before surprising her with it at home, hopefully naked. This whole plan had sounded a lot easier to pull off before the whole Richard firing thing got expedited.

Samantha stirred as she finished dressing, looking up at her with sleep-heavy eyes. "Why are you dressed? The bed misses you."

Lucinda laughed. "I'm sorry, babe. I have to iron out some stuff at the office. I was hoping if I got an early start I could end early and you and I could do some of that vacation planning we talked about."

Samantha stretched and rolled to her side, the sheet slipping down to expose her naked breasts. "Well in that case…ponder this while you're away: Tahiti, overwater bungalows, breakfast brought to us by canoe, clothing optional."

Lucinda sighed, trying to avoid the temptation to reach out and touch the newly exposed skin. "That sounds heavenly."

"I'm a genius. I know." Samantha crawled to the edge of the bed and clasped her fingers with Lucinda's. "Call me later?"

"Of course." Lucinda gave her a quick kiss on the lips and nuzzled her nose before she headed out to work.

❖

Samantha awoke with a yawn. Her hand slid across the now cold sheets beside her. She frowned, remembering that Lucinda had already left. Last night had been magical. She smiled in recollection as she stretched out, a little sore from their play. It was a pleasant reminder. As her eyes adjusted to the room she saw a note by her alarm clock. She scooped it up, standing from the bed and wandering into the kitchen to start the coffeepot. She smiled at the pink lipstick kiss on the paper, opening it carefully.

Good Morning, Beautiful,
I'm going to be hard to reach, but I will get in touch with you when I can. Thank you for last night. And every night. I love you.
PS Coffee's on, breakfast is in the microwave.
PPS You are the cutest sleeper ever.

She couldn't help but chuckle as she walked to the counter, her cup and saucer already waiting, the coffee ready to pour. She pulled out an omelet from the microwave, with fresh-cut fruit laid carefully along the edges. Her heart swelled with the amount of time and thought that went into this. She could get used to this kind of wake up, although, admittedly, she would rather make breakfast with Lucinda than eat it without her. She moved the fruit to another dish and warmed the omelet in the microwave as she dug out her phone from her purse. Since she'd started dating Lucinda, she had gotten lazy about taking her phone to the bedroom with her.

Probably because she was busy in the bedroom doing other things than checking her messages.

When her breakfast was warm, she settled onto the stool at her kitchen island. While holding her freshly poured cup of coffee, she frowned at her phone's screen. She had six missed calls from Andrew and two frantic texts telling her to answer her phone. Just as she was dialing him back, there was a rapid knock on her door.

"Just a minute," she called and pulled her bathrobe closed for good measure.

"Sam, it's me, I'm coming in," Andrew's muffled voice from the other side of the door sounded before he opened the door. "Why isn't this door locked? I didn't even need to use my key." Andrew looked a little disheveled. Well, disheveled for Andrew's standards which just meant that he had on designer-casual clothes instead of his usual dress slacks and jacket.

"Lucinda left this morning. I really ought to get her a key…" She used her fork to cut the omelet into a few small pieces before adding, "I was just calling you. What's up?"

"She's not here?" Andrew paced a bit before walking over to the cabinet and pulling down a coffee mug.

"No, she left early this morning. You're making me anxious with the pacing and ominous texts. Care to explain?"

Andrew poured himself some coffee and walked over to Samantha's bar, retrieving a bottle of Baileys which he poured generously into his cup. He marched back to her, took her fork, and took three big bites of her omelet before speaking.

"This is amazing," he mumbled as he stabbed at her plate for a fourth time.

"Andrew, slow down. Get a plate of your own. And a fork." Samantha swatted at his hand before taking back her fork.

"Did you make this? You didn't make this. It's too good." Andrew chewed loudly and took a big swig of his mug, which by color alone appeared to Samantha to be mostly Baileys and only a splash of coffee.

"I take offense to that statement." She took her first bite. He was right—this was delicious.

"Samantha, I love you, I do. But cooking is not your forte."

Samantha hated that he knew her so well; if she had made this omelet, one side would probably be burned and it definitely would have come out as scrambled eggs. "That's fair. Lucinda made it and left it in the microwave for me."

"Ah." He took a deep breath and sat across from her at the island. "Listen, we need to talk."

"We are talking." Samantha took another bite. She hadn't seen Andrew this jumpy in quite a bit, and it was a little unnerving. "Seriously, you're freaking me out a little."

"Sam, I don't even…oh fuck, here." He ran his hand through his hair nervously before handing her his phone.

The screen was open to a gossip site. In big bold letters, a blind item read: MATCHMAKER WHO CAN'T MANAGE PERSONAL LIFE HIRES PR FIRM TO SWEEP IT UNDER THE RUG WHILE GETTING BETWEEN THE SHEETS.

Samantha's jaw dropped as she clicked on the link to see more. The content was vague but the basic story was that an up-and-coming matchmaker had to seek out a PR firm to run a hush campaign on past failed indiscretions only to fall into bed with the PR exec that handled the case. The writer failed to mention a gender but did allude to the matchmaker in question making recent waves in print media and being spotted out on the town looking *friendly* with the PR exec.

This was Samantha's worst nightmare. Coming on the heels of her *Improper Bostonian* article, this would be red hot in minutes. It might already have grown legs and taken off, for all she knew.

"When did this go up?" Her voice was flat. She pushed away the plate in front of her, no longer hungry. She was nauseous.

"I got a phone call from a media outlet this morning around eight a.m. I sent them to voice mail because I figured we could set up some interviews together once we looked at our schedules on Monday. I knew we would generate some buzz but I wasn't expecting this. They were calling to see if this had anything to do with you and Eric. Sam, they asked for a comment."

The room started to spin—this was exactly what Samantha had been afraid would happen. If anyone made the connection that this was about Samantha and linked her to Lucinda, she would be ruined. How awful did it look that she was sleeping with the director of the firm she hired to hide Eric's affair? Pretty awful. She knew that. "I'm going to faint."

Andrew looked alarmed. "Don't faint yet, it gets worse. Hear all of it and if you still want to faint, I'll get a pillow for you. Maybe you should have a drink." He pushed his mug toward her; she considered it for a moment before what he said dawned on her.

"What do you mean worse? How could this get any worse?"

"That wasn't the only call. I got five more on the ride from Ben's place to here. We can only avoid this for so long. We have to release a statement, Sam."

"Do you think—?"

"It was Eric? He'd be a fool. The lawyers would eat him alive. I doubt it."

"Then who?"

"Who knows? There's plenty of competition out there. We have a target square on our backs right now." Andrew scrunched his brow with stress. "We have to call Clear View and the lawyers." He looked up with a sad expression, "You gotta call Lucinda, Sam."

The fog that had settled around Samantha's mind cleared the instant he mentioned Lucinda's name. She was supposed to protect her from this. She was supposed to keep this secret quiet. She promised this wouldn't get out. It wasn't that she thought Lucinda personally leaked this, but her proximity to the issue was dangerous. Associating with Lucinda at this point in time was career suicide and she knew it.

"Andrew"—she was shaking now—"what are we going to do?"

He looked pained. "You are going to shower and get dressed. I'm going to start making phone calls, and we are going to head over to Clear View immediately. I'll have legal meet us there. You should warn Lucinda. We're going to need all the help we can get."

Samantha nodded and walked out of the kitchen toward her bedroom. Having some semblance of a plan should have made her feel better, but it didn't. She couldn't imagine going through this with anyone else but Andrew. Or Lucinda. But she took no strength from that thought—the idea of facing Lucinda right now made her want to curl up in a ball and die. No matter how much she told herself that everything would be fine, she didn't believe it.

She stripped out of her robe and walked into the bathroom before sitting on the shower floor and letting the water wash down over her. She played back every kiss, every touch, every whispered *I love you*, all of it, wondering if it had been worth throwing her entire life's work into disarray. She knew in the back of her mind that she had been playing with fire when she got into this relationship, but it all seemed to be of little consequence when she was in Lucinda's arms. All the feelings Lucinda stirred up in her—they had been worth it, right?

Samantha sobbed under the water, trying to remember how she felt in every moment with Lucinda. Try as hard as she might not to second-guess the best thing that had happened to her in a long time, she couldn't ignore the feeling of betrayal that settled in her like a stone. This couldn't be happening again.

❖

Lucinda cracked her neck and let out a heavy sigh. She had been poring over Richard's accounts for more than three hours now. Prior to letting him go, she had reviewed his notes and client list, but currently she had the less-than-pleasant task of examining each account and seeing what deadlines matched up with whom. Furthermore, she was displeased, but not surprised, to find that Richard had been cutting corners. His work was sloppy. It was further confirmation that she had made the right call, but matching the right executive to these accounts to fix the issues and continue to provide the best service to the client was proving to be a difficult task, as this was the start of their busy season. The prospect of getting out of here by dinnertime was quickly fading.

She wearily looked at the stack of applications that had been waiting for her approval to interview new executives. It looked like she might have to start that sooner rather than later. Amanda's knock at her door drew her attention away from the endless pile in front of her.

"Brian just arrived, he'll be up shortly." Amanda had been busily syncing calendars at her desk all morning trying to help in any way possible. Lucinda was grateful she could work today—she was a lifesaver.

"Thanks. Can you close the door when you leave—it's surprisingly noisy today."

"You bet."

Working on the weekend wasn't a foreign thing for Lucinda, but having this much company was. She had asked legal to come in to review the contracts of all of Richard's accounts to estimate the risk of client loss with his departure and inform her of their options. She had also asked her three top executives to pull overtime and start the ball rolling before the week kicked off on Monday; they needed to stay ahead of this. She intended to have a finalized letter ready to be dispensed to all of Richard's clients informing them of his departure and introducing them to their new account executive before day's end and had asked each executive to give her a brief pitch of their plans for the cases she had assigned them before they left for the day.

Her phone buzzed with a text message. She smiled when Samantha's name and picture popped up. The happiness she felt dissolved into confusion when Samantha's text was short: *I'm coming into the office in about an hour. We have a problem.* Before Lucinda could type a reply, Samantha forwarded her a link, then three screenshots of emails from media outlets requesting interviews. She opened the link and stared at it in horror. Someone had reached out to the media about Samantha.

"Fuck." Lucinda called Amanda immediately. "Tell Claire to drop everything she's doing and get in here immediately."

She picked up her cell phone and called Samantha. She was sent to voice mail on the first ring. Her second attempt was met with the same fate; by call number three, the phone didn't even ring anymore, the voice mail intro cutting through her like a knife. "C'mon, Samantha, pick up," she mumbled before fumbling through her phone for Andrew's number.

Brian knocked and walked in, not waiting for her to answer. "Everybody's working on the weekend, huh?"

"Brian, oh, thank God. Come here. Close the door—we have a problem."

Brian looked surprised. "What's wrong?"

"There may have been a breach. I just got word that one of our client's confidential agreements has been teased to the press. I need you to get one of the IT guys in here to make sure no past client documents have been accessed in the last few weeks by any of the staff, particularly Richard."

He nodded, grabbing a piece of paper off her desk and jotting down some notes. "Do you think this had something to do with him?"

"I'm not sure. But the client is coming in immediately and we have to figure out how to fix this. The only way we can do that is to make sure this didn't come from a failure on our behalf. It wouldn't surprise me if that bastard had started squirreling information when he got his first warning. Let's hope he's not that smart."

"I'm on it. What are you planning on doing with the client?"

"I'm going to appropriate some of legal to sit in on the session and I'm moving Claire Moseley into lead. Keep this quiet if you can. Until we know what happened, the fewer people involved, the better."

"Will do. I'll give you an update in a few minutes."

A few minutes later, Amanda notified her that Claire was outside her door. She walked in and sat in front of Lucinda, at attention.

"Claire. Put everything else I asked you to do on the back burner and review this file." She handed Samantha and Andrew's case to her with a heavy heart. "I'm going to email you a link regarding a possible leak about this client—this could be a PR nightmare for the client and for us. I need you to handle this with the utmost confidentiality. Only recruit your most trusted peers for this. I need you to have a plan in place within the hour."

"Within the hour?" Claire looked a little panicked.

"Within the hour." Lucinda opened her tablet and put the image on the large screen to her left, pointing to the content while she talked to Claire. "Be prepared to meet in conference room *C* with legal in forty-five minutes. You can figure out the rest with them there. The client will be there shortly afterward. I'll move everyone out of this area"—she pointed to the org chart—"and reassign these tasks"—gesturing to several days of Claire's hot deadlines on the team calendar—"to Justin and call in Glenn to help cover the rest. Make sure I have an outlined plan before the client arrives."

Claire looked a little dazed but nodded, exiting Lucinda's office quickly. Lucinda called in Amanda and gave her a list of tasks and phone calls to make. After she left, Lucinda stared out the window at the gray day looming on the other side of the glass. This day had taken a sharp turn from the way it had started so blissfully this morning. She could only imagine the panic Samantha must be feeling right now. It occurred to her that it was probably similar to the panic she had herself right now: if Richard was behind this leak, this was going to come back to her. And rightly so. She had promised Samantha this would never get out—but here they were, both their careers potentially in danger. She had been so careful to make sure Richard was removed before he could access his accounts, but had she been too slow? Was she too distracted falling in love that she had mismanaged her job and let Samantha down?

The phone rang. It was Brian.

"What did you find out?"

"It's a good thing we switched over to digital records a few years ago—everything is accessible remotely by IT, which is good for us. They are confident they can figure out if the breach was internal within a few hours, but they warned me they obviously can't determine if a paper copy has been accessed."

"I figured as much. Keep me posted on the results."

Lucinda looked at her phone, feeling defeated. This could be a wild-goose chase and she knew it. Regardless of how this information got out, it was out. And she had to work her damnedest to keep it from roaring across the Internet and getting out of control. She glanced at the clock; Samantha would be here at any moment. She couldn't even imagine what she would say to her. Sorry? Sorry I let you down? I'll fix it? She wasn't sure she could.

❖

Samantha pulled the sun hat low on her forehead, her dark glasses obscuring most of her face as she stepped out of the car Andrew had hired to take them to Clear View. She was in no shape to drive, and he had spent the entire time on the phone making plans and setting up meetings. She had turned off her phone when Lucinda had called her—she wasn't sure what to say, so she decided that saying nothing was the safest approach.

Andrew checked in with security and took her elbow, leading her to the elevator. He pressed the floor to Lucinda's office and that feeling of nausea returned to her again. "You look very Jackie O in that ensemble, Sam."

She shrugged, wondering if she might actually be sick. This was awful.

The elevator doors closed and Andrew turned to her, an empathetic look on his face. "We'll figure it out. It's not the end of the world. Let's see what they have to say and move on from there."

She nodded, not trusting her voice in that moment. When they reached the floor of Clear View, she reached out and took Andrew's hand. "Okay, I'm ready."

He patted her hand and all the courage she had been trying to muster dissolved when Lucinda met them at the elevator doors. Her face was serious, intense almost. She looked tired. Her smile didn't reach her eyes—that's what Samantha noticed the most.

"Hey." Lucinda addressed Andrew. "Everything is ready in conference room C, Amanda will take you there. I'd like to have a word with Samantha."

Andrew looked at Samantha and nodded encouragingly; he stepped away from her grasp and followed Amanda down the hall, out of sight.

"Are you okay?" Lucinda's tone was gentle.

"Not really." Her voice wasn't shaking, that was good.

"We have a plan in place and will work quickly to make sure this doesn't get any bigger. We'll fix this, Samantha."

Samantha slid the sunglasses off her eyes and hoped the redness from earlier was gone. She looked at Lucinda closely, her eyes tracing over the stress lines on Lucinda's forehead, the worried way her lips twitched as she waited for Samantha to reply. She knew she should say something, but she wasn't sure what to say. She decided to be hopeful. "I believe you."

"Let's talk afterward, okay?"

"That's probably a good idea."

Lucinda nodded and motioned toward the conference room Andrew had disappeared into. She placed a gentle hand at Samantha's lower back, her apprehension clear. It felt like the warmth of Lucinda's usual contact was missing. Samantha wondered if she was imagining it or not.

❖

Samantha's head was swimming. The voices in the room were starting to blend together into this low-frequency hum. She had been pleasantly surprised at how proactive Lucinda's people had been. By the time she and Andrew had taken seats, they already had a list of options laid out in front of them. The choices ranged from denying everything to addressing the interview requests head-on with prepared statements. There was talk between Andrew and the Clear View reps about the vagueness of the blind item. No one was quite sure how much information was floating around. Everyone seemed pretty positive that if there was more to be released it would come out in the next day or so. She nodded numbly and agreed to their decision to prepare statements for the media but wait to see if anything else came to light.

She had been impressed by the account executive Lucinda placed in charge. Claire seemed knowledgeable and focused. Tenacious, even. Samantha rather liked her. But no matter how much attention she could give to the goings on around her, she was aware of Lucinda's presence at the back of the room. Outside of the small contact they'd shared by the elevator, Lucinda made no attempt to talk to her or touch her. It was glaringly obvious to her how much of their relationship revolved around touch, so even the slight absence felt like a large void. Lucinda only commented a few times throughout the meeting, always addressing the group, never Samantha or Andrew exclusively. It was as if she knew they needed to distance themselves from each other. She hoped that was the case; it would make this next conversation a lot easier.

The meeting ended and everyone filed out except the three of them. Andrew shook Lucinda's hand and hugged her, telling Samantha he would meet her in the lobby. She hated him for leaving her alone but realized she had to face this.

Lucinda closed the conference room door and leaned against it. Again not making any movement to touch Samantha—it sort of enraged her.

Lucinda spoke softly, almost whispering. "I have to stay here to work out some of the details we talked about in the meeting. I was hoping I could see you later on, maybe talk about some of this stuff a little more."

"I think we should take a little space. The last thing I need is to fuel the fire by being seen with you right now."

The hurt on Lucinda's face felt like a blow to her gut. Lucinda stepped forward, taking her hand and squeezing it gently. "Samantha, don't."

She stood her ground and shook her head. "I need to think. I have to figure some things out. I'm sorry." She squeezed Lucinda's hand and released it, stepping back.

Lucinda's expression was a mix of shock and disappointment. She opened her mouth to reply but said nothing. After a few agonizing moments, she stepped away from the door, facing Samantha as she said, "I'm sorry to hear that. I'm not ready to give up on this, on us. But I can't force you either. I love you, Samantha. I'm here to talk, when you're ready."

Samantha watched Lucinda leave the room and disappear behind her office door. She ghosted out to the elevator to meet Andrew and rode down alone without any recollection of the ride itself. She just had to get through one final car ride until she could be by herself. As much as that appealed to her, she dreaded it as well. Because she knew the minute she was alone, she would start crying and not stop.

Chapter Twenty-four

Lucinda sat on her couch, watching the video play on the screen before her. The sound was set to mute—no distractions, just the images on the screen.

It was of one of the last taped performances of her and Dominic. She could dance those steps this very day without missing a turn or a beat if asked to. This had been one of her all-time favorite choreographed dances. There was something about the liveliness that cheered her up, usually, although tonight it didn't lift her spirits at all.

The meeting at Clear View three days ago had gone as well as she could have expected. They had rallied under the pressure extremely well—her team had done everything she had asked of them. What bothered her though was her interaction with Samantha. She had seemed distant, cold even. Lucinda wondered if her perceptions were fair or if her own fears of being inadequate in her leadership position clouded her judgment of the situation.

Word from IT was inconclusive: the only person who had accessed their account digitally was Lucinda herself, the day after Connie's wedding. And as far as they could tell, Richard had not been involved at all—or at least, they couldn't link him to the leak. That was far from a 100 percent confirmation that the breach wasn't from within Clear View. It was an imperfect conclusion at best.

Lucinda realized she should probably be more upset about the whole ordeal than she was. But what was really keeping her up at night was how quickly Samantha had shut her out. It was as if at the first sign of trouble, Samantha retreated into herself. She'd pushed Lucinda away so aggressively, she felt like she had whiplash.

Lucinda stopped the DVD and stood, walking to the kitchen to pour herself a stiff drink. She settled onto the bar stool and looked out the small window to her private backyard. As she swirled the contents of her glass, letting the ice clink along the sides, she tried to ignore the way her heart felt stomped on. Samantha rejecting her after she had been so vulnerable, so willing to try, was just proof once more that everyone she loved left her, one way or another.

She drained the contents of her glass and set it in the sink, to be dealt with another day. She glanced at the calendar on the wall and felt like every bone in her body was made of sand. The anniversary of Dominic's death was tomorrow. And she realized she would spend it, like every other year since he had died, alone.

❖

Samantha had been staring at her desk without focusing on anything in particular for the last two hours. In fact, that's all she had done for days. She hadn't really slept and the amount of caffeine she had been consuming to save face was making her fingers shake. She wasn't sleeping because every time she closed her eyes she saw the slapped look on Lucinda's face when she told her that she needed space. It had taken all her strength not to apologize and beg for forgiveness in that moment. Seeing how devastated Lucinda was might have been the most difficult thing she had ever experienced. And she had been punishing herself for it every minute since.

She reached for her phone for the thousandth time in the past few days. Every time she loaded her contacts and hovered her thumb over Lucinda's name, she chickened out. A part of her wanted to be angry, to hold on to that feeling of being betrayed. She wanted to assign blame; she wanted Lucinda to save her, not be the potential cause of her problems. Not that she thought that was very fair either; she shouldn't shut her out. It was reflexive. Automatic. How easily she put her walls up and shut down. It's like she had been sort of expecting this all along, like she had prepared an emergency plan in case things got a little too intense. And yet all she had was a whole lot of doubt. And want.

She hated not talking to Lucinda every day. She hated being afraid to text her or call her. She hated living in fear of being in an honest relationship with someone for fear of the repercussions it could generate for her business. What good was this business if she denied herself the one thing she found for everyone else? She was a hypocrite if she turned her back on love for any reason at all. She was a coward. That's why she chickened out when pulling up Lucinda's name on her phone—she was a coward and she didn't deserve what Lucinda offered her. Lucinda deserved better than her and it kept her up at night. What had she done?

"Hey." Andrew was standing over her desk with a concerned look. "I've been talking to you for like three minutes and you've been in a fog."

"Oh, what's up?"

Andrew sat down across from her with a pleased expression on his face. "I have good news—well, not good news per se, but not bad news, which is something."

"I'm not following."

"Listen, I know I royally fucked up with the Lucinda and Logan thing. It was a total jerk move and I can't apologize enough, but I had a thought. After the meeting with Clear View I put in a call to Logan to do a little research into the whole blind item thing."

Samantha perked up a bit. "And?"

"And after some footwork and I'd be willing to bet a little physical violence on Logan's part, we got the intel we'd been hoping for."

"You are burying the lede here, Andrew, get on with it."

"The leak didn't come from Clear View. It didn't come from Lucinda. It came from Alec Frost."

"Are you fucking kidding me?" Samantha was out of her seat in a flash.

"That's what I said. Turns out Alec was pissed we dropped him as a client and contacted a media outlet to try and scandalize us. But since he didn't know the exact reason behind you and Eric splitting, he had to be vague. He doesn't know the details—there isn't more story coming out, Sam."

"Shit." Samantha let her head drop, her body weight supported by her hands on the desk.

"I was expecting you to be a little more enthusiastic…"

"I am such a fucking moron."

"Care to elaborate?" Andrew paused, "No, on second thought, I don't really care. Call Lucinda and tell her we figured out where the problem originated."

"I can't." Samantha slumped back into her chair, feeling deflated.

"Why can't you? Just call her and tell her the good news."

"I sort of told her we were on a break."

"A what?"

Samantha just looked at him, feeling admonished already.

"Are you serious?" Now Andrew was out of his seat, leaning over her desk with a disappointed expression on his face. "You better fix this, Samantha. You can't just push people away when you're scared."

"What if it's too late?" Samantha started to cry, a hopeless feeling settling on her shoulders.

"Can you live without her?" Andrew stepped back, a patient expression on his face.

"What?"

Samantha's whole world had changed when she met Lucinda and if she were honest with herself, she no longer considered her life without Lucinda in it. Even with all her pain and fear from her secret getting out, and pushing Lucinda away, not once had she thought about what it would be like to box up all those products in the bathroom. What it would be like to wash Lucinda's scent out of her sheets. She had not considered never being able to see bright blue eyes and hear her favorite laugh. She hadn't thought of waking up in the morning to nothing but the buzz of her alarm clock, no soft kisses to her shoulder, coffee in the pot, breakfast in the microwave, none of that. She couldn't even imagine her life without Lucinda in it. The mere mention of it brought the beginnings of a panic attack to her chest. Suddenly her throat felt like it was closing.

"What do I do?" She tried to steady her breathing.

His answer was simple. "Whatever you need to."

She nodded but didn't move, frozen in her seat.

Andrew sighed. "Find her. Apologize. Tell her she's the best thing that's ever happened to you because she is. You need to be honest with her and prove to her that you aren't going to abandon her like everyone else in this world. Stop thinking about it and go."

She grabbed her purse and hugged him, hoping that maybe it wasn't too late to make things right.

Chapter Twenty-five

Lucinda didn't answer her cell phone. All of Samantha's texts went unread. When she called Lucinda's house, her voice mail picked up.

Samantha hopped in her car after her calls to the dance studio went unanswered. Lucinda wasn't there. She wasn't at the boxing gym, and she wasn't at the park with the perfect view of the city. She wasn't at her office. Samantha looked everywhere and it was getting dark. The prospect of spending another night without Lucinda was more than she could handle.

Samantha had exhausted her resources. Panic began creeping over her when a thought crossed her mind. The aquarium. That was the only place left to look. They had had their first date there, their first kiss. Lucinda had told her she used to go there all the time. She dialed the aquarium as she drove across town, hoping to get in before they closed for the night. Something told her this was her last chance.

The teenager behind the glass at the aquarium looked at her like she had ten heads when she paid the full day's admission price to get into the building only an hour before closing. He tried to dissuade her, offering her a discount on the next day; she practically had to throw the money at him to get inside. She was dead set on finding Lucinda.

She speed walked through the penguin exhibit, winding her way up to the tropical fish section. When she found nothing, she set her sights on the top of the tank. She remembered the reverence that Lucinda'd had when she talked about Myrtle and the view from the top. From a certain angle, you could see the levels below, showcasing Lucinda's favorite sea creatures. This was Samantha's last hope; she was all out of ideas.

She was practically at a sprint when she finally got to the top of the tank, weaving between people. Divers perched on the platform, lowering themselves into the tank, one at a time, to do the nightly feeding. She would have been in awe of the display if she wasn't so desperate to find Lucinda. It's not every day you saw someone drop into a tank filled with hundreds of sea creatures.

But Lucinda wasn't here. She had failed.

Samantha walked along the curve of the tank, her eyes directed toward the water as she approached the spot Lucinda had pointed out. The divers were cleaning the tank in front of her, a few schools of shimmery silver fish frantically swimming out of their way. She sighed and glanced over to where she hoped to see Lucinda standing, her heart heavy. Then she noticed a dark mass against the glass. She picked up her pace and found Lucinda sitting on the floor, staring vacantly through the water of the tank to the exhibits below.

"Luce..." Samantha approached her slowly, fearful she might flee.

Lucinda turned her head at the sound of her name. She took in Samantha's shape before turning back to the glass, disappearing before Samantha's eyes.

"Lucy." She tried again, stepping closer before slowly sliding down and sitting next to her, close, but not touching just yet. "Hey, I'm here."

Lucinda's eyes narrowed, looking at nothing and everything all at once. She felt exposed, naked. Seeing Samantha didn't make her sad, but it didn't make her happy either. It made her feel...lost. She felt lost in those deep brown eyes; Samantha seemed sad and confused and nervous. It made sense to her.

She shifted slightly, angling her body to face Samantha and the tank at the same time. Her eyes remained on the divers in the tank, watching the stingrays glide effortlessly along the surface.

She was envious of them—they were flying, flying in peace. She wanted that in this moment, peace. Everything was so heavy and hard. She wondered how it would feel to be surrounded by water, to be weightless but secure at the same time, softly encased in water. She wondered if it would start to burn once she needed to breathe, if she could stand it.

"Do you think stingrays ever get tired of flying?" she asked quietly. "You know, like do they get bored of the continuous circles they make in the tank?"

"I don't know," Samantha answered. "It's all they know, so maybe they don't know to get bored of it."

Lucinda nodded in agreement. They didn't know what they were missing. They didn't know that there was a great wide ocean out in the real world with troubles and obstacles and predators. She did though, she knew. She knew that this contained environment was only a half life. A safe life, but half of a life all the same.

She had walled herself up after Grace. She had steeled those walls when Dominic died. She was tired of building defenses. They didn't shelter her from anything really, they just kept her from living. She was a prisoner to her walls, not protected by them. When Samantha had entered her life, she vowed to try something different. But the outcome had been the same.

She looked at Samantha, her face shimmering with the movements of the water next to them. Lucinda felt her heart rate increase slightly. Samantha was so beautiful, even when she was worried. The crease of concern on her forehead was adorable. Lucinda didn't fight the small smile that formed on her lips as she took in all of Samantha's perfect features. She wanted to remember all the details of her face. She wanted to tattoo them on her memory so she could recall them later, in case she didn't see them again.

"You're beautiful, you know that?" she whispered, her fingers hovering near Samantha's face, wanting to touch, but resisting. "You are perfect." She pulled her hand back and pressed it to the cool glass. "You should go, Samantha. Go be beautiful and perfect somewhere else."

"No."

Lucinda watched her closely for a moment. She looked back toward the water as Myrtle coasted by, sputtering water and air. "Samantha," she said, "what is it you want from me?"

"Anything you can give me. I just want you, Luce."

Lucinda let the words settle and take root. Samantha wanted her, still. She felt a pang in her chest as she thought about what that meant, about the responsibility of that statement, the weight of it. She didn't know if she trusted it. It sounded heavenly to belong to Samantha, to give herself to her that way.

Lucinda shifted so she was fully facing Samantha, her hands tapping on her lap nervously. Samantha reached across to steady them, perhaps to quiet the fear in them. The warmth of her hands was almost too much for Lucinda to bear. Her instinct told her to recoil and wrap herself up, but she knew it was time to break those old patterns. She had to break free.

"What is it about this place, Lucy?" Samantha asked. "What haunts you here?"

"Today is the anniversary of Dominic's death. I am officially older than he will ever be. We used to come here all the time. He used to clean the tank. He said it was peaceful. I spent my whole life growing around him and with him and then one day he was just gone. My only true stability in life, my rock, one day just washed out to sea without any warning."

Lucinda sighed. "I was lost and abandoned for all my life. No one wanted me, no one claimed me; there was no one to miss me. I was just a mouth to feed or a body to be clothed. I learned to swallow my emotions, to pretend to be happy and playful. You got placed in a home that way, when you didn't appear broken. But I was broken. I was unloved and broken.

"I don't ever end up on the side of happiness or love. I always seem to be just a little short, just out of reach. I want the chance to be happy, Samantha. I want the chance to have love that won't end, that won't fade. A love that won't die. I want that." She paused, wondering whether Samantha would disappear before her eyes like a dream if she spoke the truth. "I want that with you."

"Oh God, Luce. I'm so sorry. I never should have pushed you away." Samantha was crying now. "I want that too. I want all of it, please."

Lucinda brushed a tear away from Samantha's face, gently stroking her cheek for a moment as she tried to stop the trembling of her lips. "I can't live in fear that something will get too hard for you one day and you're just going to up and leave, Samantha. I've had too many good-byes to repeat that cycle."

Samantha leaned forward and pressed a chaste kiss to Lucinda's lips, holding there while Lucinda sucked in a breath, trying to slow the tremors rolling through her body. "I'm here. I'm here and I'm not leaving. I'm not leaving, Lucy." She pulled Lucinda forward into her arms and held her.

Lucinda sobbed, tucking her head against Samantha's neck, burrowing close. "I don't want to do this alone anymore. I don't want to be alone. I don't think I can take anyone else leaving again. I can't lose everything again."

Samantha saw it now; everything Lucinda had ever known in her life had been conditional and limited and not truly hers. The only unconditional love she had known in her life was from Connie and Dominic. When Dominic died, that last bit of security she had built her life around went with it. How could someone have so much hurt for so long and still learn to love? How could they be loved? When everything feels like it's not theirs to begin with. Who do they belong to?

Her. Lucinda could belong to her. She could be strong for once in her life and not run away from her feelings. Because nothing had ever been worth fighting for until she met Lucinda.

"I'm not going anywhere, Luce," Samantha said. "I'm yours. I'm here to stay. Sh, I'm here." Samantha shook her head, her own sad tears freshly falling as she looked at Lucinda's broken expression, the hurt and pain weighing down her perfect features. Samantha ran her thumbs under her eyes to catch hot tears, easing them away. "You are the love of my life, Luce. You are the happy ending I'm always finding for my clients. You are the breath of fresh air that makes me feel alive." She pulled in a deep breath and exhaled slowly. "You are all I want. All the good and the bad, I'm here, I'll help shoulder the burden, because you are worth it. All of it." Samantha shifted her position, pulling Lucinda to her knees in front of her. "I love you. I want you. I'm here."

Lucinda closed the distance between them, kissing Samantha softly on the lips, the electricity of their connection reminding her of all the great moments that awaited a life with Lucinda in it. She breathed in deeply, pressing her lips more firmly against Lucinda's as she let all the heavy emotions wash over her, cleansing her, bringing her hope.

A familiar splashing and sputtering noise nearby cut their moment short. Myrtle resurfaced on the other side of the glass, interrupting them again, just like the first time. Lucinda laughed through her tears and shook her head as Samantha giggled and pressed her face against Lucinda's neck. They stayed there for a moment, both of them watching Myrtle with amusement as she dipped her head below the surface and gulped down the food tossed to her from the divers.

Lucinda turned her head and pressed her lips to Samantha's temple as Samantha snuggled closer and allowed herself to be enveloped in Lucinda's embrace, her eyes following Myrtle's graceful journey along the top of the tank.

"The night Grace and I broke up, I came here to brood by the tank when Dominic found me. I thought he was going to feed me some bullshit line about there being more fish in the sea or something." Lucinda spoke softly. "Instead, he reminded me of a miracle that had occurred in the aquarium a few years before. One of the divers lost his wedding ring in the tank. Two hundred thousand gallons of water and fish poo and coral—everyone thought that ring was fish food for sure.

"A few months later, one of the volunteers was scrubbing the tank and vacuuming up some debris when something shiny and round caught his eye. He thought it was a coin, you know, because all of those damn tourists are accidently dropping crap in there like cell phones and cameras." She laughed. "But when he looked closer, he saw it was a ring, a man's wedding ring. I remember how

I scoffed at him and told him I remembered the story but didn't understand why in that moment he felt like I needed to be reminded of it. He just shook his head and replied as though it was the most obvious thing in the world. He said, *Sometimes it takes a little while to find what you're looking for, even if you don't know what it is.* You know, I think he was right."

"He sounds like a smart man." Samantha pulled Lucinda to standing and clasped their fingers together. "Take me home, Luce."

❖

"I still can't believe that asshole Alec was involved." Lucinda shook her head as she turned on the bedside lamp. On the ride back to Lucinda's house, Samantha had told her the entire tale of Logan digging up the goods on Alec, which made her feel a little better about the whole situation. Be that as it may, this scare was enough for her to immediately implement changes in the confidential handling of client information. While Samantha made a phone call, she shot off a quick email to Brian about the Alec bombshell and told him to start brainstorming protocol changes to be discussed on Monday and to let her know of any updates on Samantha's case. When Samantha told her about Logan's findings, she had assured Lucinda she was confident Andrew and Claire's team would sort out the details, but Lucinda figured one little email couldn't hurt, right?

"Andrew started plotting all sorts of fantastical revenge plots until I talked him out of it," Samantha called from the bathroom sink with a laugh.

Lucinda considered how much fun it would be to hear those plots over drinks. It made her happy that Andrew had used his investigative connections for good instead of evil this time. All's well that ends well, she supposed.

Lucinda lay on her bed, taking a brief moment to consider all the things that had unfolded tonight. She was tired, but it felt like a complete kind of tiredness, like she was tired for the right reasons. Samantha walked into the room and Lucinda quietly watched as she slowly undressed. Samantha walked to her bedroom window, looking over her shoulder, and beckoned Lucinda closer, extending her hand as she waited. Lucinda crawled out of bed and joined her, clasping their hands together and resting them on Samantha's abdomen from behind as she looked out at the view in front of them.

"It's beautiful here. So quiet, so peaceful."

Lucinda studied Samantha's profile; the moonlight reflected against her dark hair and illuminated her perfect features.

"It's a beautiful view."

A knowing smile spread across Samantha's face as she glanced over at Lucinda.

"Mm, I missed you."

Lucinda smiled, because truer words were never uttered. "I want to show you something."

She pulled Samantha back to the bed, playfully rolling across the sheets with her before walking to her closet. She pulled out the framed *Improper Bostonian* cover and turned it so Samantha couldn't see what it was.

"What have you got there?" Samantha's eyes shone with curiosity and affection.

Lucinda sat at the edge of the bed and ran her fingers up Samantha's arm, dancing along her clavicle before she pressed a kiss to the skin of her shoulder. "Everything got so out of hand over the past few days, I didn't get a chance to properly congratulate you." She kissed along Samantha's shoulder and up her neck, pausing under her ear and sucking on the skin gently.

Samantha let out a soft moan, closing her eyes and reaching out to touch Lucinda's face. "Congratulate me for what?"

Lucinda laughed at the clear distraction in Samantha's response. She pulled back with an impish grin and brought the frame up onto the bed, facing Samantha.

"We are celebrating your big magazine feature."

Samantha looked momentarily confused before her attention was drawn to the frame. A slight flush appeared on Samantha's face as she asked, "So I assume you read it?"

"I did. In fact, I found one bit particularly interesting. There was a part when the interviewer asked Boston's very own Miss Match if she was seeing anyone special or if she had her sights set on anyone in particular"—Lucinda reached forward to gently cup Samantha's cheek—"and I believe the exact quote you gave in response was *I think I may have finally found my own perfect match.*"

Samantha's eyes were wet with tears as she nodded.

Lucinda leaned close, her lips brushing Samantha's. "You gave that interview after our first night together, do you remember?"

Samantha closed her eyes and nodded again, her lips parted slightly.

"Did you mean it then? The way I feel it now? Do you think I'm your perfect match?"

A slow shuddering breath left Samantha's lips, ghosting across Lucinda's. "Even more now. I have never been so sure of anything, as I am of you and me."

Lucinda beamed and closed the distance, teasing her tongue along the pouty bottom lip in front of her, sucking it gently into her mouth. She savored the warmth and taste of Samantha's tongue. This moment, like all her moments with Samantha, was nothing short of magical.

"I love you." Lucinda leaned back and wiped the happy tears from Samantha's cheeks before brushing aside her own. She kept her hand cradling Samantha's jaw, gently rubbing her thumb along her perfect cheekbone.

"I love you too."

Epilogue

Samantha woke up to soft kisses being placed along her neck, over her collarbone, under her jaw, punctuated by a soft nibble to her chin, pulling her from the last of sleep's hold. "Mm," she purred. "Good morning, Luce."

Lucinda smiled against the skin of Samantha's cheek, kissing her sweetly before brushing the hair from her sleepy eyes. It was only then that she noticed the amount of light coming in through her bedroom windows and realized just how deep a sleep she must have been in.

"Morning, beautiful."

Samantha snuggled close, breathing in the smell of Lucinda's perfume and shampoo and sleepy skin, recording it to memory. The last few weeks had been magical. Samantha had never experienced this feeling, this connection with someone else. Lucinda made every moment in her life feel like one that should be celebrated. It was so refreshing that she hoped it would last forever. In fact, she planned on it. When Lucinda had told her the story of the ring in the aquarium, Samantha had decided right then and there to make sure that she and Lucinda would never be apart again.

Samantha shifted, catching the goofy, dreamy grin on Lucinda's face. "That's quite a grin for this early in the morning," she teased, pressing a kiss to Lucinda's lips.

"Early? It's after ten."

"So what?" Samantha challenged. "Do we have somewhere to be?"

"Not until our flight tomorrow. Booking this Tahitian vacation was genius. Have I told you lately you're a genius?"

Samantha winked. "Well, besides packing, I was planning on spending the whole day naked...in bed...with you. Is that okay?"

Lucinda pretended to ponder it for a moment, tapping her lip with her finger before smiling. "Sounds perfect."

Samantha had something else planned too, but she lost focus a bit when Lucinda's hand found her breast. She let out a low growl and straddled Lucinda's waist. She dragged blunt nails over Lucinda's toned stomach before placing her palm flat against Lucinda's chest, massaging as she licked a hard stripe along Lucinda's jaw.

A low humming sounded in the background, which she ignored in favor of focusing on the soft pants coming from Lucinda's mouth right by her ear as she slipped her thigh against Lucinda's core, pressing more fully into her.

"Mm, Samantha..." Lucinda whimpered as Samantha closed her fingers around a pink nipple, pulling gently while her mouth worked over Lucinda's other breast, her hand scratching down Lucinda's stomach as she pressed her thigh harder into Lucinda's wetness.

The humming stopped and the phone rang next to them, loudly, jarring Samantha momentarily from Lucinda's breast. Lucinda groaned at the loss of contact and ran her hands through Samantha's hair impatiently, pulling her back toward her chest. Samantha nodded and resumed her position, ignoring the phone. Lucinda rolled her hips against Samantha's thigh, her breathing getting ragged. She was close. The low humming rang out again, this time the sound swallowed by Lucinda's pleas.

"Please, baby, I need you..."

Samantha slid down Lucinda's body, settling between her legs and gently biting the soft flesh on the inside of her thigh, eliciting a whine of frustration from Lucinda. Samantha laughed and abandoned her teasing, kissing across Lucinda's sex slowly, before dragging her tongue over the soft, swollen lips, tasting Lucinda for the first time this morning. Lucinda let out a deep moan when Samantha flicked her tongue over her swollen clit, Samantha's hands trapping Lucinda's hips flat to the bed to hold her still while she dipped lower, thrusting her tongue deep inside Lucinda's core.

"Yes, God…" Lucinda cried out as Samantha curled her tongue and rubbed two fingers over Lucinda's clit, feeling Lucinda clench around her before finally moaning with a shudder as she climaxed.

Lucinda tried to catch her breath as Samantha continued to softly lap at her juices, cleaning her with affection, humming periodically and sending Lucinda into small shuddering fits when the vibrations neared her throbbing clit. The bedside phone rang again, just as loudly as before, refusing to be ignored this time.

"Babe, your phone…"

"Hmm?" The vibrations made Lucinda curse and grip the sheets tighter.

The ringing halted only to start back up again after a moment of quiet. Samantha groaned with irritation and refocused on her task. Lucinda quivered, feeling herself get wound up again, but the phone was so distracting. She grunted in frustration as she flailed her arm toward the annoyance. Just as she was millimeters away from swiping the receiver and silencing the noise, Samantha crawled up her body, shaking her head and slipping two fingers into her.

"Let it go to voice mail…we're busy," she husked into Lucinda's ear, kissing along her jaw.

Lucinda groaned as Samantha picked up the pace, thrusting in and out. She repositioned herself to grind along Lucinda's thigh as they moved against each other, a light sheen of sweat developing on their chests and stomachs. Lucinda started to climb too quickly, already stimulated from before, so she pressed her thigh harder against Samantha to catch her up, tugging on Samantha's hair and bringing their mouths together for a hard kiss.

Samantha moaned into her mouth, and Lucinda thought it was the hottest thing she had ever heard, her eyes rolling into her head as Samantha spread her fingers inside her, hitting all the right spots. Lucinda bucked under Samantha, her body going stiff and shuddering, the sudden movement bringing Samantha to climax as well.

She collapsed against Lucinda, laughing and panting, as the phone began ringing yet again. Samantha leaned up on her elbows, settling her hips between Lucinda's legs as she blindly reached for the phone while pressing featherlight kisses to Lucinda's still pulsing abdomen. She smiled up at Lucinda as she licked around her navel, then rested her tongue long enough to bark into the phone, "God, what?"

Lucinda watched in mild amusement when Samantha's sinfully aroused look faded as the person on the other line began speaking rapidly. Samantha shuffled up the bed to lie next to Lucinda, halfheartedly looking for her cell phone while holding the receiver to her ear. She laughed upon finding her cell phone lost in the sheets, showing Lucinda the screen flashing four missed calls. Lucinda pulled Samantha back to her side and gently stroked her fingers along her stomach, swirling indiscriminant patterns along the soft flesh.

Samantha pulled the phone from her ear, covering the mouthpiece with her hand to whisper to Lucinda, "Ugh, it's my mother."

Angry ranting could be heard in the background as Lucinda laughed and pressed a kiss to Samantha's lips. "Yeah? What does she want?"

Samantha brought the phone to her ear, listening momentarily before pulling it away again. "She's back from her three-week cruise and just saw the article. I think she's calling to chastise me for not telling her I was seeing someone." She giggled, leaning forward to kiss Lucinda, abandoning the phone entirely on the bed next to her.

"*Mija!*" A booming voice rang out on the pillow next to them, breaking apart their make-out session.

Samantha paused for a moment before flashing an evil grin to Lucinda. "Yes, Ma, I know…No, I was ignoring your calls… Because I was busy." Another pause. "Mom. Jesus. Just stop." Another pause. "Ugh, relax, don't be so dramatic. Ma. Ma. Ma. Listen! I'm dating Lucinda, Ma."

Lucinda looked over at Samantha expectantly. She pulled the phone away from her head and looked at the receiver as if it were crazy.

"What?" Lucinda asked, suddenly nervous.

Samantha shrugged. "I think she fainted."

"Should we call someone? Is she okay?"

A throaty laugh reverberated from Samantha as she hung up the phone and crawled back on top of Lucinda, pressing kiss after kiss to her face. "Meh, she'll call back when she comes to."

Lucinda smiled, deepening the kiss and running her hands along Samantha's naked torso, holding her close. She closed her eyes and let the weight of Samantha on her body warm her from the inside.

Samantha intertwined their fingers and briefly shifted out of Lucinda's grasp before snuggling close and sliding off to her side. She rejoined their lips and whispered, "I want to spend every day of my life wrapped in your arms, Luce."

Lucinda opened her eyes and looked over to find Samantha watching her intently. "I want that too."

Samantha beamed and pulled their intertwined fingers up to Lucinda's eye level, bringing her attention for the first time to the platinum band with the sparkling, flawless solitaire that Samantha must have slipped on her ring finger without her noticing.

Samantha wrapped herself in the sheet and knelt before her. "Marry me, Lucy."

Lucinda stared at her hand in disbelief. The ring was gorgeous. It was perfect and simple and stunning. She looked up at Samantha, kneeling before her in silk sheets, looking every bit the angel she had come to consider her to be. "Oh my God. Yes, of course. Yes."

Samantha squealed and was on Lucinda in a flash, kissing her face and repeating, "I love you," over and over, her happy tears mingling with Lucinda's own.

Just as Lucinda thought she might combust from all the feelings, the phone rang next to them. Samantha picked it up on the first ring, not breaking their kiss until the phone was pressed to her ear.

"Yeah, Ma?" Pause. "I love her." Pause. "No, I'm sure." She leaned back and gently nibbled Lucinda's ear, smiling into the phone once more before replying happily, "Yes, Ma, I finally found my perfect match...and we're getting married. I'll call you later."

Lucinda laughed as Samantha hung up the phone and pulled the cord out of the wall before snuggling up closer to Lucinda and asking, "Now...where were we?"

About the Author

Fiona Riley was born and raised in New England where she is a medical professional and part-time professor when she isn't bonding with her laptop over words. She went to college in Boston and never left, starting a small business that takes up all of her free time, much to the dismay of her ever patient and lovely wife. When she pulls herself away from her work, she likes to catch up on the contents of her ever-growing DVR or spend time by the ocean with her favorite people.

Fiona's love of writing started at a young age and blossomed after she was published in a poetry competition at the ripe old age of twelve. She wrote lots of short stories and poetry for many years until it was time for college and a "real job." Fiona found herself with a bachelor's, a doctorate, and a day job, but felt like she had stopped nurturing the one relationship that had always made her feel the most complete: artist, dreamer, writer.

A series of bizarre events afforded her some unexpected extra time, and she found herself reaching for her favorite blue notebook to write, never looking back.

Contact Fiona and check for updates on all her new adventures at:

Twitter: @fionarileyfic
Facebook: "Fiona Riley Fiction"
Website: http://www.fionarileyfiction.com/
Email: fionarileyfiction@gmail.com

Books Available from Bold Strokes Books

A Touch of Temptation by Julie Blair. Recent law school graduate Kate Dawson's ordained path to the perfect life gets thrown off course when handsome butch top Chris Brent initiates her to sexual pleasure. (978-1-62639-488-9)

Beneath the Waves by Ali Vali. Kai Merlin and Vivien Palmer love the water and the secrets trapped in the depths, but if Kai gives in to her feelings, it might come at a cost to her entire realm. (978-1-62639-609-8)

Girls on Campus edited by Sandy Lowe and Stacia Seaman. College: four years when rules are made to be broken. This collection is required reading for anyone looking to earn an A in sex ed. (978-1-62639-733-0)

Heart of the Pack by Jenny Frame. Human Selena Miller falls for the domineering Caden Wolfgang, but will their love survive Selena learning the Wolfgangs are werewolves? (978-1-62639-566-4)

Miss Match by Fiona Riley. Matchmaker Samantha Monteiro makes the impossible possible for everyone but herself. Is mysterious dancer Lucinda Moss her own perfect match? (978-1-62639-574-9)

Paladins of the Storm Lord by Barbara Ann Wright. Lieutenant Cordelia Ross must choose between duty and honor when a man with godlike powers forces her soldiers to provoke an alien threat. (978-1-62639-604-3)

Taking a Gamble by P.J. Trebelhorn. Storage auction buyer Cassidy Holmes and postal worker Erica Jacobs want different things out of life, but taking a gamble on love might prove lucky for them both. (978-1-62639-542-8)

The Copper Egg by Catherine Friend. Archeologist Claire Adams wants to find the buried treasure in Peru. Her ex, Sochi Castillo, wants to steal it. The last thing either of them wants is to still be in love. (978-1-62639-613-5)

The Iron Phoenix by Rebecca Harwell. Seventeen-year-old Nadya must master her unusual powers to stop a killer, prevent civil war, and rescue the girl she loves, while storms ravage her island city. (978-1-62639-744-6)

A Reunion to Remember by TJ Thomas. Reunited after a decade, Jo Adams and Rhonda Black must navigate a significant age difference, family dynamics, and their own desires and fears to explore an opportunity for love. (978-1-62639-534-3)

Built to Last by Aurora Rey. When Professor Olivia Bennett hires contractor Joss Bauer to restore her dilapidated farmhouse, she learns her heart, as much as her house, is in need of a renovation. (978-1-62639-552-7)

Capsized by Julie Cannon. What happens when a woman turns your life completely upside down? (978-1-62639-479-7)

Girls With Guns by Ali Vali, Carsen Taite, and Michelle Grubb. Three stories by three talented crime writers—Carsen Taite, Ali Vali, and Michelle Grubb—each packing her own special brand of heat. (978-1-62639-585-5)

Heartscapes by MJ Williamz. Will Odette ever recover her memory or is Jesse condemned to remember their love alone? (978-1-62639-532-9)

Murder on the Rocks by Clara Nipper. Detective Jill Rogers lives with two things on her mind: sex and murder. While an ice storm cripples Tulsa, two things stand in Jill's way: her lover and the DA. (978-1-62639-600-5)

Necromantia by Sheri Lewis Wohl. When seeing dead people is more than a movie tagline. (978-1-62639-611-1)

Salvation by I. Beacham. Claire's long-term partner now hates her, for all the wrong reasons, and she sees no future until she meets Regan, who challenges her to face the truth and find love. (978-1-62639-548-0)

Trigger by Jessica Webb. Dr. Kate Morrison races to discover how to defuse human bombs while learning to trust her increasingly strong feelings for the lead investigator, Sergeant Andy Wyles. (978-1-62639-669-2)

24/7 by Yolanda Wallace. When the trip of a lifetime becomes a pitched battle between life and death, will anyone survive? (978-1-62639-619-7)

A Return to Arms by Sheree Greer. When a police shooting makes national headlines, activists Folami and Toya struggle to balance their relationship and political allegiances, a struggle intensified after a fiery young artist enters their lives. (978-1-62639-681-4)

After the Fire by Emily Smith. Paramedic Connor Haus is convinced her time for love has come and gone, but when firefighter Logan Curtis comes into town, she learns it may not be too late after all. (978-1-62639-652-4)

Dian's Ghost by Justine Saracen. The road to genocide is paved with good intentions. (978-1-62639-594-7)

Fortunate Sum by M. Ullrich. Financial advisor Catherine Carter lives a calculated life, but after a collision with spunky Imogene Harris (her latest client) and unsolicited predictions, Catherine finds herself facing an unexpected variable: Love. (978-1-62639-530-5)

Soul to Keep by Rebekah Weatherspoon. What *won't* a vampire do for love… (978-1-62639-616-6)

When I Knew You by KE Payne. Eight letters, three friends, two lovers, one secret. Can the past ever be forgiven? (978-1-62639-562-6)

Wild Shores by Radclyffe. Can two women on opposite sides of an oil spill find a way to save both a wildlife sanctuary and their hearts? (978-1-62639-645-6)

Love on Tap by Karis Walsh. Beer and romance are brewing for Tace Lomond when archaeologist Berit Katsaros comes into her life. (987-1-62639-564-0)

Love on the Red Rocks by Lisa Moreau. An unexpected romance at a lesbian resort forces Malley to face her greatest fears where she must choose between playing it safe or taking a chance at true happiness. (987-1-62639-660-9)

Tracker and the Spy by D. Jackson Leigh. There are lessons for all when Captain Tanisha is assigned untried pyro Kyle and a lovesick dragon horse for a mission to track the leader of a dangerous cult. (987-1-62639-448-3)

Whirlwind Romance by Kris Bryant. Will chasing the girl break Tristan's heart or give her something she's never had before? (987-1-62639-581-7)

Whiskey Sunrise by Missouri Vaun. Culture and religion collide when Lovey Porter, daughter of a local Baptist minister, falls for the handsome thrill-seeking moonshine runner, Royal Duval. (987-1-62639-519-0)

Dyre: By Moon's Light by Rachel E. Bailey. A young werewolf, Des, guards the aging leader of all the Packs: the Dyre. Stable employment—nice work, if you can get it...at least until silver bullets start to fly. (978-1-62639-662-3)

Fragile Wings by Rebecca S. Buck. In Roaring Twenties London, can Evelyn Hopkins find love with Jos Singleton or will the scars of the Great War crush her dreams? (978-1-62639-546-6)

Live and Love Again by Jan Gayle. Jessica Whitney could be Sarah Jarret's second chance at love, but their differences and Sarah's grief continue to come between their budding relationship. (978-1-62639-517-6)

Starstruck by Lesley Davis. Actress Cassidy Hayes and writer Aiden Darrow find out the hard way not all life-threatening drama is confined to the TV screen or the pages of a manuscript. (978-1-62639-523-7)

Stealing Sunshine by Tina Michele. Under the Central Florida sun, two women struggle between fear and love as a dangerous plot of deception and revenge threatens to steal priceless art and lives. (978-1-62639-445-2)

The Fifth Gospel by Michelle Grubb. Hiding a Vatican secret is dangerous—sharing the secret suicidal—can Felicity survive a perilous book tour, and will her PR specialist, Anna, be there when it's all over? (978-1-62639-447-6)

Cold to the Touch by Cari Hunter. A drug addict's murder is the start of a dangerous investigation for Detective Sanne Jensen and Dr. Meg Fielding, as they try to stop a killer with no conscience. (978-1-62639-526-8)

Forsaken by Laydin Michaels. The hunt for a killer teaches one woman that she must overcome her fear in order to love, and another that success is meaningless without happiness. (978-1-62639-481-0)

Infiltration by Jackie D. When a CIA breach is imminent, a Marine instructor must stop the attack while protecting her heart from being disarmed by a recruit. (978-1-62639-521-3)

Midnight at the Orpheus by Alyssa Linn Palmer. Two women desperate to make their way in the world, a man hell-bent on revenge, and a cop risking his career: all in a day's work in Capone's Chicago. (978-1-62639-607-4)

Spirit of the Dance by Mardi Alexander. Major Sorla Reardon's return to her family farm to heal threatens Riley Johnson's safe life when small-town secrets are revealed, and love may not conquer all. (978-1-62639-583-1)